BLIND ITEMS AND BRITISH BOYS

By Melissa Gresko

ISBN: 979-8-9913968-0-6

To my family, for always encouraging my dreams

TRIGGER WARNINGS
While this book is primarily an R rated romantic comedy, there are
some mentions and depictions of heavy drinking and hard drug use.
There are also scenes including panic attacks and anxiety which could be
potentially triggering to those suffering with those afflictions.

CHAPTER ONE

DEAN

"Cheers to one year!"

Dean Coffey laughed and shook his head, cheeks flushing with embarrassment as Taylor insisted on holding out her drink for a toast across the table. The woman he worked for had also insisted on paying for dinner tonight, even though he kept telling her that they really should be celebrating *her*. *She* was the one who'd just finished a wildly successful book tour, after all.

He had simply been the puppet master, scheduling interviews, making phone calls, and booking flights behind the scenes - as he had been for the past year. Which, Taylor kept reminding him, was the true cause for celebration tonight in her eyes. This week officially marked one full year of him being her assistant. Her right-hand man. Her confidant.

"Come on, Tay, it's not that big of a deal," he chuckled, and Taylor Mullins just smirked at him, a playful gleam in her eyes as they clinked their glasses together. He took a sip of his non-alcoholic beer and watched as she flipped her golden blonde hair over her shoulder.

"Yes, it *is* and you know it. I would have died this past year without you, Dean," she replied with a shrug, as if it was the plainest thing in the world. He raised an eyebrow in her direction and tilted his head, laughing a little.

"That's a bit dramatic, don't you think? Hadn't you already written the second book in *The Jill Augustin Mysteries* before we met?" He countered, pausing and thanking the waitress as she brought a basket of bread to their table.

Taylor smiled at the waitress and thanked her as well before sipping her wine again and turning back to her assistant. The red lipstick stain she left on the glass immediately caught his attention, and he quickly snuck a peak at her broad smile before yanking his gaze back up to her bright eyes.

"Yes, but I was drowning trying to do everything myself. You did the brunt of the planning for this book tour...I never would have been able to work on the screenplay for the show if you weren't around," she pointed out, using her butter knife to point at him playfully.

"Ok, fine, I suppose I'll take some of the credit for your success," he held up his hands in mock surrender, acting like it was such a burden to take pride in his work. "But, I still argue that this dinner should be celebrating a successful book tour," he added as he took a bite of his bread roll.

He could do all the planning and behind-the-scenes work, but Taylor was the one who wrote the book. Without her, he wouldn't be sitting here across from her at this table. Her ideas were the ones that everyone instantly fell in love with. She was the one who put on a smile and did every interview like she had been born to be in front of the camera.

Sometimes he thought she was. In another life, she could have easily been an actress because people were just drawn to her and her sunny personality. He knew that wasn't what she was really meant to do, though. Taylor was a writer. Ideas bounced around in her brain at all hours of the day, and she never failed to astound him with how creative she was.

The Jill Augustin Mysteries had taken the world by storm, and he'd read the first book of the series before he interviewed with her so that he knew exactly what kind of author she was before he met her. Turns out, she was a *phenomenal* writer.

The character of Jill Augustin was relatable - a plucky heroine in Victorian England, solving mysteries and taking down the patriarchy. Throw in some spicy love scenes with her one true love Benedict Monroe, and Taylor had an instant success on her hands.

Normally, Dean wouldn't have glanced at a book in the historical mystery genre twice, but he figured it would be good to be familiar with her work before the interview - and he'd been hooked. She'd successfully converted him from a die-hard Stephen King fan to a man who was actually considering reading *more* historical mystery books.

Now the series was being turned into a show, and she had just finished the book tour for the second book in the series. It was slated to come out the next week, and in about a month, she'd be wrapping up the adaption of her first book into a screenplay. To top it all off, she somehow still found time to write new material.

The Jill Augustin Mysteries was a planned trilogy, and she was almost finished with the last book. Dean understood how much it stressed her out knowing that she had to put her work on hold to go on a press tour, but it came with the job when you became a world-famous author over the past two years.

"Soooo are you excited about Mexico?" Taylor asked with a grin just as the waitress brought out their food. She was referring to the trip they were about to embark on the next morning. It was the first time either of them was going on vacation in over a year, and after all the hard work they'd put into this tour, they both deserved it. A quick little trip before the book release was exactly what the doctor had ordered.

"*Very* excited," he confessed with a grin. "I've never been."

"That's right, I remember you telling me…well, you're going to love it! Sunny and warm, not cold and gloomy like your jolly old England," she teased as she began to cut into her filet. "You sure that alabaster skin can handle all the sun?"

"I'll have you know my skin has gotten used to the sunshine living in Los Angeles! As for that dig at my homeland…I distinctly remember someone saying they *love* the jolly old country I come from," he retorted with a laugh as he twirled his spaghetti on his fork. She rolled her eyes playfully from across the table, trying and failing to hide the smirk playing on her lips. He was referring to her history degree, of course, and the fact that she'd specialized in British history in a lot of her classes. After learning that little detail about her, it was no surprise why she'd picked Victorian London as the setting for her novel. It made him feel more connected to her in a strange way.

"I *do* love your country, yet I could do without the weather," she countered. Dean had to concede to her on that point.

"It'll be nice to have some time off for a bit," she added, and he nodded in agreement. He wasn't nearly as busy as Taylor was - she was the one in the public eye, after all - but he still could use a nice long vacation. Hell, he'd be simply delighted with a decent night's sleep at this point.

The last few weeks especially he'd been staying up into the early hours of the morning with her, making sure everything was ready for the next day to end the book tour on a positive note. They had been *very* successful, and buzz surrounding the release of the book was at an all-time high.

With just one week to go until launch, they had done everything they could to build up excitement for it - and he was fairly confident they'd see a huge payoff from it all.

Dean had also never been to an all-inclusive resort, and he had to admit he was excited to finally experience something he'd always viewed as a luxury. He'd had money growing up - lots of it - but his parents believed in spending it on education and giving back to the community, not on vacations or fancy hotels.

He felt a little weird having Taylor foot the entire bill for the trip, but she had once again insisted. When Taylor put her foot down, nine times out of ten there was no way you were going to talk her out of it, whatever *it* happened to be.

Sometimes he wondered if Taylor did too much for him. She was far too generous to him - knowing for a fact that he made *way* more than other personal assistants in the area - but she also never made him feel lesser than her.

Taylor told him many times over the past year that she liked to show appreciation and affection for people by giving gifts. It was her love language. It was her way of showing how much she cared about him and valued having him in her life, and once he viewed it that way, it made it easier. Someday, he vowed, he'd be able to pay her back somehow.

He observed her silently as she ate, taking in her appearance across from him as he slowly ate his own meal. Taylor really did *dazzle* him sometimes. She hadn't gotten *too* dressed up for this evening, but she was still wearing a shiny green and black fitted a-line dress, her hair had been straightened, and she did that fancy thing with her makeup to make her cheekbones all glittery. Her dark red lipstick was a stark contrast to her pale skin and blonde hair, but it made her look fierce. It made her look like she could take on any challenge that came her way.

She looked…simply breathtaking.

And as soon as he thought that, he chastised himself mentally, as he did every time a sneaky little thought pushed its way to the surface of his consciousness. He yanked his eyes away from her before she noticed him staring and immediately began to tease him about it.

These were thoughts he should *not* be having about Taylor Elizabeth Mullins. She was his friend. Probably his best friend, if he was being honest with himself. He should not be thinking about how gorgeous she looked tonight. Or how stunning her eye makeup looked. Or how that dress was cut low on her chest, giving her just the perfect amount of cleavage to continuously distract him all throughout the meal…

And yet…

"I'm really excited to go on a week-long vacation with you," he piped up, sipping his drink and peering at her playfully from over the rim of his glass. Taylor gazed up at him and their eyes met, and unspoken words exchanged between the two of them. He could sense the butterflies erupting in his stomach as she smirked, her blue eyes twinkling with mischief.

"I am too," she replied softly, grinning at him. "It's going to be a *great* week."

"That it is," he said in agreement, grinning at her one more time, no longer trying to hide how his face lit up at her statement before biting his lip and returning to his meal.

* * * *

A photographer had been camped out outside the restaurant all evening. Lots of celebrities regularly frequented the place, but he'd been shocked to get a call from his boss saying that they had word that some woman named Taylor Mullins was dining there.

The man had no idea who that was, so she explained that she was an up-and-coming famous author. The hostess called in the tip, and they also said she was dining with a man - they were pretty sure it was her assistant, Dean Coffey, but from his spot on the street, the photographer thought it read more like a date.

The man wasn't sure how popular this woman was, but no one else had been spotted going into the restaurant, and his boss was insistent. It was looking to be a slow night, so he had to take whatever tips came his way.

So he snapped a few pictures through the open windows of the restaurant - the hostess had likely sat them out near the patio for that exact reason - before checking his phone to see if there were any new tips to chase. He couldn't imagine this photo was going to get him much money. After all, who cared about what an *author* was doing in their free time?

CHAPTER TWO

TAYLOR

One Year and Two Weeks Ago

"You're seriously bringing in *that guy* for a second interview?"

Taylor Mullins glanced up from her paperwork and stared at her friend Caroline, wondering what the hell she was even talking about.

She peeked over at the papers Caroline had stacked in front of her and realized her friend was looking through the applications for the assistant job she had set aside for a second interview. After much deliberation, it was down to three applicants, and she was positive she knew exactly which one her friend was referring to.

Taylor sighed heavily and rolled her eyes dramatically. "It isn't like that," she insisted as she turned back to her computer. Caroline didn't need to say it, but she knew exactly what she was implying.

Caroline raised an eyebrow and stared at her

skeptically. "Oh really? The former *model* who just happens to be *British* isn't getting a call back based on his looks alone?" She asked with a tone that clearly told her that her best friend didn't believe her in the slightest.

"No! Caroline, Jesus, give me some credit," she grumbled as she snatched the papers back from her, ignoring the warm feeling creeping across her cheeks as she avoided Caroline's gaze. "He also happens to be the *only* person who applied with a communications degree who proved that he knows how to post a reel on Instagram," she added.

Out of all the people who applied, the three applications she had in her hand were the only three that showed any sort of promise at all. One of them was a forty-three-year-old background actress who never had her big break but didn't even know what blind items were. Another one was a twenty-year-old wannabe TikTok influencer who appeared to be more interested in using this job to make content for her page, and then...

Well, then it was the British former model with a communications degree.

Yes, he was good-looking, being a former model and all. Taylor certainly wasn't denying that, but that had absolutely nothing to do with her decision. She was a professional, and hot men needed jobs too, didn't they?

Truthfully, the other two applicants were coming in for second interviews to give the impression that she was giving a few people a chance. As far as she was concerned, there was no other choice. It had to be the British guy. He knew how to program an Excel sheet, schedule Facebook posts, and he was the only one who could explain what an algorithm was. If she was going to market herself seriously now that her career was taking off, she needed someone at her side who was knowledgeable about those things.

"So you're telling me that your *only* interest in this...'Dean' guy is his qualifications?" Caroline prodded, continuing to grill her as Taylor turned back to her laptop and tried to get through her emails. She was just seconds away from telling her friend to leave her condo, and would have done so already if she hadn't lovingly brought takeout from Panera for lunch.

"Yes, because thinking anything *else* of the man would be highly unprofessional," she spat back, and Caroline just smirked and made a playful tutting noise, pushing one of the dark red curls that fell in front of her eyes out of the way as she peered down at his application again.

As much as Taylor loved her friend, she was making far too big a deal out of this. Was Dean Coffey handsome? Yes, she would have been a blind woman not to notice that. Had she Googled some of his former modeling campaigns to see if his body looked as good under his sweater as she had hoped? Also yes - and she had not been disappointed. Had she maybe gotten so flushed that she slammed her laptop shut and threw it across the bed, like he would somehow sense she'd been looking at his half-naked pictures? Again, yes.

That had all been *purely* for research purposes, though. To stifle her own curiosity. Absolutely nothing else.

"Wait, his last name is Coffey? Is it actually pronounced like 'coffee'?" Caroline asked in interest. Taylor glared at her friend and snatched the applications back for the second time. She was taking up valuable time that Taylor could be using to write, going on and on about this guy who was barely a blip on her radar right now. She'd done an *excellent* job of suppressing the memories of that Google search during her current writing session, and Caroline was making it impossible to remain focused now that she kept bringing it up.

"I think it's pronounced 'caw-fae', now can you please leave me alone about this? I probably will hardly even see him," she pointed out.

Caroline was the one pushing her to hire an assistant in the first place. In addition to being her best friend, she was also her literary agent. She loved to give her a hard time about things in a lovingly joking sort of way, but she ultimately had her best interests at heart. She was the one who suggested that Taylor hire some help now that her book series, *The Jill Augustin Mysteries,* was blowing up.

If she was going to successfully launch the second book in the series, finish writing the final book in her trilogy, *and* negotiate the rights to a show, she was going to need some help. She couldn't be Superwoman forever.

Taylor hated to admit that Caroline was right. She wasn't nearly as skilled at multi-tasking as she had believed herself to be. She wasn't sure yet exactly what she'd have this man do once she hired him. She knew for sure that she wanted him to manage her schedule, planning her phone calls, interviews, and appearances. Basically, keeping track of her Outlook calendar.

Social media marketing would also be beneficial, since she was pretty terrible at keeping up with her own social media profiles and wasn't sure which platforms were considered *cool* these days. God, when had she gotten *old?*

No matter what she ended up using him for, she wanted to make sure he only focused on assisting her with her work. She didn't want to make the poor guy pick up her dry cleaning or walk her puggle, Trevor. He wasn't signing on to be her maid, after all. Besides, doing simple tasks like that was the only thing that forced her to step away from her work for a moment. She wanted him to feel like he was actually *helping* her, not doing minimal tasks like running her errands.

"Does that mean *I* have free rein to hit him up for his number?" Caroline teased, and Taylor took her bunched-up napkin from her Panera meal and threw it at her friend's head with a laugh.

"No! Absolutely *no* fraternizing with other hired help. Besides, you're married," she reminded her with a small smirk, and Caroline laughed and threw the napkin back at her.

"Unfortunately so. Look on the bright side, though. If you aren't going to bang him - and you definitely *shouldn't,* by the way, that would be a horrendous idea to mix business with pleasure - at least you'll get to look at Mister Coffee all day long," she said with a playful shrug, looking at his picture one more time before announcing her departure and finally leaving Taylor to finish her business day.

At least, that was what Taylor *attempted* to do. Unfortunately for her, all that talk about former model Dean Coffey reminded her of the pictures her Google search had unearthed. After twenty more minutes of little productivity, she sighed dramatically, shut her laptop, and decided to call it a night.

But not until she did one last thing on her to-do list. Biting her lip, she stared at the papers Caroline had left on the table before taking a deep breath, opening up her phone, and punching in the phone number at the top of Dean's resume.

"Hello, Dean? Hi, it's Taylor Mullins! Are you free

sometime this week for a second interview?”

CHAPTER THREE

TAYLOR

"How is it? Are you at the hotel yet?" Penelope asked through the phone, her naturally loud and demanding voice filling up the backseat of the car.

Taylor had it on speaker, listening to her sorority sister question her about the trip that they'd barely begun. Penelope and Betsy, her former roommates who still lived together, had called to congratulate her on the conclusion of her book tour and ask about their trip, evidently not realizing that they'd landed at the airport less than an hour ago.

"We're in the car headed there now. It's much ritzier than the place we stayed at when we came here during spring break that one year. According to the online photos, at least," she added, chuckling a little to herself as she remembered that trip fondly. There had been a *lot* of tequila involved, and somehow none of the photos from that trip remained on Facebook. She was pretty sure their sorority standards chair - who had *also* been on that trip with them - had had something to do with that, but she couldn't really remember.

It was like something had clicked inside Taylor when she got to college, and suddenly, after eighteen years of keeping to herself, she wasn't afraid to open up to her new friends. That had been where she had the confidence to start writing and she had begun to actually *show* people her work. She had always been quiet in high school, with just a few close friends whose numbers she didn't even have on her phone anymore.

None of it mattered once she got to college, joined the sorority and made her *real* friends. They encouraged her to keep writing and follow her dream of being published, and although they didn't understand her love of writing themselves, they still supported her. Penelope and Betsy were her two closest friends from college and biggest cheerleaders, aside from her dad, Dean, and Caroline.

"Spring break, huh?" Dean mouthed to her across the car, and she rolled her eyes playfully. "I know you said you *blossomed* in college but..." his questioning was cut off as she smacked him in the chest, causing him to snort with laughter as he shut his mouth.

She was sure he'd question her all about it once she hung up the phone.

"Are you sure you don't want some extra company down there? Betsy and I can come down there at a moment's notice, in case you were feeling generous and want to pay for a vacation for your *closest* friends, in addition to your assistant," Penelope teased her, emphasizing the word 'closest', and Taylor felt her cheeks heat up. Dean grinned and shook his head. It wasn't the first time her friends teased them for going on a vacation together, just the two of them.

She had to admit, to outsiders, it *was* a little weird that the two of them were going away for a little getaway. Dean was more than her assistant, though. Over the past year, he'd grown to be one of her closest friends - she hated to think it, but she was pretty sure she was closer to him now than she ever was with Caroline.

"Sure, just do all the planning for an international book tour for me and I'll book you a room," she retorted back, and she heard Penelope let out a laugh on the other end of the line.

"Don't forget to put on extra suntan lotion, you're closer to the equator down there!" Betsy chimed in from the background. Taylor was evidently not the only one who had the phone on speaker.

"Another helpful travel tip from our friendly neighborhood geography teacher," she teased her friend, who was indeed a tenth-grade geography teacher.

"And tell Dean to post some shirtless pics on Instagram!" Penelope added. Taylor tried to ignore the weird flip-flop her stomach did as her friend joked about Dean's good looks. They were always teasing him about his model past and making flippant comments about how hot he was, and she couldn't stand it sometimes. Still, she threw on a joking smile as she looked over at Dean to hide her discomfort over it.

"You're on speaker phone, Pen," Dean piped up as Taylor bit her lip to keep from chuckling. Her assistant didn't seem phased, however, and just smirked at her. He always took their joking in stride, but some protective side of her always wondered if he was ever embarrassed by it. She wondered - not for the first time in this past year - if she should maybe talk to her friends about easing up on the model jokes.

"Oh, we know! Have fun you two!" And the phone beeped, signaling the end of the call.

Taylor sighed and rested her head against the cool glass of the window. She closed her eyes, relishing the comforting feeling on her throbbing forehead as she listened to the sound of cars driving past them on the road. Dean was silent for a moment and then cleared his throat. "Are you feeling any better?" He asked quickly.

She hadn't even told him that she wasn't feeling good. He *knew* that she wasn't, because he was Dean and he knew stuff like that about her. He knew her mannerisms well enough to know when something was off, although to be fair she hadn't exactly been hiding her mood from him this afternoon. She just shrugged and he seemed to accept her answer, turning his attention out the window.

Taylor knew she was being a crab ass as soon as they got off the plane. She didn't have any reason to be, either. They'd flown first class, as they always did, and she'd taken her glass of champagne and used it to chase a melatonin tablet, and she'd quickly fallen asleep.

She'd woken up once for their snack, delighted to find Dean completely passed out next to her, his mouth hanging open as he slept through the viewing of *Inception* he'd pulled up on his phone. She hadn't been able to stop herself from snapping a pic of him to tease him with later.

All in all, it had been a great flight. But now it was hot, the time change was already wearing on her despite being only an hour difference, and champagne had always given her a headache. Why hadn't she been smart enough to request a vodka cranberry instead?

Then, their luggage had been lost, or so it had seemed. Dean worked his magic and found out that they'd actually had it picked up by the hotel and sent straight to their room. Then, they'd had to avoid paparazzi, who were camped out at the airport snapping pictures as they landed. Thankfully, she didn't think they were there for *her,* but she did catch the back of someone's head that looked vaguely familiar - she was pretty sure it was Paul Rudd - yet the sight of paparazzi still made her anxious. So now her nerves were shot for nothing, and it had been an incredibly stressful hour. Their car was waiting to pick them up, and she tried to enjoy the fact that she was speeding towards a five-star hotel to no avail.

"So I researched things to do at the resort, and we can rent a boat and go learn how to scuba dive off the coast. Does that sound like something you want to do?" He asked, clearly trying to make conversation. Taylor was hardly listening, though. Her brain was currently working overtime.

She was thinking about the paparazzi.

Taylor was still getting used to being 'famous' and being someone that everyone talked about. She had never gotten into this business to try and chase fame. She didn't ever think it was *possible* to be a famous writer unless you were someone like Stephen King.

She wanted to be a writer because she liked *writing.* She thought she had fun ideas for stories, and she wanted people to be entertained. She wanted people to love Jill Augustin the way she did, and she would have honestly been content with just a few five-star reviews on Goodreads and making it on the Amazon best seller list. Taylor had never expected Jill to capture the hearts of so many people worldwide. Now she had people wanting to make her book into a *show,* with people like Jennifer Lawrence and Elizabeth Olsen scrambling and bugging Dean to get an audition.

The first time that had happened, Emma Roberts' manager had called them to see if she could get her an audition, and Dean dropped the phone and almost hung up on her he was so startled. She still couldn't believe it. Over a dozen starlets had reached out to her since.

Nothing gave someone imposter syndrome quite like an A-List celebrity wanting to play a character *you* created in a show.

Authors didn't become celebrities. Authors didn't have people reporting on where they went and what they were doing. So why was she different? Why was she the one under the magnifying glass?

It was new, and it was different. She liked being noticed and appreciated for her work. If she was being honest with herself, though - she liked being *liked.* The publishing industry itself did nothing to help her underlying self-esteem issues, since rejection happened more often than not, especially when you were just starting out and querying agents.

As rejection after rejection had rolled into her inbox, her fears continued to mount, and she was convinced she would be always on the outside looking in, wishing she would be the one who was picked. Instead, she had to face her worst nightmare over and over again as agent after agent passed on her pitch.

The exclusion was something Taylor had experienced for as long as she could remember, and she was desperate to avoid it at all costs. Now, she had the whole world watching her, and one mistake would be all it took for everyone to decide that they hated her. Public opinion changed *that* quickly.

She could care less if people knew her name or recognized her on the streets, but if she messed up and her writing career was over, she'd be devastated.

This was what she was meant to do. The fame itself wasn't what she was worried about - in fact, she kind of hated it, especially now since things were really taking off with the release of the second book. Shit, did she need to start looking into hiring a security guard or something?

There were far too many thoughts for her jet-lagged brain to process currently. Dean nudged her and she blinked, having almost forgotten he was there.

"I asked if you wanted to learn to scuba dive. Are you ok? You've got that look on your face that you get when you're disassociating."

Taylor sighed heavily, looking back out the window as she chewed on her lip. "Maybe we shouldn't have come here," she grumbled softly.

"What?" Dean asked, and she sighed again. She was probably giving her poor assistant whiplash, changing the subject and her mood so quickly. She rested her chin on her palm and looked out the window. Her thoughts were spiraling thanks to her underlying anxiety, and she could feel the suffocating feeling of doubt starting to creep up to her chest.

She knew she was a moment away from questioning her every move in life, and for what? All because she'd seen the paparazzi hounding a Marvel star at the airport? It was laughable how easy it was for her to lose focus on what was important, which only made her even *more* anxious.

"Cancun. Maybe we should have just stayed in New York. Or run away to Europe. I should have at least tried to learn some Spanish before we came, I hate not knowing at least a *little* of the local language before…"

"Hey," Dean cut her off and put his hand on hers, giving it a reassuring squeeze that he had done many times before. His hand wrapped around hers strongly, and she instantly grew a bit calmer. Like someone had dumped cold water over her and brought her back to Earth. Butterflies erupted in her stomach as their skin touched and she felt her face flush. She avoided his gaze so he didn't see how pink she was. How was it that he was able to do *that* so easily? A simple touch, and a moment later she was a puddle of goo. "Just say the word and I'll turn the car around. I'll cancel the reservation. Whatever you want to do, ok?"

Taylor nodded, knowing she was being ridiculous, and she sighed. She closed her eyes and once again rested her forehead on the window, peering out at the Mexican billboards they passed as they headed to the resort area of Cancun. "No, it's ok. I know this is good for me. I know I'm…spinning, letting the intrusive thoughts win. I have *so* much going on, and I'm tired and cranky…"

Dean chuckled a little and squeezed her hand again, and she noticed he wasn't letting go any time soon. The longer he held her hand, the calmer she felt herself becoming. "Taylor, the world is not going to end because you take *one week* off from working, ok?" He assured her. She took a deep breath and smiled a little to herself. Naturally, Dean had gotten straight to the root of the issue and knew exactly what was *truly* bothering her. "No one is going to forget who you are, or think you're a bad writer for taking time off, ok?"

She swallowed a lump that was forming in her throat and turned back to him, smiling at him. He was eyeing her tentatively with those dark brown eyes as if he were afraid she was going to go into a full-blown panic attack, but she wasn't. She didn't *feel* like she was, at least.

She nodded at him and then chuckled a little, staring at their clasped hands as she blushed even harder. Taylor hated to admit it, but she'd always had a thing for strong hands - the kind that men had where you could see every small vein and tendon, not in a gross sinewy way, but in the way that you knew he'd protect you if it came down to it.

Dean's hands were her favorite. His thumb brushed against hers delicately, like he was trying to slowly coax the anxiety from her. All her close friends - and her dad - knew about her anxiety. She'd had to start meds in college and had attended therapy for a while because of it. Yet none of them had been able to actually *calm* her during the midst of an attack like Dean. He had a gift.

"Sometimes I think you should be a writer, Dean. You have a way with words and always know exactly what to say," she admitted to him, and he chuckled, shooting her that classic grin that she loved so much. It was kind of a shame his modeling career never took off. That grin could sell anything, she was sure of it.

"Nah, I just think I can read you like a book," he retorted, winking at her playfully, and she nodded. He really *could* read her like no one else. It was what made them so great together. "You're the writer, I'm the reader."

"That was corny," she teased him with a playful arm punch, the corner of her mouth pulling up into a smirk. He smiled and then shrugged, dropping her hand as if he just remembered that he had been holding it. This time, she was quite certain *he* was the one blushing.

"It's true. Whatever you do though - please promise me you'll try and *relax,* ok?" he asked. Dean had been berating her for overworking herself for the past month. He'd gone above and beyond trying to help her with the workload, easily putting in 60-hour weeks to help her get everything done on the press tour. He was right. It was time for her to relax and take a break before going back to the real world. She'd accomplished some amazing things this year. It was time to celebrate.

"And don't worry about not knowing any Spanish. I can speak for us," he assured her, grinning at her. Taylor blinked and felt her mouth open slightly in surprise.

"You can speak Spanish?" She asked, and he nodded as if he hadn't just casually dropped the fact on her that he was bilingual.

"And French," he added. She *really* opened her mouth in surprise for that one, because they'd *been* to France and she couldn't remember him speaking French even one time. Aside from the typical greetings, and asking where the bathroom was.

"How am I just now finding this out?" She asked with an astonished laugh, and he shrugged and chuckled.

"Well, everyone we encountered in France started speaking English the second they clocked us as tourists...and the Spanish bit never came up I suppose," he replied with another smirk. She scoffed and rolled her eyes playfully.

"Uh, when I proposed coming on a trip to Mexico, that might have been a good time to bring it up," she pointed out, and he just shrugged. Dean never liked to brag about himself. Taylor found it absolutely adorable.

"How is it that I'm still learning new things about you?" She asked quietly, leaning back and looking at him thoughtfully. His face flushed again at that, and he peered out the window with a small smile, avoiding her gaze as he cleared his throat.

"Maybe I just like to keep you guessing," he responded, but she wasn't sure that was the true reason.

She was sure it was because Dean had thrown himself into this assistant job and made his primary focus learning about her. He'd done such a good job at it, that sometimes he forgot she wanted to learn about *him* too.

Or maybe Dean was just such an amazing person, that she could know him for the rest of her life and still never know everything there was to know about him - and she liked that. She liked that a lot.

CHAPTER FOUR

DEAN

Dean could tell that by the time they finally reached the hotel, Taylor was drained. Whenever a big stressful event came up, she always fell victim to a post-event fatigue that he couldn't quite figure out. It was like all the stress was gone, so her body had nothing to do with that excess energy and manifested it in a headache. He made a mental note to see if the hotel shop had migraine meds later - he couldn't remember if he'd packed any for her or not.

Finishing a multi-week book tour *definitely* qualified as a stressful event, so he wasn't surprised that she was dealing with quite a few emotions. He wouldn't bring it up to her now, though, because she might snap at him for treating her like a baby, packing her meds for her like she couldn't manage it herself.

Snippy Taylor was his *least* favorite Taylor and he tried to avoid her as much as possible. Unfortunately, ever since they'd gotten off the plane, he knew that was what he was dealing with. It was like walking on eggshells around her when she got in one of these moods.

He tried to give her some grace, knowing her anxiety really got under her skin sometimes, but he'd also gotten good at reminding her that her worries were often not the end of the world, and he could usually coax her back into a better mood.

Dean had the suspicion that no one in Taylor's life had ever truly cracked the code on how to break through to her during an anxiety attack. He felt an odd sort of pride knowing that *he* was the only one who seemed to know how to calm her nerves and bring her back to reality.

After the kind concierge employee helped them unload their things onto a luggage cart, they approached the front desk and Taylor set her purse on the floor with a sigh, like she'd just trekked a whole mountain to get here. He needed to get her upstairs and get her to bed soon. Or at least get some caffeine in her. He slid next to her, nudging her gently with the side of his arm to try and let her know that it was ok, and they were here now. She could relax.

He might have been imagining it, but he was pretty sure he felt her tension ease up *just* slightly next to him.

"Checking in under Taylor Mullins," she announced as the front desk woman walked up to them. The woman appeared to be a little older than them, probably in her forties, but she had that grace and command about her that let you know she knew this hotel like the back of her hand. Dean read her name tag and made a mental note that her name was Maria, and the word 'manager' was etched in small font underneath her name. That would explain the demanding presence.

Maria smiled at them and looked between the two of them before she turned to Dean.

"Ah, yes, we heard there was a celebrity staying here! Welcome to the Royal Cancun Resort, Mister Mullins," she said, addressing him as she spoke. Dean simply blinked at her, confused as to why she was addressing *him*. The reservation wasn't under *his* name after all, and she probably thought he looked like a complete idiot staring at her with a befuddled expression. At first, it didn't even occur to him *why* she was talking to him until he replayed what she'd said back in his head.

Oh shit. She thought *he* was Taylor Mullins. Yikes - he already knew this wasn't going to end well. He turned to Taylor while shaking head, and he saw the color drain from her face as she realized what mix-up was happening. *Shit.* This was the kind of thing that could send her into a spiral, and she was already tired as it was from the flight. Carefully, he reached over and squeezed her hand as he cleared his throat.

"Actually, my name is Dean Coffey, *this* is Taylor Mullins," he corrected her, gesturing at Taylor. The manager's face paled and he could see her processing her mistake, and Taylor tensed next to him. His heart began to race and he gave her hand another reassuring squeeze, and even though she squeezed his hand in return, he had a sinking feeling in his gut that the spiraling had already started.

"Oh! I am so sorry, I..."

"Assumed the *man* was the rich, successful author?" Taylor asked, and Dean shot her a dirty look as his face flushed in secondhand embarrassment.

"Tay!" He hissed under her breath. That was highly unlike her. Even on her worst days, she was never impolite to people, especially the wait staff. As he stared at her, he could see the realization dawning on her of what she had just done, and her face paled. She quickly opened her mouth and started to apologize, but the poor manager was worked up in a tizzy now.

"No no no, I...I thought...I am so very sorry. I was not aware that you..." Maria trailed off and for a second looked like she might cry. Dean swallowed as his heart plummeted to the pit of his stomach. Great. Just great. What a way to start off the trip. By making the manager of the hotel *cry*.

"I see you two are staying in our Grand Imperial Suite. Excellent choice, most expensive one we have," the woman prattled on, clearly flustered. Taylor tried to speak up again to apologize but the woman was running off, saying something about getting them the keys to their room. He turned to Taylor once she left and nudged her with a frown.

"What the fuck?" He whispered, and she bit her lip, looking like she might burst into tears just like Maria.

"I know, that was so rude of me. Shit," she grumbled under her breath.

"It was an honest mistake, I'm sure. It's not your fault you have a unisex name," he reminded her, and she nodded, still looking extremely upset with herself. She began to wring her hands nervously together as the woman hurried back a moment later. Maria seemed to have taken a moment to compose herself, much to Dean's relief.

"I would like to personally escort you to your room if you please," Maria offered, flashing them an eager smile. Clearly she was overcompensating for the mistake, but the least they could do at this point was humor her. Taylor looked like she might protest but then thought better of it, blushing.

"That would be lovely, thank you so much, Maria," she said, and Maria went on and on as she came out from behind the desk, informing them that she had called to have something special delivered to the room as she gestured for them follow her. Dean wanted to crawl into a hole and hide as they began their tour of the hotel, and he had a feeling Taylor wanted to sink away into the floor as well. He didn't blame her. She *had* made a scene for nothing.

"Are you ok?" He asked her quietly as Maria started pointing out all the points of interest in the resort, such as the bar, the main dining room, the buffet, and the exercise room as they passed.

She sighed. "I'm just tired Dean," she insisted. He nodded, thinking about what he could do to try and make her relax. He had an idea, of course, but he wouldn't be able to implement that until they were finally alone in their suite. Right now, he would let her sit there and think about her actions as they walked, letting her feel ashamed about her behavior for a few minutes. He would do anything for Taylor, but he also wasn't afraid to point out when she was wrong.

Taylor Mullins was only human and made mistakes, just like the rest of them. Unfortunately for her, she wasn't going to escape this mistake any time soon, as Maria announced that she was going to personally take them up to their room once they reached the elevator bank.

The next three moments passed in extremely awkward silence as they took the stuffy elevator up to the third floor, and Dean just hoped and prayed that the rest of this vacation would go off without a hitch.

It certainly couldn't get much worse than this, could it?

CHAPTER FIVE

TAYLOR

"Are you sure you wouldn't like a separate suite for your assistant?" Maria asked again, and Taylor bit her lip sheepishly as she nodded in response.

She figured the manager was trying to be nice and do her job after the incident in the lobby. The incident that Taylor was still personally mortified about. Still, Maria had asked *three* times already if she wanted to book a separate room for Dean - how many times did Taylor have to politely decline before she got the hint?

"No, thank you, this is quite alright. I can see there is more than enough room here for both of us to have our privacy," she pointed out once again, taking in the large entryway they were currently standing in. Dean nodded at her, looking around at the kitchen and the living room area that broke off into two rooms - one for him, and one for her.

"Well, then, by all means, do make yourself at home," Maria said with an obviously fake grin. Taylor didn't blame her for putting on a show for them after she snapped her out at the front desk. She felt awful about it and was trying not to get annoyed as Maria tried her best to be as overly accommodating of them as possible to make up for her blunder.

This was no one's fault but Taylor's. She was well aware of that fact. She kept trying to interject and apologize for earlier, but Maria was determined to fill every moment of silence with more facts about the hotel and their stay, and it was hard to get a word in edgewise.

"As you can see, your bags have already been delivered. Also, please accept this as a welcome gift. Our treat, from the hotel," she continued, gesturing to a bottle of champagne that was chilling in a large ice bucket on the table in the entryway. Taylor didn't need to hear her say it, but the unsaid implications of the gift hung in the air. *It's also an apology for accidentally assuming Taylor was the man checking in.*

"That was very kind of you, thank you," she replied politely. Out of the corner of her eye, she saw Dean eyeing the champagne, knowing full well he wouldn't be drinking any of it once the manager left. Maria wouldn't have had any idea why *Dean* wouldn't appreciate the champagne, of course, but it was yet another little hiccup in their trip that had just barely begun.

Dean was clearly just as eager to put this whole awkward mess behind them as Taylor was, heading to the door of the room and opening it. "Thank you again for showing us to our suite, Maria, I'm sure we'll see you later at dinner," he said quickly, grinning at her and giving her a look that very clearly told her - in the nicest way possible - to get out.

Maria stared at him for a moment, biting her lip as she walked to the door. The older woman looked at both of them uncertainly as she made her way to the doorway. "I didn't get a chance to show you your private pool..." she began, but Dean shook his head, a piece of blonde hair falling in front of his glasses.

"That is quite alright, I think we can find it ourselves," Taylor told her. "And Maria...I'm so sorry about my attitude downstairs," she added quickly, feeling her face flush with embarrassment as she addressed the elephant in the room. Maria looked surprised that Taylor had bothered to apologize at all, but she quickly regained her composure and smiled back at her.

"No apology necessary, please, Miss Mullins, it was my mistake...and I want to make sure we do whatever we can to make this trip perfect for the two of you," she assured her, which just made Taylor feel even more embarrassed. Maria was so sweet and polite and clearly loved her job.

"Thank you again, Maria...I mean, *gracias,*" Dean said with a grin as Maria gave a little chuckle, clearly won over by his charms as he closed the door behind her retreating form. As soon as the door was closed, Taylor let out a low groan and rubbed her temples.

"Ugh, she hates me," she grumbled as she headed into her room. She knew it was hers because it was advertised as being the bigger of the two, and Dean had insisted on giving her the larger room as always. She headed to the bathroom and immediately kicked off her black heels, pulling her button-down shirt out of her slacks and letting out a soft sigh. She missed the days when she could wear comfy clothes like yoga pants on airplanes and didn't need to look like she was trying so hard all the time.

Taylor couldn't *wait* to change into sweats and take a

nice nap. She wanted to crawl into bed, pull the covers over her head and cry about how she'd made a fool of herself in front of a woman who was just trying to do her damn job.

"I have no clue why I'm so jet lagged but I seriously need a long nap," she called out, continuing her one-sided conversation with her assistant, who was probably unpacking in his own room and not even listening to her anymore. "That's definitely why I snapped at her. I must remember to make a point to thank her personally for everything she's done at the end of the trip, I don't want her to get the wrong idea of me," she rambled on. Or worse, the woman could go to the press and sell a story for a nice penny to the local tabloids. *Famous author treats hotel staff like shit*...that would get magazines flying off the shelves. Not that Maria seemed the type to do that. She seemed very sweet, actually.

She slipped out of her slacks and kicked them aside over her discarded shoes, and she pulled her bracelets off and tossed them haphazardly on the bathroom counter. She walked out to the bedroom, her fingers working to take her large hoop earrings out as she went.

"I think this proves that you're right, and I really need a fucking vaca..."

Her words trailed off as she walked into the bedroom, taking in the large king-sized bed in front of her. It was exactly as advertised on the website, looking like a snapshot straight from the travel brochures with light yellow and white sheets that complimented the green and tan colors of the palm fan wallpaper.

The wicker furniture might have seemed dated but it fit the theme of the room perfectly, and the entire far wall was clear floor-to-ceiling windows and a sliding glass door overlooking their private pool and patio. Yes, it was decorated exactly as it had been when she'd fallen in love with the suite and booked the room without a second thought, except for one addition.

Her assistant, Dean, lying completely naked on the bed.

He was propped up on his arm, facing her as he lay on his side and shot her that cheeky lopsided grin of his. He'd taken the champagne from the other room - and the ice bucket - and had placed it propped up on the bed, strategically covering one very important body part of his from her view. He'd also taken off his glasses, and as she walked into the room and stopped in her tracks, his grin grew even wider.

"Fancy meeting you here."

* * * *

Taylor stared at him for a second, blinking as she took in the picture in front of her, and then...let out a laugh and grinned.

"Shit, you got naked fast," she teased him, walking over to the bed and tossing her hoop earrings on the ground. She hopped on the bed and immediately moved to straddle him as she had done dozens of times before, pushing the champagne bucket out of their way.

"Oi! You'll spill the ice on the bed!" He laughed as he grabbed the bucket out of her hands and moved to put it on the nightstand, turning his attention back to her and gripping her thighs as she hooked her leg over him. She immediately felt the familiar butterflies going bananas in her stomach as his strong hands rested on her legs, and he stared up at her like she was the prettiest thing he had ever seen.

"Have I mentioned I love when you use British slang around me?" She asked him, her hand snaking into his blond hair and tugging playfully. He laughed and bit his lip as he rocked his hips up into hers. Her heart practically skipped a beat as she felt him rub against her, turning her into putty in his lap with a single movement.

"You might have, but go ahead and tell me again, just in case," he joked back, causing her to giggle as she started to unbutton her shirt to reveal her light beige bra. He smiled up at her, flashing her that amazing grin, and her heart started to race as it always did when she had him in her bed.

Taylor had lost track of how many months they'd been doing this now. It had to be at least six...she'd just taken him out to celebrate one year of him being her assistant, so it was somewhere close to that. It had started out innocent enough - some back-and forth-flirting for a bit. Playful inside jokes between the two of them. Both of them tip-toeing that line and trying to figure out how far was too far.

It all peaked one night in London when in a mixture of club shots, revealing outfits, and EDM had made them drop their reservations long enough to cross the line and leave it far behind.

She had known as soon as he touched her that night that this wasn't going to be a one
-time thing. Yet, deep in their hearts, they also both knew that this was all it could be. Just sex - because he was her assistant, she was his boss, and the mess they would make trying to sort this out while she was in the public eye would make both of their lives a living hell.

When she'd hired Dean, she never once thought she'd

go so far as to sleep with him. She truly didn't have any ulterior motives when she'd offered him the job - at least, none that she'd been consciously aware of. She thought he was cute, yes. Who *wouldn't* think Dean was cute? But she'd never intended to act on it.

They'd gotten along in their interview, and over the past few months, she'd come to view him as one of her best friends. In fact, he might actually be her best friend…it's not like she saw many other people besides Caroline, Betsy, and Penelope.

Dean understood her. She realized quickly that it wasn't just his desire to be a good assistant, but he wanted to be a good *friend* to her as well. He knew so much about her that it scared her sometimes but in the best possible way. He not only knew her as a person but as a lover as well.

Six months later, she still got goosebumps when he gave her bedroom eyes from across a crowded room, giving her that glance that was reserved only for her. It was a look that others wouldn't pick up on as they both put on smiles and continued to face the world as boss and assistant.

His touch ignited a fire in her, and there had been more than a few times when he lightly brushed against her at a function or leaned in a little *too* close to whisper in her ear with his hot breath on her skin, and she'd snapped. She would squeeze his hand, tell him to meet her at the coat closet down the hall and sneak away from the party to do all sorts of deliciously wicked things to him.

"So, is this what you had in mind when you said I need to relax?" She asked cheekily, raising an eyebrow as she rolled them, pushing her lacy pink panties off and down her legs once she was under him. He smiled and leaned down to kiss her softly. She absolutely loved it when he kissed her hard and passionately, but sometimes the slower, softer kisses made her even more flustered than the rough ones. She couldn't get enough of his lips. She didn't know what he did, but they were always so incredibly soft, and his tongue...damnit, his tongue could do downright god-like things to her if he was feeling particularly generous that day.

"Certainly seems like it would help, doesn't it?" He teased as he propped her legs up on his shoulders. Oh, she liked this position. Especially since it was still light out, so she could see every line of his body as she stared up at him.

Her breathing started to quicken in anticipation, knowing that all he had to do was look down at her with those piercing brown eyes and she turned into a puddle of desire for him. Even now she squirmed a little, desperate for him, her body aching and craving his in an almost painful way.

"Someone is already loosening up on this vacation," she said with a smirk, and he playfully pinched her thigh as he settled into her, groaning her name as he pushed into her with his length. She moaned loudly and bucked her hips up to meet his, her desire to be as close as humanely possible to him taking over.

"And now we need *you* to loosen up," he muttered softly under his breath as he got in position, gripping her legs around him for support and moving slowly, agonizingly slowly, and making her bite her lip as he worked.

"How many times is it going to take, hmm? One? Two? Five? I'm in no rush," he teased as he squeezed her thighs playfully, and she laughed, which turned into a deep moan as he increased his pace.

"How about we...play it by ear..." she giggled, her breath hitching as he moved. Her voice trailed off and she was certain she didn't know what words were anymore - the thought of Dean Coffey taking her *five* times this evening had completely turned her brain to mush. It simply wasn't *fair* how he could move so perfectly inside her. He always had her crumbling in a matter of minutes.

She also appreciated this angle more than she realized, because now she was able to stare up at him, taking in his muscular body and watching his face succumb to pleasure as he moved. Taylor could watch his face while they had sex for hours. She loved watching him lose himself in the passion, and she loved that she was the only one who got to see him like this.

Once he had moved his hand down to her clit and began to stroke her, it was over for her. She barely lasted more than another minute before she fell apart underneath him, bucking her hips off the bed to meet him as he moved roughly, and then she felt him release. He groaned her name as his hands dug into her thighs, and once he was spent, he rolled off of her and plopped down on the bed next to her, pulling her into his arms.

She nuzzled her face into the crook of his neck, kissing his collarbone softly - he had such a beautiful collarbone - and she teasingly ran her fingers along his abs, causing him to chuckle underneath her.

"Tired already?" She panted playfully as he lay next to her, and he laughed again.

"Just a bit," he admitted, and she playfully smacked his chest.

"I believe you promised me five times," she smirked at him, and he raised an eyebrow and grinned at her.

"I did say that, didn't I?" He growled, rolling on top

of her and kissing her gently.

She kissed him back and sighed contently into his lips. "We can take a nap first if you want, though," she added, because that *had* been her original intention before she fell to his charms.

Despite how riled up they seemed to get each other, they weren't teenagers anymore, and now that he'd just given her heart and body a good workout, the exhaustion was weighing on her heavily, and she could tell he was getting tired too.

He nodded slowly against her and sat up, pushing himself back on the bed so he could slide the covers off from underneath them. He got into bed and she followed him, crawling under the plush white blankets. She curled up next to him, sighing contently into his shoulder and falling into a familiar position next to him.

"Should we set an alarm for dinner?" He grumbled into her hair, already sounding half asleep, and she shook her head.

"Nah, let's pass out and wake up when we're hungry," she suggested. She was on vacation mode now. She didn't need to set an alarm or adhere to a schedule, and he nodded before kissing the top of her head.

"Sounds perfect," he whispered, and when she looked up at him, he already had his eyes closed, his perfect mouth open just the slightest bit as he started to drift off to sleep.

Taylor smiled to herself and rested her head on his chest again, her own fatigue started to overtake her as she fell asleep listening to the rhythm of his heart.

CHAPTER SIX

DEAN

One Year Ago

Dean had that familiar feeling of nervousness that he always got when he was at a job interview. Doing the modeling gigs to get extra money had really screwed with his self-esteem. He knew he was a good-looking guy with a chiseled body, but when you are in a room with fifty other guys who *also* have great bodies, it takes a toll on you.

He didn't live at the gym and obsess about his macros and protein like those guys did. Now, he couldn't help but feel like he was being judged every time he walked into a room based purely on his looks. It was why he had started wearing his glasses again as of late. Like it would maybe take him down a peg or two in the looks department and people would judge him for his mind instead of his looks, which he knew was stupid, but he did it anyway. Who did he think he was, Clark Kent?!

He had a good feeling about this job, though. He liked Taylor Mullins. As soon as he'd gotten the call for the interview, he'd been a good little boy and done all his research on her. He read about her book series, *The Jill Augustin Mysteries,* and had even ordered a copy of the book so he could read it.

It didn't exactly sound like something he'd usually go for, especially since he'd read online that there was a bit of smut in some of the later chapters, but he ended up devouring the whole thing in two days.

A small part of him wondered if he'd get to read her second book before it made its way to the shelves, which would be a fun job perk. He'd have to make sure he still had time to read and hang out with his friends now that he was, hopefully, about to be a personal assistant to a famous author. Hopefully, she wouldn't overwork him.

He had the feeling she wasn't like that, though. He'd expected her to be a bit more...*cold* towards him. Professional to a T. That was the vibe he got from her in all the interviews he'd watched of her on talk shows and news stories that had brought her on to talk about her book.

Yes, she was poised and charming and threw a joke into the conversation at all the right times, but he felt like it *had* to be an act. Someone who was as smart as she was couldn't also be insanely beautiful, charming, *and* witty at the same time, right?

Dean knew that she had gone to school at USC, been in a sorority, and graduated with a double degree in history and creative writing, and had worked at a museum as a tour guide for a bit - ok, for longer than a bit, almost ten years - before her book was finally published. He knew that her titular character Jill had been growing in her mind since the 10th grade, and it was obvious when she spoke that she viewed the woman as an actual person and one of her closest friends.

She was everything you'd expect a writer to be.

Yet when he met her in person, she was just as charming and graceful, and kind of hilarious. He'd never laughed so much in an interview before. She asked him a bit about the modeling, but mostly she wanted to know what he would do if he was her assistant. How would he put his communications degree to good use for her? She made it clear she wasn't looking for someone to get her coffee each morning. In fact, she didn't even make a joke about how he had the word 'coffee' in his name, which he'd heard more than enough times when he told his friends he'd interviewed for an assistant job. Never mind the fact that his name wasn't even pronounced like that!

It was clear that she wanted someone who would be willing to work close with her and guide her through this crazy world. It seemed like it was new territory for her, but she wasn't letting anyone in on that fact. There was a wall there for sure, a carefully planned persona that she was putting out in the world, and he got the distinct impression she wanted to be able to drop that wall around her assistant.

After one meeting with her, Dean was determined to be that person. He wanted to know the real Taylor Mullins behind the wall. He was downright *eager* to break it down.

The fact that she was stunningly gorgeous wasn't bad either. Not that that made a real difference to him. She'd be his boss and it would be highly unprofessional to think of her that way! He wasn't some horny teenager, he could push aside any lustful feelings he had for her easily, he was sure of it. His intense attraction to her had to be due to the fact that he hadn't had a serious girlfriend in almost two years, and the last girl he'd dated had been over a month ago now.

He was simply starved for intimacy, that was all.

She didn't have an actual *office* per-say, but her agent, Caroline, had agreed to let her use a conference room at her literary agency to host interviews. He reached into his pocket and pulled out the small bottle of hand sanitizer he always had on him and reapplied, mostly to give his hands something to do, but also because he couldn't remember if he'd done so after taking the elevator or not. A moment later, Taylor appeared in the doorway and grinned at him, calling him inside, and once again the nerves started up.

"So, I'm going to be blunt Dean," she began as she sat down across the table from him, and Dean suddenly felt his heart rate skyrocket. He'd been nervous, but to hear the interview opened up with *that?* Shit, this wasn't a great start.

"Not a single person I interviewed holds a candle to you. You're the only one with qualifications, and also the only one I can actually hold a conversation with," she told him. Dean blinked and then let out a sigh of relief, chuckling a little as he relaxed in his swivel chair.

"Wow, uh, thank you, I was…I gotta be honest, you had me nervous," he admitted, and she laughed, biting her lip and pushing her hair over her shoulder. His eyes flickered to her mouth, suddenly wishing *he* were biting her lip before he shoved that thought *far* away and refocused on the interview.

"Damn, yeah, I kind of came in hot with that intro, didn't I?" She laughed, and he felt himself easing into the conversation, his momentary lapse in judgment when he'd daydreamed about biting her lip completely forgotten. If this interview was going the way he *thought* it was going to go, he now had a very *very* good feeling about all of this.

"So, what I'm getting at is - the position is yours, if

you want it," she offered with a kind smile, and Dean found himself beaming. He didn't want to seem too overeager but he *did* want the job. Badly.

True, he'd applied first to make sure he could get his foot in the door when it came to the administrative side of communications, and to earn a steady paycheck now that the modeling gigs had dried up after the pandemic. But after meeting Taylor and reading about her work, he was actually convinced this would be a good fit.

Which still had nothing to do with her killer looks! Nothing!

"I've already told you what you'll do on a day-to-day basis," she continued, waving her hand nonchalantly as she spoke. It was true - at the first interview, she'd told him about some of the things she had in mind for him to do, but his duties would change from day to day.

The crux of the job was essentially to be her helper. Plan out her meetings, her phone calls, and let her loosen up so she could focus on her real work - writing. "Basically, we'll meet up most days at my condo and work out of there, but if it's a slow day and I don't have much scheduled, you can hang out at home and work from there. If I have an interview or something I expect you to tag along but other than that...well, I've never done this before," she added with a small laugh.

"Well, whatever you need from me, consider it done," he told her, pushing his glasses up the bridge of his nose, and she smiled at him.

"So that means you accept the position?" She asked, and he nodded, trying not to seem too excited in his acceptance. She grinned and clapped her hands excitedly.

"Well, great! That's awesome! Caroline said she'd

help me draw up some sort of employment agreement…thing to have you sign, so we can officially have you start with me next week sometime, once all the tax shit and legalities are taken care of," she explained. He simply nodded, knowing that whatever she told him he had to do, he would simply be along for the ride. Since he wasn't familiar enough with the American tax system, he was more than happy to let her handle it all.

"That sounds fantastic. Thank you so much, Ms. Mullins," he began, and she quickly held up a manicured hand to stop him.

"First off - it's Taylor. Absolutely *no* Ms. Mullins, got it?" She asked, raising a brow, and he nodded with a smile. "Unless you're talking about me to other people, I suppose. Also…I only have one ask of you, Dean. On a personal level," she told him, biting her lip again. Dean realized that he was about to see some of that wall come down, and he was eager to get a glimpse behind it. He nodded, showing he was listening, and definitely *not* staring at her bottom lip that she currently held between her teeth…

"Don't ever lie to me, ok? This world…it fucking sucks sometimes, and I'm moving into uncharted territory and I simply don't have time or patience for bullshit," she explained. He nodded, appreciating her candor. He had to agree that all the bullshit, as she so delicately put it, was grating and something he had no interest in either.

"I want to know I have at least *one* person in my corner who isn't going to fuck around with me. If I ask you to read something I wrote and it sucks, tell me. If I'm making a colossal mistake, step up and say something. I might not listen," she added with a small smirk, "but if it blows up in my face, at least I know someone tried to stop me."

Dean understood exactly what she was asking of him. He nodded in agreement, even though he still felt like she was putting on a bit more a confident front for him than she was letting on. "Taylor...I promise you, I will never lie to you. I'll have your back. It's what I'm here for."

She smiled, a slight blush creeping over her cheeks before looking down at the papers in front of him, which he assumed was his resume. "You know, your resume is impressive - especially compared to the garbage I had to go through with all the other resumes - but that's not why I'm hiring you," she told him.

Dean paused for a moment, worried that she might tell him that she just hired him for his pretty boy looks. Damnit! He should have known - Ricky, his old roommate, had been *convinced* she just wanted to sleep with him when Dean had told him he got called back for a second interview. It was his greatest fear and for a second, he wondered if that might be coming to life.

"I hired you because I know you mean it when you say you won't lie," she informed him, the corner of her mouth curving up into a small smile. "I didn't need to ask you that to know...don't ask me how, but I just do...and that's my only real ask of you. Everything else is just...administrative bullshit," she chuckled, and he found himself laughing along with her.

"Well, thank you again...Taylor. I'm looking forward to being your assistant," he told her, and he found as he spoke, he truly did mean it. They both stood up and she held out her hand, which he took without hesitation, gripping it firmly and giving her a shake.

Damn, she had really soft, dainty hands.

She smiled back at him, and this time when she smiled, it was different, and Dean had a feeling he was seeing her *really* smile for the first time. "I'm looking forward to it too."

CHAPTER SEVEN

DEAN

Taylor slid the little container of hand sanitizer across the table for him and, without much thought, he picked up and squirted some in his hands. The usual pre-meal routine whenever they were out...whenever Dean used a public restroom...and whenever he had to touch a stranger's hand. She never used it herself, but she always had one in her purse for him. He hadn't even asked her to do it, she just did. She was thoughtful like that.

"To our first night in paradise?" She suggested with a grin as she held up her water glass. He laughed and nodded, clinking her glass with his.

"Always a toast with you," he teased and she shrugged.

"I like celebrating things!"

He was just about to agree that they had a lot to celebrate when the manager of the hotel, Maria, popped up next to them.

"Hola! How are you two settling in?" She asked with

a friendly smile. Taylor blushed and he knew she was recalling the incident from earlier, and Dean flashed the woman a grin.

"Fantastic, thank you. Everything has been just lovely so far," he assured her. He didn't want this woman thinking they were going to be expecting a ton of freebies after their little run-in at the front desk. She was probably only checking in to make sure she didn't have to do any more damage control.

"We wanted to bring this over to you. It's the couple's menu, there are a few things on there that the regular menu doesn't have. Especially for dessert," she explained, handing them each a menu that was decorated with pink and red paper hearts. Dean blinked up at the woman and looked at Taylor, who tensed.

Oh no, he hadn't been expecting *that*.

Poor Maria could not stop putting her foot in her mouth and she didn't even realize it.

He gulped and felt his face blushing, staring down at the ludicrously decorated menu. "Oh, that's very...thank you Maria, but we're not..." he began, fumbling over his words as he tried to spit the words out, which were some reason evading him.

"We're not a couple," Taylor clarified, her face just as red as his as she pointed back and forth between them, as if to emphasize her point. This time it was Maria who gawked at them and turned pale.

"Oh! Perdon! I am...I just assumed, after you didn't want to get a separate room..."

Dean couldn't help but feel like they'd ruined this woman's entire day. Possibly her week.

Taylor shook her head quickly. "No no, *I'm* the one who's sorry, you've been nothing but nice to us since we got here."

"And it's an easy mistake to make," Dean assured her. It was true - they got mistaken for a couple all the time. Even before they'd started sleeping together. He wasn't sure why he was so flustered by it *this* particular time, although for some reason he didn't think the menu with the paper hearts had helped matters at all. It was probably just because poor Maria had already been on the receiving end of them having to correct her once today. He felt awful about having to do it again.

Maria blushed and Taylor reached into her bag and pulled at a hundred-dollar bill. "Please, take this tip, Maria. As an apology for earlier, and a thank you for being so generous to us."

Dean smiled a little at the kind gesture. Yes, it could be argued that Taylor was tipping her to try and buy back her affection since the thought of anyone not liking her sent her anxiety skyrocketing. Yet he also knew she genuinely felt bad for snapping at her earlier. He had seen her get eaten up like that before when she was having a bad day and was less than nice to someone.

Taylor was never one to demand to speak to a manager, but she could get snippy, and then she often spent the next two or three hours obsessing over it and feeling mortified by her behavior.

"Oh, Miss, I can't..." Maria insisted, but Taylor shook her head, pushing the money towards her.

"Please Maria, you deserve it. You really do," she told her, and after a moment of hesitation, the manager took the tip with a smile. "You've been very kind to us, and I'm afraid I didn't return the favor this afternoon."

"Thank you so much, Ms. Mullins," she muttered, blushing as she looked down at the money in her hand. "If you need anything at all while you're here..."

"We'll be sure to ask for you personally," she assured Maria with a smile, and the manager thanked her again before clearing her throat and hurrying off to check on the next table, taking the menus with her.

Taylor sighed and leaned back in her chair with a groan once the woman was out of earshot. She ran her hands over her face as she stared up at the darkening night sky dramatically. Dean tried not to laugh, but the whole situation with Maria was a *little* funny now that the moment had passed. It wasn't a big deal and no one else on Earth would take it as seriously as Taylor did. In fact, Maria would probably forget about it by the time they checked out next week.

"She is going to personally hand deliver us breakfast in bed every day that we're here now, I would be willing to bet good money on that," he teased her. She laughed and rolled her eyes, glancing at him with the smallest of smiles.

"She hates me."

"I think she's positively your biggest fan, now."

"You make it sound like I bought her off."

"You *kind of* did," he pointed out, unable to stop a small giggle from escaping his lips.

"She deserves a generous tip! I'll leave her another one too before we leave," she added, and Dean knew without a doubt that even if there hadn't been a mix-up with her earlier, she would have left Maria and everyone else at the resort a big fat tip before they left. She always did. She was also very adamant about leaving glowing reviews for places online.

"So, back to that *relaxation* thing I was talking about..." he reminded her, and she sighed heavily and smirked at him, taking a sip of her water.

"Dean..."

"I'm just saying...you get anxious after you've accomplished something big," he pointed out. She paused and he could tell she was surprised that he picked up on that. Dean wasn't sure why she was so surprised. It was his job to do that, after all. It was his job to know her.

"After you finish a project you always get stressed for a day or two afterwards. Like you can't figure out what to do with that pent-up energy. You need a break, big time, and I'm going to make sure you take it," he told her with a small smile.

She blushed and played with the straw in her water before looking back at him, batting her eyelashes slightly.

"Are you sure you're just my assistant? I feel like at this point, you're kind of more like my life manager," she joked, and he felt himself chuckling at that. Life manager was a title he kind of liked, to be very honest. Especially being the life manager to Taylor. He shrugged, leaning back and crossing his arms as he stared out at the ocean view from the balcony of the dining room.

"Life Manager Dean Coffey does have a nice ring to it," he replied, and she grinned.

"I feel like you're the only one looking out for my well-being sometimes, including myself...so yeah. Maybe that's your new title," she said softly. It had started out as a joke, but as he looked at her now, he could tell she was being genuine in her sentiments towards him.

He was very tempted to take out his phone and take a picture of her right now. She was blushing slightly, looking out at the ocean with him as she avoided his gaze. She was lost in her thoughts, a small smile on her face from their conversation, and with the sun setting behind her and her blonde hair blowing softly in the wind - *wow.* He was taken aback by how beautiful she looked.

So he did. He took his phone and snapped a quick pic, and she giggled when she realized what he'd done. She turned even redder as he texted her the picture, pausing to favorite it in his albums so he could find it later.

"Well, it's my job to look out for you. But…I'd do it for free any day of the week," he joked with her.

She playfully pouted and sighed heavily.

"I promise I'll relax on this trip. Cross my heart."

"Good, because I'm going to make you," he insisted. Feeling bold, he surveyed the restaurant, making sure no eyes were on them - especially Maria - before he playfully ran his foot down her calf under the table. She laughed, trying to keep her face neutral.

"Behave!" She warned him as he beamed at her. He couldn't help it. Something about this trip was turning on all sorts of switches inside him. He was being reckless and he knew it. They weren't supposed to be acting this…*coupley* around each other. Not here, not at home…most of the time, not even in private.

Because they weren't a couple.

They were friends. Friends who occasionally slept together. That was it.

Yet he noticed she wasn't stopping him either.

"I still have…four more opportunities to make you relax today, if I recall our earlier conversation correctly," he reminded her, dropping his voice low and trying to sound as sexy and alluring as possible. She inhaled sharply and her cheeks flushed, and he said a silent thankful prayer that American women found British accents so attractive. She could deny it all she wanted, but he knew she turned weak in the knees when he tried to sound extra posh.

"Just four?" She asked playfully.

Oh good, she was in on this game with him. Thank *God*.

"I said that was *today*. I intend on doing far more than that this trip, believe me," he replied playfully, his gaze dropping to her lips. Shit, he needed to stop, or he was going to start getting hard right here at the dinner table.

She squirmed a little in her chair, which didn't help the situation at all, and giggled. "Who the hell is this guy, Dean Coffey?" She teased, her face turning pink as she glanced around to make sure no one was listening in on them.

"This is Vacation Dean. He's *very* randy," he joked, still keeping his voice low as he teased her.

She giggled and rolled her eyes playfully.

"Oh stop. I'm about five seconds away from throwing my water on you," she jested with him, twirling her straw again as she eyed him up from across the table.

"To cool me off?"

"No, to give us an excuse to leave the dinner table and go back to the room," she whispered.

He blinked at her, his mouth open just the slightest bit as he tried to figure out what to say in response to *that*. Apparently, he couldn't form words at the moment. That was happening a *lot* today. Finally, after a moment of his brain short-circuiting, he cleared his throat and bit his lip.

"Room service for dinner instead tonight?"

"I think that's a good idea."

"Maybe we could order hot fudge sundaes for dessert."

"An even *better* idea."

He couldn't ever remember leaving a dinner faster than they did that night.

CHAPTER EIGHT

TAYLOR

Eleven months ago

"So, tell me about yourself, Dean Coffey," Taylor said with a smile as she took a sip of her latte. She made sure to put extra emphasis on pronouncing it "Caw-Fae" as he had instructed when they first met - since that was the *appropriate* way to pronounce his insufferably posh last name.

People constantly got it wrong, and he admitted that he eventually stopped correcting them, so when he smirked at her and playfully rolled his eyes, she felt herself beaming with pride at the fact that they had an actual inside joke between the two of them now.

They were sitting in her living room, having just gotten off the phone with Caroline who was sending them the final details on book tour dates from her publisher. It wasn't for another eight months, so that gave Dean plenty of time to start booking things for them - flights, interviews, hotels, and all the other fun logistical stuff that he was in charge of.

It had been a nerve-wracking phone call, because every time she had a business phone call, she imagined the person on the other line telling her that there had been some huge mistake. Her biggest fear was that they'd suddenly decide they hated everything about Jill Augustin, and her book sales from the first novel had been a big prank all along.

Dramatic and unrealistic? Absolutely. She knew it was her anxiety talking, whispering those thoughts in her ear, but she couldn't shut it off sometimes. Of course, the phone call had been just fine, no one revealed that they hated her guts, and business proceeded as usual. As it always did. Now she was able to focus on relaxing for the rest of the day - and she decided that the way she wanted to relax was by getting to know her assistant a little bit better.

Dean just shrugged in response to her question. She rolled her eyes and shook her head as she tucked her legs under her on her couch. Trevor hopped up and settled himself next to her, resting his head on her knees. That certainly would not due. She needed actual answers, with actual words.

"No, no shrugging. Tell me about your childhood. Your family. Are you a dog or a cat person?" She asked with a grin and he laughed. She loved it when he laughed. He had such a naturally serious-looking face, but when he beamed like that, his whole face lit up.

"Dog person, definitely," he assured her, glancing at Trevor before looking back at her. He tilted his head, blinking at her, and took a sip of his own drink. "Why do you ask? Are you looking to write my biography as your next book?"

She grinned and shook her head. This was why she liked having Dean as her assistant. Other than the fact that he was great at what he did - she had had no idea how many apps existed to organize your life and social media posts until he came along - but he was funny and witty, and when they joked around she felt like she'd known him for years, not a month.

But that was exactly it - she *didn't* know all that much about him. She knew he was British, of course, and that he'd moved to Los Angeles and went to UCLA as an international student to study communications. She knew all that from his resume, though. Other than a few little nuggets of information over the past month, she realized the man that she was spending more time with than her dog was still a stranger to her.

"I just...we spend all day together, most days. I want you to feel like we can be friends," she explained, hoping that he didn't think that sounded silly. Some people had no interest in being friendly with co-workers, no matter how much time they spend together.

Thankfully, he nodded in understanding and placed his coffee on the nearby coffee table, making sure to use a coaster - which she appreciated - and looked back at her. He leaned against the couch, propping his cheek upon his hand.

"Ok. So...*friend*...if you had to choose any book to live in, which one would it be and why?" He quizzed her with a grin. She beamed back at him, thrilled that he was deciding to play along with her game. Forget the rest of the afternoon she had planned - she would be willing to bet she could sit here and talk to Dean Coffey for hours.

"Ugh, good one! That's tough," she conceded with a laugh, screwing her face up in thought as she pondered over all the amazing books she'd read over the years. "Ok, this is going to sound cheesy, and feel free to judge me all you want for it but... the *Bridgerton* series," she admitted, a soft blush creeping across her face.

He laughed and looked at her with wide eyes, which she'd expected. "Oh god, aren't those those smutty books that they made into a show on Netflix?" He asked, and she nodded, her face turning even redder.

"Come on Dean, are you *really* surprised? Don't you remember the scene from *my* book where Jill and Benedict get locked in a closet together and can't get help for hours?" She asked with a cheeky eyebrow raise. Yes, Taylor Mullins liked to read smut. What thirty-year-old woman *didn't* like to indulge in a steamy romance novel from time to time?

This time *he* blushed, which made her grin with pride, and he cleared his throat as he clearly tried to brush it off. "I try not to think about the fact that something so *filthy* came out of your brain," he teased, and she took her pillow and threw it at him. He laughed and caught it with ease, taking it in his arms and hugging it to his chest.

"Ok, ok, so why *Bridgerton*?" He asked, continuing his line of questioning as he peered at her from over the pillow.

She shrugged. "I guess it has everything I'd want to just live a comfortable life. Money, pretty dresses, never wanting for anything - and of course a loving husband with a smoking hot bod who wants to have sex with his wife constantly," she reminded him with a smile. Ignore the fact that women couldn't hold jobs or vote in Regency London. In her fantasy land, none of that would matter.

"Is that why you named your love interest Benedict? After the character?" He asked curiously. She opened her mouth and was about to answer and say yes, she *had* named her Benedict after the character from the popular series, when she paused and raised an eyebrow.

"Wait, how did you know that was a character in the books?" She asked him.

His face started to flush and she had to stop herself from cackling with glee. Oh, this was perfect! He was never going to live this down.

"I didn't," he insisted. Taylor smirked at him and began to giggle, watching him struggle to hold back laughter, causing him to snort a little in the end.

"You've watched the show!" She laughed, pointing at him accusatorially, and he shook his head insistently.

"No no no! I've...read the books actually," he admitted, and her mouth fell open in shock. "Only some of them! My sister Vicky had one last time I visited her flat and I was intrigued so..."

"You read *smut*, Dean Coffey!?" She exclaimed. This conversation was turning out wonderfully. She never would have imagined learning all *this* about him when she started her ridiculous line of questioning. He blushed again and this time, *he* was throwing the pillow at her.

"It was one time!" He confessed, but he was laughing playfully now, and she realized just how much she loved his laugh as she cackled in delight, holding out her arms to shield herself from the pillow onslaught.

After they finished their little pillow fight - which Trevor abandoned, obviously deciding it was safer on the floor in his kennel - she grabbed her coffee again and crossed her legs, smirking over at him. She wasn't sure what info she'd get out of him that was better than *'reads steamy regency-era romance novels'* but she would take what she could get.

She hated that her face was heating up as she thought about the fact that Dean read romance novels. Actually, now that she thought about it, it was kind of embarrassing to know that he'd read *her* romance scenes in her books. She hadn't left out many details in Jill and Benedict's steamy affair - a lot of people seemed to agree it was her best writing - but knowing *he* read it? The thought suddenly mortified her for some reason and she tried to will away the blush creeping along her face.

"OK, my turn to ask you a question…why did you move here? Why not go to school in London?" She asked, changing the conversation. Dean seemed grateful for the change of subject. He nodded thoughtfully as he sipped his drink before setting it aside and sighing.

"Well, I dunno…L.A. has always fascinated me. The entertainment industry - movies, music, books, art, it just - has always brought me so much joy. Music, movies, reading, all of it has gotten me through hard times. It sounds silly, but I always wondered what goes on behind the scenes. I researched directing, production, sound editing, all that stuff, and I just knew I wanted to be involved in it *somehow*. I'm not an actor by any means, or a singer, so working behind the scenes, managing things to make all the pieces come together, it seemed like the best option. I don't have to put myself out there in front of a camera or in a recording student. Yet I can still have a hand in creating it."

"I wanted to be part of that magic, part of building that world so people can continue to enjoy art even if the world is falling to shit around them," he explained. He paused after that and looked at his coffee, smiling softly to himself as if reflecting on his journey to get to this point, and Taylor ate up every word he'd said.

She listened intently, a strange feeling erupting in her chest. That was so...*poetic.* She could certainly relate to the bit about art helping her through hard times, except for her, it was books. Her love of reading had taken a natural turn into a love of writing, and to this day, when things became too much, she usually ended up turning it into a story somehow.

Jill Augustin had always been her favorite, but she had whole file folders on her computer of unfinished first drafts. Most only chapter or two long...but still, it was a seed to be planted into something bigger someday. Sometimes, Taylor daydreamed about all the books she could write with those little snippets she'd written on her bad days. She tried not to think about that, though, because it was easier to focus on Jill.

If she thought about her unfinished novels, she'd start to think about the fact that she probably would never be able to finish them all, and her fear of running out of time to be great would start creeping to the surface again.

"Also, have you ever been to England? The weather sucks. It's *much* nicer here," Dean joked, yanking her from her thoughts and back into the conversation.

"I actually have *not* been to England but I'd love to go," she informed him with a smile. He beamed at her.

"Really? Well, I'll take you sometime. Show you all the sights!" He said, and she had a feeling that he was genuine in that offer.

"Yeah? You'll take me everywhere? Westminster Abbey? The Tower of London?"

"I'll even go in that stupid London Eye thing for you too," he promised her, and she chuckled and grinned back at him.

"Well start planning an amazing trip to England,

Dean Coffey, because I'm holding you to that," she replied with a smirk. "Actually...in all seriousness...Caroline *did* just say they want me to do some stops in Europe for the book tour. I would imagine England would be one, considering the book takes place there."

"That's right! The book takes place there, yet you haven't been there. I can't believe it. You're a fraud, Taylor Mullins!" He joked, and she snorted and took the pillow, throwing it at him again, which he once again caught like they were playing a game of catch.

"Where else would you want to go in Europe, if you got the chance?" He asked.

"Planning our itinerary?" She responded, raising an eyebrow questioningly.

"Possibly," he smirked.

"Hmm, well...England, France, Germany, and Sweden I suppose. Or Denmark. Depends how many stops we're allowed and how much time we have," she pointed out. He nodded, a thoughtful look on his face.

"Ok...got it. Committing it to memory right now," he assured her with a smile.

Taylor blushed a little at that statement because she knew for a fact he wasn't joking and probably *was* really committing that to memory. Was Dean really *that* dedicated to being her assistant? Or was he simply a good person?

"Ok...what are your parents names?" She asked, continuing their little game, only to realize a moment later that that might be too personal a question. Taylor tended to be a bit too open once she became comfortable around someone and she often forgot other people might not feel as open on their end.

He didn't seem phased though. "Emerson and Florence," he told her with a smile. "You?"

"Maggie and Erik, but we don't talk about Maggie," she added quickly. When he gave her a confused look, she shrugged. "She left when I was three. Haven't heard from her since," she explained. Which was sort of shocking to her now that everyone knew her name. She'd thought that the woman might reach out looking to try and cash in on her newfound fame, but nothing. She was grateful for it, though. It saved her the awkwardness of having to deal with that trauma.

Taylor had to admit that it stung to know that even with her success, the woman who gave birth to her seemed to want nothing to do with her life.

Dean's eyes widened and he looked horrified he'd even asked, even though *she* had been the one to pose the question first. "Shit, I'm sorry."

She shrugged again. "It's fine," she insisted. No, it wasn't, but at the same time...it was because she'd accepted it. It was just one of those facts of her life.

"Any siblings?" She countered, and he nodded.

"A little sister, Vicky. You?"

"No, but I do have thousands of sorority sisters across the country," she reminded him with a grin, and he laughed and rolled his eyes.

"I am never going to understand this Greek life tradition you lot seem to have here in America," he admitted as he looked down and started to play with the corner of the pillow.

"No frats at UCLA tried to recruit you?" She asked, raising an eyebrow. He had the frat boy look down pat, and she knew from experience that frat boys were notorious for trying to recruit any guy that they sensed could party on their level.

"Oh, they tried, I just refused," he retorted with a cheeky grin. "I was hazed enough on the rugby team in school, I did *not* need to go through all that again."

They volleyed back and forth like this for about an hour, learning random facts about each other. He told her all about rugby, she told him about her swim team. Then she learned that he had been on the swim team too, but almost got held back a year due to his grades. They talked about their former roommates - he still hung out with Ricky regularly, and she obviously still kept in touch with Betsy and Penelope. She quite liked spending the afternoon like this, just making conversation, but as the day wore on, she felt herself getting antsy again, especially as a new idea popped into her head for her final book. She got that overwhelming urge to run to her laptop and jot it down before she forgot, like she always did whenever something just *came* to her.

She really needed to start utilizing the notes app on her phone more often.

"Hey Dean?" She piped up as he announced he was leaving for the day, grabbing his keys and wallet off the coffee table as he paused to look at her.

"Yeah?" He asked, looking at her like he expected her to ask for something last minute before he left.

She smiled at him and tucked her legs under her as she settled into the couch with her MacBook. "Thanks for doing this with me. Just...hanging out I mean."

He smiled and chuckled a little. "Of course, Tay. You're kind of cool to hang around. And I'm not just saying that to get a raise," he added with a wink.

Taylor felt unfamiliar butterflies erupt in her stomach

when he did that, but she quickly squashed them and rolled her eyes. "Good, because it's not working," she retorted, and he laughed again and shoved his wallet in his back pocket.

"Night, Tay," he told her before giving her a small wave, and after she watched the spot where he'd stood, where the closed door now remained, she shook her head, trying to get rid of her muddled thoughts as she returned to her work.

* * * *

After that, Taylor learned a lot more about Dean. She wasn't necessarily *trying* to learn all his little idiosyncrasies, but she found herself studying him almost as if she had an upcoming quiz on all things Dean Coffey.

For one, she learned that when he got nervous, he always picked at the skin on his thumb. Just the one on his right hand. Whenever she noticed him doing that, she tried to grab his hand and squeeze it, letting him know know he didn't need to worry.

He was also a germaphobe, even though he didn't come outright and say it, but she saw how he was always using hand sanitizer, and he told her that he panicked if he wasn't able to shower every day. He tried to play it off like he was being dramatic but she had a feeling there was an element of truth there. As an anxiety sufferer herself, she saw the signs. Regardless, that showed that he took care of himself and took his health seriously, and she appreciated that.

She learned that his favorite movie was *Lord of the Rings,* and he could recite the whole thing by memory, but he'd never actually read the books despite being a generally well-read person. She teased him mercilessly about it for a whole week after she learned that, and then got him the box set for Christmas.

He loved to communicate in text messages with gifs, which was so corny it almost made her gag. Although she liked to overuse emojis, so maybe it evened out. She hated to admit that she would get as giddy as a schoolgirl sometimes when he'd text her late at night about something stupid - usually whatever Food Network show he was watching - and they'd end up having whole conversations, gifs vs. emojis, back and forth into the early morning hours.

And he didn't have to say it, but she knew that he was getting to know her more too.

He learned quickly that her favorite types of pens were the felt-tipped ones with the caps. Preferably in bright colors. She often hurriedly removed the cap from her pen with her teeth, keeping it in her mouth as she hastily scribbled down any passing thought before she forget it, especially if her computer wasn't nearby. So, every once in a while, she'd come home and find a new package of them sitting on her kitchen counter.

One time, when she had been on the verge of a panic attack about a nasty review she read online, Dean hadn't said anything, he'd quietly gone over to the DVD player, popped in a disc, and started her favorite movie - *Clueless* - and sat down on the opposite end of the couch from her after gently taking her phone from her. Not a single word was uttered, but before she knew it, she was relaxed, cuddled under the blanket as her panic attack slowly subsided. She took note of how he pointedly tried to avoid looking at her from the other end of the couch, but she knew he kept glancing at her, making sure she was ok.

She hadn't been able to sleep that night. Not because of the panic attack, but because of the thought that someone knew her so well, that he knew what to do to calm her down without even asking - it was terrifying and exhilarating and it made her heart race in a way she'd never experienced before. She knew she had mentioned her love for the movie in passing, and how it always calmed her down. It made her heart race to think that someone was actually listening and taking note of those things.

And when they threw her a surprise birthday party, with Caroline and Betsy and Penelope and some of their friends, she knew it had been his idea to make it *The Great Gatsby* themed. He didn't have to say it, and she knew Caroline would happily take all the credit, but she knew it was him. Who else spent so much time with her that he would have inevitably noticed the poster of the cover she had hanging in her office, or the fact that she had not one, but *five* different copies of the book scattered in various parts of her house?

Dean Coffey was an incredible human being, and by some miracle, he was becoming her best friend. What had she done to be so lucky?

CHAPTER NINE

TAYLOR

"Wake up, Tay!"

Taylor had slept in her own bed the evening before, even though they'd both stayed up late into the evening clawing at each other on various surfaces of their suite. She was a night owl, though, and did some of her best writing in the evening and she didn't want to keep him up with her typing.

After their shower together - to get the lingering hot fudge off of their sticky bodies - Dean had retired for the evening on his side of the suite and she worked until 1 AM on the ideas she had circulating her brain for the final novel. Now she was being *rudely* awakened by her assistant as he jumped on the bed next to her like an over-excited golden retriever.

"What time is it?" She grumbled as she tugged the comforter over her head.

"10 AM, I let you sleep in a little," he told her, and she groaned. Their definitions of *sleeping in* were very different. "Come on, put your swimsuit on, we have to go in the ocean!"

She raised an eyebrow and peeked at him from under her duvet. "We *have* to? What, is it going somewhere?" Dean responded by playfully throwing one of the decorative pillows at her head.

"No - I went on a walk this morning and learned more about the hotel. They've got these flags out on the beach that let you know how strong the waves are. Green means the wind is tame so the waves won't be too bad, yellow is not so great and then red is obviously 'don't go swimming' but I'm sure people do anyways...and there are green flags all along the shore. So let's go!" He playfully yanked the covers away from her and she tried to roll away, and he dove and grabbed her arm to pull her up to sitting as she finally gave in and chuckled a little.

"Why are you so excited?" She asked with a small smirk, and he blushed a little.

"I've never been swimming in the ocean before," he admitted with a small shrug. She tilted her head at him in confusion as he pulled away from her.

"Don't you have beaches in England?" She asked, and he snorted playfully.

"Those don't count. It's cold and gross most of the time and you can't see down to the bottom like you can here. So come on! Chop chop!" He teased her, clapping his hands at her as she sighed heavily and ran a hand through her messy bed head of hair.

"How long have you been up?" She asked as she headed to her dresser, digging through the various swimsuits she'd brought and trying to figure out which one she wanted to wear that day. It was only their second day there, and she still had so many to debut!

Each one had been picked specifically based on

whether or not she thought Dean would like the pattern. It was a difficult decision.

"Only since 8. I went down to the hotel coffee bar and got you a coffee and bagel, by the way. They make an absolutely fantastic Americano, too, in case you were wondering," he added, heading into the other room and returning a moment later with an iced coffee and bagel for her, and sipping from a nearly empty cup of espresso himself.

"Ah. That explains a few things," she teased, and he playfully grabbed her flip-flops, throwing them at her with a grin.

"Come on, before the flags change colors!"

Taylor groaned again playfully as she took a bite of her bagel and finally decided on a swimsuit, a black and gold floral string bikini. She took note of the fact that Dean was already wearing his swim trunks, and she allowed herself to admire his backside as he walked away from her.

"Enough checking me out, I'm here as more than just eye candy, you know," Dean teased her, as if he knew exactly what she was doing even though he wasn't facing her, and Taylor laughed before changing into her swimsuit. After she'd dressed, she grabbed a white mesh cover up and hastily pulled it over her before she followed him into their shared kitchen and wrapped her arms around him from behind as he looked over a brochure for parasailing.

"That is true. You're here as eye candy *and* to make sure I relax," she reminded him, and she could feel him chuckling against her. His hands lightly rested over her arms, his fingertips grazing against her skin. She could feel goosebumps rising as he touched her, and even though she was sore from yesterday's activities, she felt the familiar ache growing between her legs.

"And to admire you in bikinis. That is also a very

important duty of mine," he joked, and she giggled into his shirt, burying her face in the soft cotton fabric.

He smelled nice. Dean *always* smelled nice, but she rarely got the chance to bury her face in the essence of him like she was now. She knew it was a Ralph Lauren scent that he liked and she'd already bought a new bottle for him for Christmas - which was months away. She'd been tempted to open it and spray it on something, *anything* in her house so she could smell him all the time, but came to her sense before she'd ripped open the packaging.

His hands continued to lightly run along her arms, and she wasn't sure how long they stayed there in that position. It had to have been only a minute or two, but she felt like it was an eternity. An eternity that would eventually have to come to an end when they walked out of their room and faced the real world once again.

"This is nice," Dean whispered, and she nodded against his back.

"It is," she whispered in agreement. He took one of her hands and gently brought it to his lips, kissing her knuckles softly before peeling her arms from him so he could turn to face her.

"Oh my...*this* is even nicer," he teased, his eyes growing wide as he took in the sight of her wearing her bikini and see-through cover up. She smirked and bent her leg slightly, putting her hand on her hip in a pose.

"This old thing?" She joked, and he beamed at her, greedily taking in the view in front of him. "I thought you were eager to get in the ocean?" She reminded him, and he shook his head.

"Well, that was before this far more pressing matter came to my attention," he told her.

Smirking with satisfaction, Taylor put her sunglasses on and grabbed her beach bag from where she had discarded it on the kitchen table. She reached over and gave his hand a playful squeeze before tossing her hair over her shoulder. "You can do your job of admiring my bathing suit and showering me with compliments once we're out in the sunlight. Then you can *really* admire it properly," she said, pointedly looking away from the obvious sign of his excitement growing in the front of his trunks. If she slipped up, she might end up taking him back to her room, and then they'd *never* make it down to the beach.

"Showering you with compliments?" He asked playfully, readjusting his trunks before grabbing his room key off the counter.

"Yes, I've just added it to your duties," she informed him with a quick cheek peek before opening the door to the hall with a grin. "Come on, before the flags change color!"

CHAPTER TEN

DEAN

"Ok, is it everything you wanted it to be and more?" Taylor teased Dean as they bobbed in the ocean.

They'd wandered out together, hand in hand under the guise of wanting to keep their balance, but his heart had been racing the whole time. He never got to hold hands with Taylor in public. It was...*thrilling*. That alone had made his first beach experience well worth it. Holding hands with her was definitely a feeling he could get used to.

They'd wandered out far enough that the water came to their shoulders, but they were able to still touch the sandy ocean floor and brace themselves for each wave as it came. He grinned and playfully splashed her.

"Even better. Because you're here in a bikini as well," he replied with a smirk. She blushed, ducking her head under the water as a wave came up behind them. He watched her bob back to the surface and smiled at her before he closed his eyes and leaned his head up to the sky, taking in the sun.

It *was* spectacular here. The salty smell of the ocean was far more relaxing than he'd ever imagined, and being here with Taylor...yeah, it really *was* better than he'd ever imagined. It amazed him how beautiful this planet was - they hardly ever got a chance to just relax and enjoy the breathtaking views of the world, they were always working and hustling and trying to make progress in their careers.

They'd done so much traveling the past few months for her book, but rarely had any time to do touristy things. He made a mental note to make sure they planned for more leisure time in the future - and not just the sexy kind of leisure time. Dean was certain it would do both of them some good to add more relaxation time into their schedules.

"I love just...being here," he muttered, and she swam up to him and playfully kissed his shoulder. He felt his heart race slightly as he felt her lips on his wet skin. They were still in public, and although they were far out into the ocean, and the chances of her being recognized were slim to none...she was being bold.

He liked it. He liked it a lot.

"I do too. Thank you for being here with me," she added, and he smiled at her.

"Anything for you," he whispered, and she chuckled and blushed. *God*, he loved it when she blushed. He reached forward and playfully kicked his leg against hers under the water.

Just as he did that, a huge wave came up behind them, taking him unprepared as he'd been focused purely on her. He gasped and didn't have time to brace himself before he was knocked over by the wave, feeling the water carry him away as he was pushed under. He rose to the surface and coughed, taking in a deep breath of air as he heard Taylor yelling for him.

"Dean! Dean, are you ok!?" She was yelling as he rubbed his eyes, trying to get the salt water out of them. Another wave hit him and he stumbled a bit, but then Taylor was there, holding onto his arm, and once he got his footing again, he burst into laughter, still sputtering and coughing a little.

"Jesus, Dean!" She laughed when she realized that he was ok, slapping his chest playfully and making the water splash around them. "I thought you were going to drown!"

"What? That wasn't sexy?" He teased back between coughs, still blinking his eyes furiously and trying to get rid of the burning sensation.

"I think your beloved flags lied to you, Dean. Maybe today is *not* the best day to be swimming in the ocean," she suggested, and he when finally was able to open his eyes for longer than a few seconds, he saw Taylor...he began to laugh hysterically all over again.

"What?!" She demanded, and he grinned at her.

"Your hair is a *disaster*," he teased her. The wave must have hit her hard too, because her ponytail had come loose, and her blonde hair was sticking out at odd angles now at the base of her neck. She reached up and felt for her hair, a small look of horror forming on her face.

"Oh shit, that's gonna suck to brush out later," she laughed as another wave made them stumble a bit, and he playfully splashed water at her.

"I think it's a good look for you. Very hot," he smirked, and she rolled her eyes playfully as she tugged the ponytail out and gave up on it entirely.

Dean glanced back at the beach and realized how far

out they were, and how there weren't many other brave tourists in the ocean around them. He swam up to her and put his hands on her waist, pulling her close to him, and she settled into his arms easily. Her arms snaked around his neck and she smiled at him. Even with her hair a mess and her eyelashes dripping with ocean water, she was the most gorgeous creature he'd ever seen.

He hated how much he loved this. It was all so... normal holding her like this. Like they were an actual...

No. He had to stop himself. Those thoughts were dangerous.

"How hard do you think it would be to have sex in the ocean?" He asked her with a teasing grin. She rolled her eyes and tightened her hold on him slightly, moving her body closer to him as the waves rocked them back and forth. His breath hitched and he tightened his grip on her.

"Based on how well you've been able to handle the waves out here, I'd say pretty difficult. For you, at least," she replied, her hand moving to his hair and lightly running her fingers on the back of his neck. Goosebumps prickled up all over his body, and it wasn't because the ocean was cold. "You seem extra horny this trip," she added with a chuckle, and he blushed. He had to admit, even he had noticed how he seemed extra turned out since they'd gotten to the resort.

"I can't help it. I'm in a tropical paradise with my favorite person," he whispered. She blushed and bit her lip, and he tucked a piece of her wild blonde hair behind her ear. "She happens to be sexy as hell too, so maybe I *am* a little incorrigible right now," he added with a smile.

Taylor let out a content sigh and rested her head on his shoulder. He pulled her close, cradling her as they swayed gently with the waves. He closed his eyes, trying to memorize the feel of her curves under his hands.

"I sometimes wish we could just...be normal people again," she admitted softly, her voice barely more than a whisper over the sound of the rushing water.

Dean squeezed her and kissed her cheek, running his arms softly over her lower back. He thought that too - he thought that all the time. Yet he couldn't let her know that he wanted that too. He had tried to bring up the subject once, asking what would happen if the world knew about them - and she had promptly shut him down. Because she viewed him as a friend with benefits, nothing more, and he just had to accept that.

He pulled back to look at her, studying her for a moment before he cleared his throat and smiled playfully at her.

"I *am* a normal person, so speak for yourself," he teased, and she chuckled before burying her face in his shoulder again.

"You're seriously such a nerd sometimes," she grumbled, and he pretended to act shocked and grabbed his heart as if she'd stabbed him.

"You wound me, my dear!" He responded and she laughed and gave him a light kiss on the lips. She pulled away and ran her hand through his hair again, and he bit his lip. God, she was gorgeous. Her bright blonde hair gleamed in the sunlight, and her freckles were starting to pop on her face the longer she was out in the sun. The softest blush appeared on her cheeks as she watched him study her, turning bashful, and he leaned forward and kissed her gently before giving her a playful squeeze.

"I have an idea. A much, um...*safer* idea," he told her with a wicked grin, and she smirked back at him.

"I'm listening."

CHAPTER ELEVEN

TAYLOR

They couldn't stop giggling as they ran into the nearby supply hut. She was positive no one had seen them, as only hotel employees came around this area, but Dean was obviously thinking ahead. He grabbed a nearby broom and slid it through the door handle, locking it from the inside so they could have privacy. Her heart was practically beating out of her chest. This was by far one of the riskiest things they had ever done.

"What has gotten into you?" She giggled as he approached her and pulled her close, kissing her deeply and cupping her face with his hands. He pushed her against the wall of the hut, nearly tripping over a fishing net that was lying across the floor.

Taylor caught him and they both burst into laughter. She helped him steady himself and ran her fingers along his chest playfully, watching him suck in a breath as she did so. His perfect abdominal muscles flexed as he looked down at her hand like it was burning his skin.

"This might be dangerous," she pointed out with a grin, gesturing to the fish net on the ground that had almost just taken him out. He smirked down at her and kissed her again, taking her leg and hooking it around his thigh. She instantly wrapped her leg tighter around him, pulling herself as close to his body as possible.

"Good, that's what makes it fun," he muttered into her lips. She groaned softly and he propped her up against the wall again.

"If you break an ankle, don't blame me," she teased him, and he smacked her butt playfully, causing her to laugh loudly. Shit, she had to be careful. They'd get caught if she was too loud - but the thought of that was making her body hum with desire in a way she hadn't experienced before. She should be running far in the other direction right now, not taking this chance with him...yet the idea of being risky and possibly being discovered was keeping her tethered to him.

"It'll be worth it," he assured her before kissing her harder. She felt her breath leave her body as he kissed her like his life depended on it. Dean always made her feel so wanted. She pressed herself against him, reveling in the feel of his wet skin on hers. Her hands ran down his chest, her fingertips lightly grazing the soft blond hair curling over his pectoral muscles as he groaned softly into her lips.

They made out for a few moments, their hands running up and down their damp, sandy bodies before she managed to shove his swim trunks down and he peeled her bikini off of her. He tasted salty from the ocean, and his hair was still damp as she ran her hands through it, tugging slightly.

Dean pressed her against the wall of the shack, lifting her and holding her up by her thighs, while using the wall for leverage. She opened her legs wide and gasped softly as he positioned himself, pressing lightly against her with a soft whimper.

He had just been about to slide into her when they heard someone trying to get into the hut.

They both paused, eyes wide as they stared at each other, holding their breaths. The door rattled and thankfully the broom they had used to keep the door closed was staying put. Taylor could hear a man calling out to someone in Spanish, and then tugging at the door again. She bit her lip to stop herself from giggling, and Dean looked like he was about to burst out in laughter as well, his forehead pressed against hers as he gripped her thighs tightly.

Thank God Dean was a man who could laugh at the absurdity of this situation, and he wasn't panicking. It would be *so* easy for them to freak out right now. If they got caught, they would be packing their bags and finding a new hotel within the hour, and she doubted Maria would come to their aid on this one.

"Shush!" Dean hissed, a small snort of laughter escaping from him as she buried her face in his neck. The co-worker called out to someone again, but suddenly she had a deliciously wicked idea. She probably shouldn't do it, but she couldn't help herself. The temptation was too strong, and her desire for him was too great right now. She had to do *something*.

Taylor reached down and started to stroke him slowly with her hand, causing him to groan softly and his eyelids fluttered closed as he lost himself in the feel of her hand. He bucked into her hand on impulse, his breathing getting heavier and his hot breath against her face as she worked him.

"Tay..." he moaned, his mouth curling at the corners

into a soft smile as he tried to act like he was chastising her, but she could tell his brain was only on one thing, and that thing was her hand.

"Better be quiet, or we might get caught," she continued before licking his earlobe, playing with him, and he shuddered. She loved watching him get so turned on by her that his whole body reacted. She could feel it in her hand as plainly as she could see it in his face.

"That might be kind of hot," he volleyed back, and she grinned, leaning in and nipping his earlobe this time. He grunted, his desperation evident as he tried to keep silent.

"*This* is kind of hot," she replied, and she increased her pace as she stroked him. He groaned again, and she knew he was doing his best to be as quiet as he could. He was trying to resist, but she felt him moving his hips into her hand as she worked him. She loved watching him lose control like this, and it spurred her on.

"I'm so turned on right now," she whimpered, and he bit his lip, grunting as his grip on her tightened. To make her point known, she took her other hand and clasped it in his, dragging it between her legs so he could feel the wetness between her thighs. She smirked to herself with pride as she heard him let out a strangled little moan that she'd never heard before, and she thought for a second he might just fling her to the ground and take her right there.

The voices at the door started to fade away, and they both paused, listening to the workers as they appeared to have retreated. Now that the coast was seemingly clear, they stared at each other and then burst into laughter.

"Are you trying to get us caught?" He chuckled at her as he hoisted her leg further up his thigh, positioning himself once more at her entrance. She bit her lip and gasped a little as he propped her up against the wall, readjusting as he picked up right where they'd left off before they were interrupted.

"I'm trying to get you all hot and bothered," she whispered, and he kissed her roughly. He didn't have to tell her that she'd been successful. His every mannerism told her as much.

He thrust into her and she moaned his name, and he began to move, but only got a few thrusts in before a nearby broom fell on them. Seriously, why did this resort need so many brooms on hand?? It was the yellow plastic handle that hit them both in the head, causing them to laugh and he paused to playfully kicked the broom out of the way.

"I thought this was the safer option compared to the ocean," she teased into his lips and he chuckled. He sighed and, despite her whining in protest, he helped her off of him as he stepped away from the wall. He grabbed her wrist and took a few steps back, laying down on the floor of the hut over the fishing net that was spread over the wood. She climbed on him and had him inside her a second later, and he groaned as she wasted no time and began to ride him.

"Taylor...*fuck* that's good," he gasped, his hands moving to her thighs and squeezing. She grinned down at him, her hips grinding hard and fast down into his. For her, seeing him let loose was a delight. Dirty talk wasn't her forte, but when she did get the courage to do it, she had him turning into Jell-O in her hands and it was totally arousing.

"God, you look so good when I'm riding you," she whispered, and he moaned loudly. She really *really* hoped those hotel workers were gone, or they were about to hear a lot more than they probably bargained for.

"Seeing your face when I touched you earlier...it was so hot," she groaned as she leaned down to kiss him. He bit her lip, bucking his hips up to meet her. She could tell by the way he flushed and the way his brown eyes fluttered softly shut that he was getting close.

Usually, *he* was the one who had her falling apart in front of him with just a simple brush of his hand against her skin, but when she was able to turn him into a whimpering mess of a man - her entire body was ablaze. The satisfaction that she could not sum up into words flowed through her, and all she could think of was making him feel as good as he constantly made her feel.

"I love touching you, it gets me so hot, so *wet* for you," she growled in his ear, and sure enough, he let out a strangled moan and she felt him grab her hips tightly, bucking into her once, twice, and then he snapped. He threw his head back against the floor of the shack, moaning her name as he unloaded into her, and she continued riding him, chasing her own release, which didn't take more than a few more seconds.

She collapsed on top of him after riding out the pleasurable waves, and he clung to her tightly. He was gripping her so hard she was afraid she might have bruises, but damn if that wasn't also such a hot thing to imagine. They panted into each other, their skin hot and sticky from the humidity, as they caught their breath. Her body was tingling all over, not just from her orgasm but from the way he was holding her and breathing heavily against her.

"How...how is it you can get me...discombobulated like that?" He laughed in her ear, and she grinned and kissed his rough cheek.

"And that isn't even some of my best work," she playfully teased. He smirked up at her and pinched her thigh, making her squeal and wiggle on top of him.

"Oh, I know. I have the texts to prove it."

Taylor smiled and climbed off of him, picking their swimsuits off the floor and tossing his to him. He grinned and stood up, pulling his trunks on as she got back into her bikini. She could feel his eyes on her body the whole time, making her heart race.

They both checked to make sure they didn't look like total disasters before he pulled the broom from the door handle and slowly peeked outside. She was half expecting the workers from the hotel to still be there, having heard the whole thing, but the coast was clear. Dean grinned at her and motioned for her to follow him out, and they both started strolling down the beach back to their hotel like nothing happened.

She couldn't help but giggle, though, as she watched him walk a few steps ahead of her, and he turned to her and raised an eyebrow.

"What?"

"I think we should go into the ocean, or have you lay down in the sand...otherwise it's going to be a bit obvious what we were doing," she told him. At least, obvious to anyone who knew there were nets stored in the shack where they kept the beach supplies. Dean tilted his head at her in confusion, unsure of what she meant.

"What?" He repeated, clearly confused.

"Babe...you've got fishnet indents *all* along your back," she revealed, and he looked over his back in horror. Sure enough, the netting they'd been laying on had sunk into his skin, causing deep red indents on his back and the backs of his legs.

Whoops.

"Shit," he laughed, running for her and grabbing her hand. "Come on, back in the ocean before someone sees!" He teased her, dragging her into the water before he let go and playfully jumped into a wave that crested just as they got knee-deep in the ocean.

Taylor laughed and ran after him, but her face was flushed and her heart was threatening to beat out of her chest. She tried to focus on how playful he was being as he gestured for her to follow him deeper into the water and trying not to think about the fact that she'd just slipped and called him *babe,* and hopefully, he hadn't realized it.

CHAPTER TWELVE

TAYLOR

Six Months Ago

Taylor had never intended for things to escalate as fast as they did.

Dean had been working for her for six months. They finally got their trip to England planned, and as promised, he showed her the sights that she had been dying to see since childhood. The Tower of London, Big Ben, Buckingham Palace... he made sure to make sure they crammed as much sightseeing into the trip as possible. She insisted they meet up with his family at some point while they were there as well. She was eager to meet them, and thankfully he didn't protest and told her it was a great idea.

She wasn't sure when he'd last visited his childhood home. He talked about his family enough for her to know that they didn't exactly understand why their son had wanted to move to L.A. and get into the public relations business, and he never talked about *them* coming out to see *him*. She had been hesitant to bring it up, fearing that maybe he wouldn't want to visit them because their relationship wasn't as strong as she assumed it was.

Taylor was worried for nothing. Florence and Emerson Coffey were kind and welcoming and thrilled that she'd insisted on working in a visit to them during their trip. She had been slightly disappointed that his sister Vicky had been busy and unable to meet up with them, but Dean assured her that he was going to fly her out to visit him in L.A. soon and she'd be able to meet her then.

It had overall been a very pleasant night, and they'd entertained her to no end with stories of Dean's childhood. Despite being embarrassed as his parents recounted his days as a rebellious student who kept getting detention for mouthing off to the teachers - something that she certainly had *not* expected - he happily laughed along with them and made sure to clarify certain points to make himself look better.

After a lovely evening of having dinner with his family, he'd offered to take her out to a local club down the street from their hotel. He knew she liked to party, and she *had* gotten all those cute new skirts that she'd brought with her, just in case she had an opportunity to show off.

Dean had never struck her as someone who would want to frequent a dance club, but she was excited to see this different side of him. She hadn't gone dancing in forever and was excited to have a fun night out for a change, instead of sitting in her hotel room, going over the next day's schedule or stressing over the draft of her final book.

He met her in the lobby, wearing a simple black t-shirt and jeans, and she felt a little overdressed next to him. Especially when she saw the scuffed-up Converse that he was wearing. Maybe this wasn't so much a club as it was a pub, in which case she would stick out like a sore thumb. She had chosen a tight red and black skirt, with a black crop top that had two thick straps with heart-shaped silver buckles adorning them. She'd worn her long blonde hair down and opted for comfy platform sandals instead of heels.

All doubts about her outfit disappeared when she saw the way Dean looked at her as she approached.

Taylor could only describe it as the look that someone had when they got the wind knocked out of them. His mouth opened a bit in surprise as he took in her outfit, and he looked like he might say something…but thought better of it. His brown eyes looked her up and down, and she felt goosebumps erupt on her skin. For a moment she felt like she might burst into flames from the fire in his eyes as he looked at her. He was looking at her the way Prince Charming fawned over Cinderella the first time he saw her, and it took her breath away.

Then he opened his mouth again and cleared his throat a bit. Whatever trance she'd seemed to have cast over him, a moment later it was broken as he composed himself.

"Hey…you look good," he said simply, shooting her a small smile and clearly trying to brush past whatever had just happened. She wasn't sure what to make of that. Did that mean she looked *good* good, or was he saying that because she *had* overdressed and he was trying not to make a big deal out of it?

Damn this man. He was usually easy to read, but for some reason tonight she couldn't gauge his emotions whatsoever. But why the hell did she even care? Did she really want to know if Dean thought her outfit was nice or not?

"Thanks, so do you," she offered a compliment in return, and he chuckled and shook his head as if he didn't really believe her. Just like that, whatever moment had transpired between the two of them passed just as quickly as it had come.

He led her out of the hotel and down the street, asking if she'd be able to walk a few blocks in those platform sandals, which she assured him she could with a teasing eye roll. She loved these sandals. They were comfy and reminiscent of her summers as a child in the early 2000s. At first, she thought it was lame that late 90's trends were coming back in style, but today was one of the days when she was grateful for them. Plus, it gave her just enough added height for her to look Dean more squarely in the eyes. He was still taller than her - as most people were, even with her heels, but she felt like she was on a more even playing field with him.

It wasn't until that moment that she realized he'd ditched his glasses.

"You're wearing contacts," she observed with a small head tilt, and he laughed and nodded.

"Yeah, that's about as dressed up as I get. Nothing like...I mean, everyone is going to be looking at *you* when we get there, so it doesn't matter," he joked, but she noticed the softest hint of a blush on his fair cheeks as he spoke. He was pointedly not looking at her, focused ahead on the crowded street in front of them.

They didn't say much aside from some small talk until they got to the club. After introducing herself, the bouncer let them both in without question. She wasn't sure if it was because she was an up-and-coming famous author, or if she was just an attractive girl an American accent. Dean made some joking remark about how he wouldn't have been looked at twice if he hadn't been with her, and then quickly steered them towards the bar. He ordered them drinks - his treat, he insisted - and now, surrounded by the dark interior and the loud club music blasting overhead, Taylor felt like she was back in her element.

This is what she lived for. To be the center of attention in a crowded room without actually being too loud and obnoxious about it. She could feel men gazing at her, and women staring at her in jealously. It reminded her of her college days and made her feel like just another girl out on the town.

One could definitely argue that she loved being admired in clubs because she rarely felt admired elsewhere, but that was a load of baggage she didn't want to unpack any time soon. But she knew they were admiring her because she was dressed up and had put effort into her appearance. They weren't admiring her because she was *Taylor Mullins,* hot author on the scene, and that was a welcome change.

She hadn't realized how much she had valued anonymity until she'd lost it.

The loud music vibrated through the floors and up to the bar they were sitting at, as if fueling her and giving her energy. Work was done for now, and it was time to lose herself in the music and the familiar atmosphere of a party.

As the night dragged on, Taylor slowly realized that something strange was happening. For once, she didn't care as much about other people in the club. That was...new and unexpected. There was only one person here who mattered, and he was sitting right next to her, drinking a *Negroni* of all things.

Somehow, even through the loud music, she could hear every word Dean said as he talked to her, their conversation getting more and more relaxed the more drinks they pounded back. A fan approached them about three drinks in and recognized her, insisting they buy them shots. How she was recognized in the dim light of the crowd, she had no idea, but she appreciated their kind gesture and thanked them. Another fan bought them a round of drinks a few minutes later, and before Taylor knew it, she was more than a little inebriated.

She dragged Dean to the dance floor, despite his protests, and she felt like she was smiling wider than she had in weeks. She couldn't remember the last time she'd danced - her life recently had been a swirling mass of book signings, interviews, and contract negotiations. All of it was made infinitely easier with Dean by her side now. How she had ever survived with an assistant before now was a mystery.

How she had ever survived without *Dean* was a mystery.

She was a sucker for EDM, which the club provided plenty of, and was now shaking her head and wiping her hair wildly like she was in a dramatic British teen series. Dean was laughing at her, yelling at her something about looking like she was in a shampoo commercial. He was slowly warming up as each song played and breaking out of his shell more.

He started out very stiff, hardly doing more than bobbing along to the music, but she grabbed his hands and made him move his hips. She yelled at him over the music to loosen up, and he slowly began to get more and more into the music. He didn't have *much* rhythm, being a stuck-up kid from the posh part of London, but it was endearing to watch him try and keep up with her on the floor, belting out the lyrics to the songs with reckless abandon.

Even in her drunken state, she took note of all the men watching him jealously as she danced with him - and couldn't help but shoot a glare at a few women in the crowd that she caught eyeing him.

Whoa, where had *that* come from? Dean Coffey was not *hers* to stake any sort of claim over. Yet why did she want to rip the eyes out of anyone who so much as looked his way? Why was she tempted to run up to all the women and tell them that Dean was much more than just a good-looking man? He was one of the best men she'd ever met, and none of them deserved him.

A waitress was passing out shots, making her way through the crowd and handing them to the wealthy patrons who were too drunk to care if she added another shot or two to their tabs. Taylor grabbed two and handed one to Dean with a grin, both of them pounding them back as they burst into drunken laughter.

She wasn't sure how much time had passed - it could have been an hour, or it could have been four - but she was having the time of her life. She never wanted it to end.

In the blink of an eye, everything started to get more...*intense*. Dean's hand was intertwined with hers now, pulling her close to him. She could tell he was past the point of being tipsy, just as she was, but that look in his eyes from earlier was back.

The way he was looking at her, allowing himself to eagerly check her out...made butterflies erupt in her stomach. Normally she felt weird when men checked her out so blatantly, but Dean's gaze on her body was more intimate than that. He wasn't just checking her out - he was looking at her as if he had never seen someone so beautiful. It was intoxicating. Even better than the shots they'd just had.

Alcohol certainly hadn't been involved earlier in the evening when he'd first seen her, and now that she gazed up into those brown eyes, she recognized it. He'd shot her that same look a few times over the past six months, but she'd never realized just how much those eyes burned into her soul until this very moment.

Taylor Mullins was wanted by most men she encountered. But Dean...he *wanted* her. Probably for some time now. She could read it plain as day on his face. And she was terrified to realize in that moment that she might want him too. The look in his eyes was stirring something awake inside her, and desire started coursing through her veins as she pressed up against him.

Some part of her brain knew she was playing with fire. This was a bad idea - she thought back to Caroline warning her months ago when she hired the hot British man as her assistant that this could end in disaster. Yet she didn't stop herself from allowing herself to be pulled closer to him. She didn't stop his hands from traveling to her hips as she moved her hands to his hair. His body was warm and inviting, and she felt like she belonged there in his arms.

The black t-shirt he was wearing clung to his sweaty body, and she felt such a strong urge to tear it off that she moved her hands to the small of his back, gripping the fabric tightly in her fists.

His lips were close to hers now, his breath hot on her face, and suddenly she remembered where they were. They were in *public*. Anyone could see them, even in the darkness of the club. If she could be recognized by a handful of patrons earlier, then who was to say she wouldn't be recognized as she flirted with Dean on the dance floor?

For a moment she wondered if anyone cared if she was caught making out with her assistant. When she first started out in the publishing world, probably not. But she'd struck gold, and she wasn't just any other author. She was now Taylor Mullins, best-selling author of *The Jill Augustin Mysteries,* soon to be a popular television show, and she had to be aware of these types of things. Most authors never had paparazzi camped out in the bushes across from their condos. Most authors never had their faces recognized in public. Most authors never saw the success she did - and that made everything different.

Still, she had no desire to pull away from him, so she found herself turning her body so that her backside was pressed against him. The truth was, she didn't trust herself to look into those eyes anymore without drowning. His gaze was boring into her soul, making her body ache for him so badly she didn't think she could trust herself to not jump on him if she kept staring at him.

She could feel Dean tense as she backed into him, and she wondered for a second if he was going to let go of her. To her delight, she found that he was pulling her close to him, his hands still on her hips as his grip tightened. Boldly, she began to move her hips in time with the music, grinding against him.

Taylor could feel his hot breath against her neck as he leaned closer to her and he moved his hips against hers. She bit her lip as she felt the bulge in his jeans digging into her ass, and she moved her hands to rest on top of his. Their fingers snaked together, as if they both signaling to the other that they were caving in to...*whatever* this was between them.

Two songs later, his lips lightly kissed the spot under her ear on her neck, and she shuddered. She had never been touched so delicately before, and her self-control was reaching the breaking point. She was so close to something so...*magical* with him. She just knew it. She knew if she gave in to temptation, if she turned around and captured his lips with hers, it would be so amazing that it would steal the breath from her lungs. It would shatter her whole world. She would be kissed in a way she had never been kissed before, and the thought both terrified her and exhilarated her.

She should end this right now, because something told her that this was it. They were to the point of no return, and if she put a single toe over that line...they were done for. The doors would open, and everything would change between them.

Taylor should stop herself from going over that line.

She should step away from him, untangle their hands, and walk out of this club without a single look back at him.

That was what she *should* do. But what Taylor Mullins *should* do and what she was *going* to do were two very different things, she knew that for certain.

She walked out of the club after that song - but she was tugging him by the hand as she did so.

CHAPTER THIRTEEN

DEAN

Five months, six days and twenty-three hours ago

The hotel room door barely had shut behind them before he was on her.

Dean pushed her up against the wall, his lips finding hers and immediately capturing them in a deep kiss. He knew that his brain was still muddled with alcohol, but he was thinking clearly enough to know that he wanted this more than he'd ever wanted anything else. Fuck, he'd fantasized about this for weeks without ever thinking it could possibly be *real*.

Taylor always dressed like a knockout. Even when she was meeting with publicists or doing interviews, wearing business casual clothing, he had the urge to rip everything off of her and kiss every inch of her body. It was stupid - so incredibly stupid - to have sexual feelings towards his boss. That was crossing so many professional lines it was ridiculous.

He had told himself when he first got the job that he wouldn't let the fact that he worked for a smoking hot woman derail him. This was a *huge* opportunity to get his foot in the door. Taylor had connections, and with her upcoming TV deal for her book series, she was about to be even more well-connected. He couldn't have asked for a better opportunity.

Plus, he actually *liked* working for her. Dean liked keeping track of things like her social calendar and emails, and making phone calls on her behalf - he liked helping her. It was relief for her to have some of the burden off her shoulders, he could tell.

He just…*liked* Taylor.

As he had suspected when he first got the job, Taylor Mullins had a wall around her. He was one of the few people who got to see behind that wall, and somehow, without him really realizing it, he'd come to care deeply for the person behind it.

For him, it wasn't just about his desire to fuck her senseless. He got to see a side of Taylor that not many people saw. She put a very carefully crafted persona out into the world, and he knew it was because she felt she had to be perfect or somehow, everything would get taken from her. Everything she'd worked for and all the acceptance she finally won would be gone in an instant if she did one wrong thing.

That and all the shit with her mother running off on them, which she refused to talk about. He knew being liked and well-received was important to her. She wanted to be the center of attention *without* jumping up and yelling 'Look at me!' and waving her hands around. He had no idea why she felt like people didn't like her. She was funny, witty, and creative. Sometimes a little dramatic. She was extremely kind and generous - he saw her credit card statements, he *knew* she paid her dad's mortgage and donated to her sorority's charity regularly, but she never said a word about it.

She didn't want to show any signs of weakness, but one of her biggest weaknesses was thinking that being herself would make her seem soft.

He knew the real Taylor Mullins. He noticed how much she struggled whenever she snapped at someone working for her, replaying the incident in her mind until she sent that person a bouquet to make amends. He saw how her favorite thing to do when she wasn't writing was to curl up on the couch with her crocheting project and rewatch episodes of *New Girl* for the 100th time. He saw her scrutinize herself, watched her scroll endlessly on social media sites, reading about what people had to say about her.

Dean was the only one who ever thought to come over and close the laptop, reminding her to not think about what everyone else had to say about her.

Maybe that was why she was letting him into this part of her. A part that he should stay far, *far* away from, but damnit, it felt so good to succumb to his desire. His lips stayed glued to hers as his hands ran up her thighs, cupping her ass under her skirt as she moaned into his mouth. Her kisses were like oxygen to him in that moment. He couldn't get enough. He needed more, *much* more, to stay alive. To keep breathing.

"Bed. Now," she panted against his lips, and as always, he was a slave to anything she requested. He moved his hands back to her thighs and hoisted her up so she could wrap her legs around her waist, which she did instantly, her arms wrapping around his neck as they kissed hungrily.

She tasted sweet, like whatever sugary alcoholic drinks she'd been drinking at the club. He had a feeling part of that was just her, though. He'd imagined that kissing her would be a world changing experience, and he hadn't been wrong. In fact, it was somehow even better than that. He instinctively knew every head tilt to make, every brush of his lips against hers that made her moan softly into his mouth. It was like his body just *knew* what to do with her.

He headed to the bed and dropped her playfully on the large king-sized bed, and she giggled as she leaned up to grab his t-shirt, pulling him down on top of her. He kissed her again as he felt her hands eagerly pushing under the fabric of his shirt, and he leaned back to pull it off and toss the plain shirt aside. She stared up at him and bit her lip, and he felt himself getting nervous. Was she having second thoughts? Shit. This was a bad idea. He knew it was a bad idea, someone should stop it...

"Fuck, you're hot," she whimpered, and before he could even respond, she grabbed him by the back of the neck and pulled him back down to her, kissing him passionately. He felt so lightheaded, so over the moon that this was all happening that he could barely even process that she'd just called him *hot*.

She, Taylor, thought *he* was hot...he was going to hear her saying that in his memory on replay for the rest of his life. He was sure of it.

As his hands played with her skirt, eagerly tugging it down over her hips, she broke away from him for just a moment, although her lips were still centimeters away from his, and her hands were gripping his shoulders tightly.

"Before we do this...we should probably...set up some expectations...for when we do this," she managed to pant out as she peppered kisses all along his jaw. He moaned softly, his eyes closing as he reveled in the feel of her lips along his scruffy jaw.

The flame that had been simmering deep inside him for Taylor all these months was threatening to burn him up, and he tried desperately to keep his focus on her.

Because he was currently making out with his boss. The woman who employed him.

Shit, he was making out with his boss!

This was wrong, so so wrong...but fuck, he couldn't stop himself. She didn't seem to have any interest in stopping him either, and who was he to deny her what she wanted? She could have asked him to commit capital crimes for her in this moment, and he'd do it in a heartbeat.

"Right...like what?" He asked, amazed he could even *form* words as his hands moved up to her cute little crop top now that her skirt had been kicked away. He groped her chest and she moaned into his lips, apparently forgetting their conversation for the time being. His hand ran down her stomach, admiring each curve of her body before he paused, looking down at her.

"Fuck, you have a belly button ring?" He managed to squeak out as he took note of the little silver diamond bar she had in her naval. How had he not known that?! She looked up at him in confusion and he laughed, leaning down and nipping her lip. "That's so fucking sexy," he groaned into her lips, and he heard her laugh into his mouth as she kissed him.

"*You're* sexy, Dean," she moaned, and he didn't realize until that moment how much he wanted to hear his name drip from her lips. It was intoxicating, just as much as the Negronis he had been pounding back in the club earlier. He needed to feel more of her, kiss more of her...

"But this...no one can know about this..." she whispered. As much as it pained his heart to hear those words, he knew she was right. This was highly inappropriate and crossed all sorts of lines. Just as he had for months, he would keep his mouth shut.

"Not a word to anyone," he replied, letting her know that he understood. This had to stay a secret. They had no other choice. They had to keep this simple - just physical. Not only would this complicate things if word were to get out, but Taylor was in the public eye now. *Any* man who dated her - not just him - would be entering a world where their every move was monitored.

Not that he was thinking of *dating* her. Not in the slightest. Right now, all he could think about was getting the rest of these infernal clothes off so he could shag her senseless. He pushed the crop top off of her, reveling in the fact that she, apparently, hadn't been wearing a bra underneath her shirt, and tossed it aside. He'd always imagined that she looked amazing naked, but fuck - why wasn't *she* the one who had been a model out of the two of them?

Taylor was like an angel, laying there on the bed, ready for him to take her. He was straining so badly against his jeans that he wasn't sure how he hadn't passed out from wanting her so much.

"God, you're beautiful," he groaned as he kissed her, his hand moving to her exposed breasts and kneading hungrily. She whimpered under him, her hands playing with the zipper of his jeans. Impatient, he pulled back for a moment to help, stripping himself of his jeans and kicking aside his beat-up Converse he'd been wearing and his socks before pouncing on her again.

He kissed her as she wiggled underneath him, and he

ground his hips into hers. The only fabric remaining between the two of them now was their underwear, and she was already anxiously playing with the waistband of his boxer briefs to try and get him completely bare. His heart was pounding in his ears, trying to memorize every moment of this. He needed to sear this into his brain for all eternity because he didn't know if he'd ever...

Wait. What had she said?

"Wait...are you saying you'll want to do this again?" He asked softly, pulling away for just a moment to look down at her in confusion. She'd said they had to come up with expectations for *when* they did this...which, to him, implied that there might be *more* liaisons in hotel rooms that they would have to keep secret.

Fuck, his head was spinning. His whole body was warm as she looked up at him, a small smile forming on her face. This couldn't be real, could it? There was no way his dream girl was actually under him right now, coming up with a plan to be fuck buddies with him on the down low?

"That depends on how well this goes," she replied coyly, smirking up at him before she leaned up and captured his lips in another kiss. He groaned as he felt her hands on his ass, pushing his briefs down, and he lifted his hips to help her shrug them off before kicking them aside. His hand was tugging at her black lace panties, trying to pull them down and over her legs.

As soon as he was completely bare, Taylor lifted her hips against him and pushed her underwear down, kicking them off the bed, and just like that, they were both completely naked, pressed into each other. Dean's heart continued to race, his mind screaming at him that he was so close to her, so close to victory and having everything that his heart desired, and all he had to do was take the plunge.

It was like something had switched all of a sudden and they realized that they were pressed against each other, completely exposed. Not just physically, but emotionally too. They had both just crossed the line and changed things between them forever. Even if they woke up tomorrow and agreed to just be friends and never sleep together again, they both knew it wouldn't be the same. He could see it in her eyes. He wanted her more than he'd ever wanted another woman, and she wanted *him*. Fuck it - they were done holding back.

They were both completely flushed and breathless, just staring at each other and panting heavily. He knew his hard-on was digging into her thigh, as her legs had opened of their own accord to make room for him, but he wanted to just sit and just *be* in this moment for a minute. She gazed up at him and smiled, her hand moving to his hair and softly running her fingernails along the back of his neck. He was certain he had never been touched so delicately before, and he instantly felt his nerves melting away.

Dean shuddered slightly, his hips pressing into her on reflex as he took in her beautiful face. Her lips were puffed and red from kissing, and her hair was messy and sprawled out on the pillow behind her like a halo.

"Just sex, right?" He asked softly, and she nodded.

He could do just sex. He was sure of it.

"Just sex," she confirmed, biting her lip in anticipation as she looked up at him. He leaned down and kissed her again, gentler this time, before he pulled away with a small groan.

"Shit, hold on, I have to get a condom," he said,

moving to get up and head over to his discarded jeans. He was 99.9% certain he had a condom in his wallet, and if he didn't... well, he wasn't gonna think of that just yet...

To his surprise, Taylor tugged him back and shook her head. "No no, it's ok...I'm on the pill, and I haven't been with anyone since I was last tested," she assured him quickly. He blinked down at her in awe before he kissed her roughly, chuckling a little as he pulled away.

"Holy fuck, I think you might be trying to kill me, Tay," he whispered, laughing against her lips as she giggled up at him. She leaned up to kiss him and playfully bit his lip, tugging softly on his hair.

"I like it when you do that," she whimpered, and he looked at her in confusion. She was going to need to be more specific.

"What?" He asked.

"Call me Tay," she admitted, her cheeks flushing softly. He grinned and laughed a little. He didn't know when he'd started doing that, but now that he thought about it, he didn't think anyone else called her Tay. it was his little pet name for her. And she *liked* it.

Dean liked a whole lot of things about Taylor, and he hoped she liked a lot of things about him too.

He positioned himself at her entrance, groaning softly when he felt her arousal against him. He couldn't hold back anymore. He slid in slowly and she groaned loudly, her long nails digging into his back. Her hips jutted up into his as he slid into her fully, groaning in the crook of her neck as he felt her wet heat around him. It was everything he had imagined and so much more at the same time. It was like they were two pieces of a puzzle, brought together and fitting into place perfectly. He wasn't sure how any other woman would compare to her after this, and he hadn't even fucking *moved* yet. It just all felt so... so...

No, he couldn't think that. He couldn't think about how *right* this felt. Because that was a door that had to remain closed, and locked, and he had to throw away the key and never look back. It was so hard to do, though, when it felt like absolute heaven to be nestled inside her. She leaned up and kissed his cheek gently, and he closed his eyes as he tried to memorize everything about this moment. Her lips on his skin, her arms around him, the feel of her skin against his...he needed it engrained in his memory forever.

He lost himself after that. There were no other thoughts in his brain except the feel of Taylor wrapped around him. Her legs held him to her tightly as she groaned, her hips meeting him at every thrust. How was it that this was everything he'd imagined it would be and yet so much better at the same time?

Her blue eyes met his as they moved together, getting closer and closer to that edge, and when he felt her walls tighten around him and she yelled out his name, the thread holding him together snapped. He cried out and released and moaned her name into the crook of her neck, his body moving roughly against her as he pulsed and they rode out the waves of pleasure together.

When they finished, he propped himself over her, gazing down at her with a soft smile on his face. She grinned up at him, pushing his hair out of his eyes, and he swore he felt sparks of electricity where her fingers brushed against his skin. The room was still spinning, and alcohol was still pushing down the voice in his brain that was screaming at him, insisting he'd made a colossal mistake. As they tried to catch their breath, he gently kissed her and cupped her cheek with his hand.

"That was...wow," he whispered as he softly ran his thumb along her cheek, and she giggled playfully.

"Yeah...wow," she replied back. They both continued to look intently at each other, as if they were studying each other's faces for the first time. His heart was still racing, and he knew he should be thinking about what tomorrow would bring. Dean knew he should be trying to figure out what this meant for his future, for *her* future, but he couldn't.

He only thought of her, and how beautiful she looked underneath him. How amazing she felt still wrapped around him. How his heart felt like it was going to explode as he'd watched her come apart underneath him, crying out his name and bringing every fantasy he'd ever had about her to life.

It was Taylor who spoke first, and when she did, all his fears and worries melted away for the umpteenth time that night.

"Wanna do it again?" She asked softly with a cheeky grin.

Even though he knew that he should say no, and insist this was a one-time thing, and to tell her this might have all been a big mistake...that wasn't what he said. Instead, he looked down at her and grinned right back, and when he spoke, his voice sounded more like a growl than anything else.

"Abso-fucking-lutely."

CHAPTER FOURTEEN

TAYLOR

Five months, six days, and eighteen hours ago

The next morning, Taylor blinked and looked around as she rubbed her eyes. Her head felt like a weighed ten pounds, and the bright light streaming in from the windows felt extra blinding this morning. Her mouth was fuzzy with the aftertaste of vodka cranberries, and she felt...sticky. Like she'd been sweating a lot. She couldn't remember where she was at first - she could tell that she was in the hotel, but she didn't think she was in *her* room. So whose room was...

She turned to her left and saw the broad back of a man facing her, and she remembered. She remembered *everything*.

That wasn't any man. That was *Dean* lying in bed next to her.

Her eyes widened and she threw her hand over her mouth to stop herself from gasping loudly. Shit, they'd actually done it. They'd actually *slept together* last night! As she stared at his back, her mind raced as she tried to figure out the implications of this. The first thing that popped into her brain was just how inappropriate this all was.

He *worked* for her! This could derail her entire career, and for what? One night of passion with her - admittedly - extremely hot, British assistant? She was in *London* for Christ's sake, she couldn't have just picked up any other British bloke while she was here if she'd been horny? Dean could probably sue her for sexual harassment if he really wanted to, take her for all that she was worth...but she knew deep in her heart that he would never do that.

Still, she remembered, through the blur of her memories, insinuating that she wanted *more* hookups with him after last night. Almost the very definition of a quid-pro-quo, except she'd never actually offered him better pay, or implied that she'd fire him if he didn't comply. So, she was *probably* fine, but really, she shouldn't take the risk...

And yet, if she was being honest with herself...fuck, last night had been amazing. So yeah, she really *really* wanted to do that again...

No, she shouldn't. It was a bad idea. Right? Yes, it was absolutely a *terrible* idea and she shouldn't let herself fall to her temptations. She shouldn't be thinking about sleeping with him again or kissing him, and she probably shouldn't be staring at his muscular back, trying to commit the map of his moles and freckles to her memory...

Taylor went back and forth with her own internal struggles over the situation for about twenty minutes, even debating whether or not she should sneak out and return to her room, until he stirred next to her. He rolled on his back and rubbed his face, groaning loudly as he blinked and stared up at the ceiling. She could see the gears working in that blond head of his, and he softly swore under his breath.

"Yeah, same here," she piped up softly, and he jumped, shooting up in bed as he looked at her with wide eyes. He grabbed for the comforter and pulled it over his chest, like he was trying to hide anything too revealing.

She knew she shouldn't find it funny or charming or endearing…but she did, and she bit her lip to keep from laughing. His blond hair was sticking up at odd angles, and she realized as she studied his face that she had left a hickey on his bare collarbone. Oops.

"Taylor! Oh *fuck*…oh my god, oh my god, what did we *do*…" he grumbled, running a hand through his hair as his whole body flushed with embarrassment. She had to admit, she was a little surprised at how he was reacting. She knew he had been drunk, but he had been more than a willing participant last night. He'd been downright *enthusiastic*.

And there was that look he had given her when he first saw her in the lobby…he hadn't been drunk then…

"It's ok, Dean…" She sat up, hugging the sheets to herself, thinking about how he had desperately been trying to cover himself up a few seconds earlier. She wasn't sure why *she* was doing it, though, because she was wearing his shirt. Perhaps it was because she instantly felt extremely vulnerable. The way he was reacting was making her nervous, and not in a good way. She was starting to think she'd read this situation completely wrong.

"We must have been *so* shit-faced last night," he continued, looking like he was on the verge of being sick. She wondered for a moment if she should get up and go get the trash can, just to be safe. "I can't believe…"

"Did you not want to do it?" she asked, cutting him off and biting her lip, turning red. Maybe she had horribly miscalculated this whole thing. Hell, she didn't even *date,* was it possible that her brain had somehow manufactured a romantic look in his eyes simply because she'd been desperate for affection?

"What?" he blinked and stared at her, shaking his head. "No, I did, *lord* knows I did..." he trailed off, blushing again. She smiled a little to herself. He had just admitted that he *did* want to sleep with her last night, which instantly made her feel a little bit better.

"Ok, so...why are you freaking out so much?" she asked hesitantly.

Dean paused, looking at her before focusing his attention on his hands. He looked like he was trying to figure out the right words to say. She wondered again if she'd misjudged this situation. They'd said just friends, but what if he was about to tell her that he couldn't do *just friends?* That he wanted more and he couldn't be with her now knowing that they could never be, and she was about to lose the best thing that had ever happened to her?

"I...don't make smart decisions when I drink," he explained quietly. She dared to scoot a little closer to him, reaching out to take his hand in hers. She wondered for a moment if he might pull away, but he didn't. Instead, his fingers intertwined with hers, and she felt her heart racing. They held hands all the time, but after last night, it was different. This was *all* different.

"Dean, it's really ok. We both were drunk, and I don't regret it at all," she assured him. He shook his head.

"No, no, I don't just mean last night," he told her

with a heavy sigh. "I mean...I used to be really bad. I'd get into some bad shit at school when I got drunk. Random sex. Drugs... the heavy kind, I mean...it got out of control," he explained, his voice getting quieter as he spoke. "That was the first time I fell off the wagon in...a while."

Taylor's mouth fell open softly and she stared at him. She had absolutely no idea that he'd had issues with substance abuse in the past. Dean Coffey was the last person she had suspected of being a wild party boy, but everyone had a past. Taylor was certainly not one to judge him because of it.

Come to think of it, last night was the first time she'd ever noticed him going out to a club...had he ever had drinks at dinner around her? She couldn't remember.

"Why didn't you tell me?" She asked, squeezing his hand. He blushed again, avoiding her gaze. "I never would have had you go out with me if I knew," she added.

"I know," he admitted with a heavy sigh. "That's why I didn't say anything," he added, his voice barely more than a whisper. He finally looked at her, his brown eyes boring into hers. She felt her heart racing, and he bit his lip. Fuck, he had nice, plump lips. She shouldn't be worried about that right now, but she couldn't help it. She *should* be worried about the fact that he had been so desperate to go out with her that he'd willingly put his sobriety at risk just so *she* would have a good time.

"Listen to me right now, Dean Coffey," she said, scooting close to him and throwing her leg over him, straddling him and cupping his face in her hands. She was wearing his shirt from the night before and nothing else - she couldn't remember when she'd put it on, but she found she quite liked wearing his clothes. She also liked the incredulous look he was giving her right now as she climbed on top of him. His hands snapped to her hips as if on instinct, but his face still plainly showed the shock at her actions.

"I don't want you *ever* putting yourself in a situation where you might be tempted by that ever again," she instructed him. "Especially for me."

Dean looked like he might argue, so she took her finger and put it to his lips. "Because…you didn't need to go out last night and get drunk to get me in your bed," she admitted softly.

She hadn't realized just how true her words were until she spoke. He looked up at her, his brown eyes wide in awe as if he couldn't believe what she was saying.

Something in his eyes…should concern her. They had both determined last night that this was just going to be a fuck buddy's situation, and she wondered for the briefest of seconds if he wanted more than that.

Taylor couldn't give that to him, and he couldn't ask for it. She knew that, and she knew he did too. But he nodded slowly up at her, and she pushed those worries aside.

"I mean what I said last night though…" she added, and he quickly nodded.

"I understand. Completely. Just sex," he reiterated, and she was relieved that he remembered that from last night. The fact of the matter was, despite her pounding headache from all the vodka cranberries she'd had last night, she realized she was just as ready to jump his bones again as she had last night. To drive her point home, she rocked her hips against him, her heart racing as he moaned and his eyelids fluttered. She felt him twitching underneath her and she said a silent thankful prayer for morning wood.

She smirked at him, and butterflies erupted in her stomach when he grinned back up at her. "Last night *was* really fun," she whispered. She was thrilled that after all this, and after realizing that alcohol had definitely played a role in their actions last night, he still seemed like an eager participant in all of this.

Dean chuckled, his hands moving up to the hem of his shirt that she'd stolen and playing with it carefully, his fingers just barely brushing over the fabric. "It was a little more than fun, I'd say," he admitted with a laugh, and she leaned in and kissed his cheek.

"And uh…as your employer, I feel like I should make it clear that this isn't going to be, um…*expected* of you or anything," she added quickly, and this time it was him who put his finger to her lips.

"Don't worry about that at all. I know," he assured her with a soft smile. His hands continued to play with the shirt, slipping underneath the fabric and up her sides.

"So…does this make us friends with benefits, then?" She asked with a smirk as she leaned in, her lips hovering over his as her arms went around his neck. He laughed a little and beamed at her, and she realized just how much she enjoyed his smile. He really was a good-looking man, but that wasn't the only reason she felt comfortable doing all this with him.

"I mean, if you insist on putting a label on it," he whispered back, his lips itching ever closer to hers.

She finally closed the gap between them and kissed him. There was only a moment of hesitation on his part before she felt his hands move further up her sides, cupping her breasts and squeezing as she groaned softly into him. She leaned back for a moment to yank the shirt off and throw it aside, and her heart raced as she watched him look up at her.

"Shit...you look even more beautiful in the light of day," he whispered. Taylor's stomach flip-flopped with excitement at his words. Somewhere in her brain, something yelled at her that she shouldn't be excited at the fact he thought she was beautiful. He shouldn't be saying things like that. Yet she charged forward, leaning down to kiss him as she lifted her hips and adjusted herself, taking him in her hand and guiding him inside her.

She moaned into his lips and pulled back as she settled on top of him, and her heart raced even more as she looked down at him. His hands dug into her thighs, his mouth open slightly as he groaned, and he was looking at her like... like...

Like he couldn't believe she was actually real and actually riding him right now.

There was far too much emotion in that gaze of his, and she should climb off of him right now and walk away.

But fuck it. She'd already crossed the line and left it behind her - might as well keep going.

* * * *

They came up with ground rules after their second... or maybe their third...bout of sex that morning. They ordered McDonald's to the room, gorging themselves in order to try and cure their hangovers as they formulated what this was going to mean for them going forward.

The ground rules were simple and they figured they could abide by them easily. They both knew that a relationship between them wasn't possible, but neither of them could have a serious relationship right now, so this 'situationship' would be ideal for both of them. Not only that, but they were both going to be extremely busy for the next six months - romance was definitely not on the agenda for either of them. But who was to say they couldn't enjoy a little pleasure on the side? As a sort of stress relief?

The *first rule* was that work was off-limits. When Dean came over to help her with her daily routine, sex was not allowed. They had to focus on getting shit done for the book tour in a few months, and she needed to set aside time to write each day. They couldn't lose sight of the real reason they'd come together, and her career literally depended on her having a successful tour and finishing up her series. They couldn't afford distractions on the clock - plus, Dean insisted that having sex with her when he was technically working for her made him feel a bit like a prostitute, and she couldn't argue with that logic.

Naturally, they lasted about five weeks before she found herself muting herself a call with Caroline as Dean took her roughly on her living room couch. She knew it was an important phone call, something about the cover art for the new limited edition release of the first book, but he'd looked at her with those burning brown eyes, and before she knew it, she'd jumped on him. Some days, those plump lips and that bright blond hair combined with his stupidly hot British accent were too much for her to resist. So Caroline prattled away, unaware of the debauchery happening on the other line.

The *second rule* was no hot tubs. Dean had come up with that. He said that he wasn't a fan of hot tubs in general - going back to that whole germaphobe thing - so if that was one of her fantasies, she needed to count him out. It was silly, but wasn't this *whole thing* silly to begin with? They added it to the list, and then Dean went on a tangent about how unhygienic the whole idea of hot tubs was in general.

That one lasted only three weeks because the hotel they were staying at in New York happened to have a private hot tub in her room. She hadn't even planned on him joining her, but when he walked into her room and saw her wearing a bikini and climbing into the tub, he suddenly overcame his fear of dingy pipes and bacteria. Two minutes later he had her pressed against the edge of the tube, untying the strings on her swimsuit.

The next rule was no hickeys. That would open up way too many cans of worms to count. Eventually, after some light-hearted negotiation, they agreed to keep any hickeys out of site - stomachs, thighs, anything that would be covered on a day-to-day basis with clothes was considered a safe zone. Two and a half weeks in, though, she'd gotten carried away and gnawed at his neck so much it looked like he'd been attacked by a vampire. She couldn't stop herself. He was too damn delicious for her to resist.

They agreed to have him work from home that day.

She'd told him not to expect any blow jobs from her. She wasn't a huge fan of going down on guys, and it made her feel self-conscious because she knew it was due to her tiny mouth that she didn't enjoy it. He promised he would never force her to do something she was uncomfortable with, and that was fine by him if she never sucked him off. It certainly wouldn't deter him from using his mouth on her, if that was what she was worried about.

Well, he didn't have to *make* her do anything, because she found about two weeks into their fling that she actually really liked giving head when it was Dean. Watching him was the best part - he looked like a Greek statue when his head was thrown back, eyes fluttered close and his mouth opened in pleasure. The little whimpering noises he made were the best part.

Dean also suggested that they should make time to spend time with their friends. As tempting as it was to close up shop and immediately jump into bed once 5 PM hit every day, he pointed out that people would likely figure out what was going on quickly if they kept up that schedule. They had *some* self-control, right? He'd make sure to hang out with his former roommate, Ricky, and even go out a few times and *try* to act like he was single when in public. Taylor agreed and made sure she spent time with Caroline and her other girlfriends so no one would suspect a thing.

After about a week and a half, though, they found they both couldn't seem to drop their phones when they weren't together. Both of them were teased mercilessly by their friends until they revealed they were just texting each other, and it was all business. They all seemed to buy it, and none of them seemed to have any clue that their texting back and forth had little to do with business and *everything* to do with pleasure. In graphic detail, most of the time.

Dean Coffey, as it turns out, was *very* good at sexting.

Their final rule, and the most important, was no sleepovers. Just a quick bang, and then whoever had come over would leave and go back to their own apartment. Sleepovers would make things too complicated and domesticated. They were not about to become the people who had breakfast in bed or woke up in the morning next to each other with stupid grins on their faces. If they became two people who slept over, spooning each other well into the morning, then they would be lying to themselves if they said this was just a sexual relationship, nothing more. It would be a sign that they were too comfortable, too close, muddying the waters too much - and there wouldn't be a clear way out of it that didn't end in disaster. This morning was an obvious exception, but after this, no more.

They lasted four days.

CHAPTER FIFTEEN

TAYLOR

"Please tell me it isn't true."

"What isn't true?"

"Oh my god, you haven't seen?!"

"Seen *what* Caroline?"

Taylor really hoped that whatever she was going to tell her was worth the international data plan she'd gotten for this trip. Her agent groaned as if she couldn't believe her friend didn't know *exactly* what she was talking about, and she could practically hear her rolling her eyes all the way across the phone in L.A.

"There's a blind item about you!" She hissed. Taylor blinked, pausing the folding of her swimsuit as she absorbed what her agent had just said.

"Wait, a blind item? About *me?*" She asked. Surely she'd heard her incorrectly. Caroline huffed.

"Yes! 'The A-list author who *didn't* write a book

about a magical preteen British wizard is definitely shacking up with her assistant. Let's hope the sex inspires her to write something steamier in her final novel of the trilogy,'" her agent rattled off the blind item to her, and Taylor listened, speechless. "And then there's a link to a trashy gossip website that has a picture of you and Dean out at dinner in New York last week," she added.

Taylor closed her eyes and rubbed her temples as she balanced the phone on her shoulder. There was so much to unpack there, she didn't even know where to begin. "Who the fuck writes blind items about *authors?*" She grumbled. "Seriously? Like, Tom Cruise hasn't done anything scandalous lately so they have to resort to the publishing industry? How boring."

"Is it true or not, Taylor?" Caroline asked, cutting straight to the point. Taylor felt that same pang of guilt in her chest she felt every time she lied to her friend, or anyone when it came to her and Dean and shook her head.

"No, it's not true. I took him out as a thank you for working for me for a year," she explained. Caroline let out an audible breath of relief on the other line, and Taylor chastised herself for not realizing earlier that the paparazzi might have been around, and they might have looked into it more than they should have.

Naturally people would assume it was a date - but it really *had* been a nice outing between friends to celebrate their achievements that year.

The fact that they were fucking had nothing to do with that.

"So how do we damage control this?" Caroline

continued. Taylor blinked, looking down at her phone as if she hadn't quite heard the words coming out of her mouth.

"Damage control? Do we *need* to do damage control? I mean, how many people read blind items these days? Or even believe them?"

"A TON of people, Taylor! There are whole TikTok accounts devoted to speculating on these things!" Caroline exclaimed. Taylor sighed and glanced at the cracked door of the bathroom, where the shower could still be heard as Dean finished up his morning routine. He would probably know more about that than she did. She knew social media was important, and she loved scrolling on TikTok and Instagram mindlessly to pass the time, but Dean was the one who made her look good online. He would probably have some ideas.

"Look, I'll try and think of something. I'll ask Dean when he's done getting ready if he has any ideas as well. I'm exhausted and we have to get breakfast...once I've had my coffee I can come up with a game plan," she assured her.

"Ok. And be careful! Any more pictures like that and you'll have a hard time selling that you're just friends," Caroline warned her. Taylor groaned in response.

"Ok *Mom* I'll be sure to look for the paps in the bushes hiding in their camouflage," she grumbled, and she didn't get a chance to hear Caroline's witty comeback before she hung up the phone. She hadn't even had a chance to ask her friend about the dig at her writing - but that was hardly the pressing issue at the moment.

Perfect timing, as Dean stepped out of the bathroom, his blond hair wet and plastered against his face and a white towel wrapped around his waist. She couldn't stop herself from eyeing him as he stood there in nothing but a towel, reminding herself that she had bigger problems to worry about right now. Jumping Dean's bones right after he got out of the shower should *not* be high on her priority list right now, even though her body was screaming at her to do so.

"Caroline?" He asked, knowing full well that the only people she'd be talking to right now were him and her agent. She nodded.

"There was, uh, a blind item posted about me," she explained. He paused and then ran a hand through his wet hair.

"You sure it's about you?" He asked. She nodded. She was still trying to process that she'd been referred to as an 'A-list' author. Did people really follow her career that closely? She got that weird feeling in her stomach that she always got when she thought about how paparazzi now sometimes hid outside her condo across the street. Like she was on display, and not in a good way.

"And uh...you," she told him, ripping off the band-aid quickly. He'd walked over to the dresser to throw on a pair of underwear and paused, one leg through his boxer briefs and his other leg balanced in the air like a flamingo.

"Me?" He asked in shock as he finished pulling them, coming over and sitting next to her on the bed as she pulled it up on her phone. She bit her lip as she scrolled, trying not to think about how his ocean spray body wash smelled amazing when he was this close to her. His skin was hot and sticky from the shower, and it was like he'd picked her favorite pair of boxer briefs that he owned on purpose. She couldn't stop glancing down at him, taking in the hard lines of his body through the black material.

He read the blind item and let out a low whistle. "Fuck. That is...damning."

"Caroline says we have to do damage control," she told him. He wrinkled his nose in confusion and looked at her.

"Damage control?"

"That's what I said!"

He chuckled and shook his head. "I don't think anyone even really cares if these are true or not."

"They do, though," she said with a sigh, running a hand through her hair. The more she thought about this, the more anxious she got. She knew deep down that Caroline was right. People talked, and not all press was good press.

"So..did you have any ideas in mind for damage control?" He asked, raising an eyebrow at her. Taylor shook her head and leaned back on the bed, staring up at the ceiling.

"No. Nothing," she admitted. He leaned back and laid down next to her, and she felt her heart race as she realized he'd reached over and grabbed her hand.

"We can come up with something. It'll be ok. I promise," he assured her softly. She smiled and looked at him, and he turned to look at her and returned her smile. There was something reassuring in his eyes, and she knew that it would all be ok.

"I just…still have a hard time dealing with the fact that people actually care enough about me to make me famous," she admitted with a whisper. He raised his eyebrows and turned on his side to face her, and she followed suit, lying on her side as he looked at her with a frown.

"Why?" He asked curiously.

Taylor wasn't exactly sure if she could put into words why it gave her so much anxiety. Perhaps it was the fact that she didn't think her writing was good enough to be that popular. Maybe it was because it made her feel like a circus act being watched this much. Or maybe it was because she feared it would just get even worse if her career kept skyrocketing, and more people knew her name.

"I just don't know what's so special about me. Why am *I* the one whose book sold so well? Why do I get a show and a huge book tour and…"

"Taylor, stop," Dean said softly, reaching out and lightly setting his hand on her forearm. She paused, staring into his brown eyes and blushing. She was doing it again. She was spiraling. His touch on her grounded her though, keeping her tied down to Earth. She focused on studying his face, keeping her anxiety at bay as she looked over his handsome features. The way his nose came to a dainty little point, his long, bright blond lashes, the tiny little birthmark on his cheek…

"Why *not* you, Taylor? You're beautiful and talented, and people enjoy your books. They enjoy *you*. Why *shouldn't* you be one of the lucky ones?" He asked her quietly.

Her heart started to race and she realized she had no answer for him. Did he really think she deserved all this? The money, the fame, the notoriety…would she ever truly feel like she earned any of it?

She muttered a small thank you, and he smiled, his hand gently running up and down her arm in a comforting way. She felt herself relaxing a little, and she thought back to how Caroline would react if she had somehow, magically, been able to witness what had just happened. She felt herself starting to chuckle under her breath.

"Imagine how Caroline would freak if she knew it was all true," she added with a small smirk, and he laughed and shook his head.

"I think her head would implode."

"I'm pretty sure she'd threaten to get you deported," she added, nudging his arm playfully, and he leaned forward and lightly kissed the tip of her nose. Whenever he did that, she could feel the warmth of his lips all the way down in her heart. It was so…tender. She loved when he got rough with her, but when he was delicate with her? That was almost better.

"How about we get dressed, go get breakfast, and forget about this for a few minutes, ok?" He suggested, and she smiled and nodded in agreement.

"That sounds lovely," she said as she sat up. She hopped to her feet and held out a hand for him and he stood up, and she grinned as she eyed his naked torso.

"You're ready to go, yeah? You're just wearing these to breakfast?" She teased, gesturing to his boxer briefs. He rolled his eyes with a grin before heading over to the wardrobe.

"I thought the idea was to get attention *off* of us sleeping together," he retorted, and she beamed at him.

"What? I thought we could give all the single ladies at breakfast a show," she smirked, and he raised an eyebrow at her as he laughed and pulled on his jeans.

"Starting a riot at breakfast? Classy," he teased her before taking his towel and tossing it playfully at her.

"Oh, you think you'd start a *riot* walking around like that? Someone thinks highly of himself," she teased, and he grinned again before he tackled her playfully to the bed. She cackled, letting loose a loud laugh that she very rarely ever uttered as he tickled her sides.

"Dean!"

"What? You started it!" He exclaimed as he blew a

raspberry in the crook of her neck. Her heart fluttered with excitement as she giggled, wrapping her arms tightly around him before he pulled away with a smirk. She lightly smacked his chest and he hopped off of her before heading over to the nightstand and grabbing his glasses before going to get a shirt out of the dresser.

"Getting out all your flirting before we head out into public?" She asked with a playful grin, but she realized as soon as she said it that she meant what she had said. She liked it when Dean flirted with her. She knew she shouldn't, and that was bringing them closer and closer to a place they couldn't come back from, but it made her feel…appreciated. Admired.

He paused and bit his lip, nodding. "A little bit, yeah."

He walked over after throwing on his t-shirt, taking her by the hips and staring down at her. She liked when he wore his glasses, even if it meant she sometimes bumped them while they were kissing. He looked like a hot professor when he wore them.

"It'll be fine, we'll figure something out," she said with a soft sigh as she cupped his face in her hands. He nodded softly and nipped her lip playfully, squeezing her hips one more time before taking a big sigh and stepping back.

"Alright. Friend mode commencing now," he declared as he headed for the door, and she rolled her eyes playfully as she grabbed her purse.

"Nerd," she teased him as she walked out the door after him.

CHAPTER SIXTEEN

TAYLOR

"Stop looking at your phone, or I'm going to chuck it in the ocean."

Taylor looked up at him and raised her eyebrow, pushing her phone to the edge of the table and focusing on her breakfast again. She knew that Dean could tell she was still on edge, though, and no amount of screen-free time was going to get her mind off the blind item.

She hated that she was obsessing over this so much. With every passing moment, her obsession continued to grow. She shouldn't care. Blind items weren't even true half the time, and most people knew that. Why was she stressing so much?

"I can't tell if you're happy or upset about this whole blind item thing," he pointed out, and she glanced at him in confusion.

"Why would I be *happy* about it?" She asked, and he shrugged as he took a bite of his eggs.

"Well, that means people are talking about you.

You're making it to the big time, right? Something like that?" He suggested, and she paused as she thought about it. He had a point, but she didn't think she was *pleased* that this was what people were talking about. Taylor didn't want this to overshadow her career and her writing. That was what really mattered, not what she did in her bed, but she knew how people were. She was a woman - the lens they used to study her was far more critical than a man.

"Or is it bothering your imposter syndrome?" He asked, giving her a pointed look from across the table, and she sighed heavily.

"I *don't* have imposter syndrome. And no, I'm not happy. It makes me look like...like...like I hired you just because you're handsome," she admitted as she angrily dug into her pancakes.

Dean smirked at her and she knew exactly what he was going to say, so she kicked him under the table with a small smirk.

"Don't even say it. Yes, I think you're handsome, ok?" She whispered, and he grinned, his eyes sparkling playfully behind his glasses. They had to remember they were still in public, and with the blind item coming out this morning, they had to be extra careful.

They were getting reckless, and if they had another slip up here, there was no way they'd be able to brush this whole thing under the rug. Not that she thought any of these vacationing couples around them even knew who she was. Sometimes she got stopped by fans for pictures or autographs, but no one had come up to her here, which she was grateful for. It made her forget the lens she was under for a quick minute and allowed her to just let loose.

Taylor *had* been letting loose, at least, until this whole blind item fiasco. Now her anxiety was back in full force.

"I think we just need to let it blow over," Dean suggested, and she nodded thoughtfully as she took a sip of her juice. "Once your book is released next week, the sales will speak for themselves. No one will care about us once all they can talk about is Jill Augustin."

She bit her lip, unsure if she really believed him. "You think so?" She asked sheepishly.

He shrugged. Ok, there was her answer. "Perhaps. I mean, I'm not sure. I just don't see anything else we can do to pivot attention away from it, short of creating *another* scandal," he added. She frowned a little at that. She hated it when Dean didn't have all the answers.

She shook her head. "And I definitely do *not* want to do that," she assured him.

"Ok then for now…let's just eat, enjoy ourselves, and maybe wait until Caroline calls us with updates. And *no* checking Twitter or Instagram or anything else today, ok?" He asked. "I will not hesitate to take that phone from you."

She smiled and shot him an appreciative look.

"What do you want to do today? Snorkeling? Shopping? We can see if they have a guide that can take us to those Mayan ruins you wanted to visit," Dean suggested, and she felt an odd flutter in her heart as he spoke. He was probably deflecting, trying to figure out anything to keep her thoughts away from the blind item. Yet she also appreciated that he knew she wanted to go to the ruins - she'd just mentioned it in passing, and naturally, he'd taken note of it. He was always doing things like that. Learning about her and studying her.

"I could go for some shopping. You know I love to spend money when I'm stressed," she teased.

"As someone with access to your credit card statements, I can attest to this," he replied with a joking laugh.

They managed to make it through the rest of the breakfast without a single mention of the blind item, but both of them knew it was weighing heavily on the back of her mind. She really wished she knew how to shut off her brain in these instances, but that just wasn't possible.

She could only hope that they came up with something to get the heat off of them, and fast, so she could go back to enjoying her vacation.

****

"Oh god, do you think my dad heard about it?!"

"Taylor, do you *really* think your dad reads blind items? Or gossip magazines?" Dean questioned her with an eyebrow raised.

"Probably not but...ugh, that would be so embarrassing if he found out about us that way," she grumbled. He pretended to act offended and grabbed his chest as they entered the lobby, heading for the elevators.

"Oh, you're embarrassed by me? I see how it is," he joked, and she playfully punched him in the arm.

"Absolutely not. I'd be honored to date you," she retorted, and then blushed when she realized what she'd said. If he noticed how awkward that statement was, he didn't let on which she appreciated - but she saw the hint of a blush creep up his cheeks.

"But uh, I'm pretty sure my dad likes you more than he likes me, so come to think of it, he actually wouldn't care," she joked, pushing past her little blunder, which made Dean laugh.

He looked like he was going to say something else when they both realized all of a sudden that there was a small crowd gathering in the lobby of the hotel. There were a handful of employees huddled in a corner, watching a man check in at the front desk. Even more alarming, there was a paparazzi outside the hotel, shooting pictures of the man from outside the large glass entryway.

Great, just what she needed. More paparazzi sniffing around the place.

The man in question was wearing a leisurely pair of golf trousers and a light purple polo, which made his tan skin pop. He looked a little older than her, maybe only by a few years, and as he chatted away with the front desk staff he ran a hand through his chestnut hair, golden rings glittering on his thumb and middle finger.

The man didn't seem phased by the camera as it clicked away pictures, and Taylor turned to Dean and poked him in the side, drawing his attention away from the paparazzi. She gestured towards the man, tilting her head to try and make it not so obvious that she was looking at him.

"Who's that?" She asked. She knew that he was trying to break into the management business, so he knew of a lot more actors and actresses than she did. He glanced at the man and stared at him for a second before his eyes widened and he let out a low laugh.

"Holy shit. That's Alex Campano. Haven't seen him in ages."

Taylor blinked. The name didn't ring any bells for her. "Who?"

Dean looked back at her. "He's a famous British

socialite. Well, technically Italian I guess. His family is loaded and has distant ties to the Italian royal family," he explained. "Like, the real *old* monarchs, from before Napoleon."

Taylor was going to have to take his word for it since Italian politics had not been one of the things she'd studied in college. She nodded at him and glanced back at the man, who was still checking in. "That would explain the paparazzi."

"Yeah, they always followed him around school."

She paused, looking at him in shock as his words sank in. "Wait, you went to school with him?" She hissed. They'd talked about all manner of things this past year, and for some reason, the fact that he'd gone to school with a man whose family had once literally been royalty in Italy had never come up.

He shook his head. "Well, not really. Technically yes, but he was three years older than me, and I never spoke to him," he added. Still, she couldn't believe how he'd just dropped that bomb on her so casually in conversation. She always forgot Dean came from a relatively wealthy family.

"Is that all he's famous for, then? Money?" She asked, and Dean shrugged.

"Yeah, pretty much. I'm not sure what he does for a living besides travel and take pictures of himself shirtless on the beach," he added. "Heard he was a nice guy in school, though."

She nodded, absorbing it all as an idea started to form in her head. She watched the man intently as Dean scrolled on his phone, clearly unimpressed with the new arrival at the resort. A minute later, before she could really process what she was doing, she brushed off the skirt of her wrap dress and started across the lobby to him.

She heard Dean call out to her to come back, but she didn't listen. If she stopped she'd chicken out, and she saw no other option here for her current dilemma so…she had to just jump in. Taylor confidently approached the man as he wrapped up at the counter and put on her best smile for him.

"I knew this hotel was known for attracting the best guests from across the globe, but I had no idea Alex Campano would be staying here when I booked," she eased into the conversation with a smile as Dean caught up to her. She could practically feel the nerves radiating off of her assistant as he approached her from behind, but she ignored him.

Alex smiled at her and she took a moment to really take in his appearance. He had long dark hair - not so long that he could tie it in a ponytail, but long enough to tuck behind his ears - and a few days' worth of growth on his face. He was tanned and had dark smile lines on his face as he grinned, as well as lines near his eyes that told her he smiled at people quite a bit - a good sign. The softest smattering of freckles dusted over his nose and cheeks, and he held out a hand for a shake.

"I hope you're including yourself in that group," he shot back with an effortless grin. His voice was thick with an elegant posh accent, similar to Dean's, which made sense if they'd both gone to the same school. Somewhere in the distance, she heard a click of a camera as their hands met. Pieces were falling into place exactly how she wanted them. "Taylor Mullins, isn't it? Author extraordinaire taking the world by storm?"

She simply blinked at him for a moment, taken aback. She had to admit, he surprised her. She hadn't expected to be recognized by him and had anticipated having to do some schmoozing to warm him up to her.

"That's me," she said, blushing a little. Alex seemed to notice and flashed her another smile. Oh, man. He was good at this.

"At this rate, I think you'll be as recognized as George R.R. Martin, so get used to it," he flirted back. She bit her lip, wondering if he *truly* thought that or if he was just buttering her up, and then she heard Dean clear his throat next to her.

"Hello. Dean Coffey. I'm her assistant," he said, reaching out his hand for a shake. The way he was moving his body next to hers, and crossing his arm over her, it was like he was trying to shield her from the guy. Jesus, why didn't he just start rubbing himself all over her and claiming his territory? Dean had never struck her as a guy who got jealous. What was his problem?

"Coffey," Alex repeated, and she noticed the slightest bit of recognition in his eyes. Dean seemed to notice too and jumped on it.

"Yes, we actually both attended Bergdorf Academy," he explained. Alex made a little 'ah' face as the memory came back to him.

"What a small world," he chuckled. He turned back to Taylor and grinned at her. "So are you two here together? Or with others?"

She knew what he was asking. It was just a friendly question, on the outside at least - but she caught the undertones in his words. She was about to open her mouth and answer when Dean jumped in at the bit first.

"Together. Just us two," he told him plainly with a smile. He looked to be grinning, but Taylor had never seen that smile on him before. It was the fakest smile she'd ever seen, and she was *so* tempted to smack it right off his face.

What was he doing?! She had a solution to their problem right here in the palm of her hands, and he was ruining it by acting like a damn peacock, trying to one-up Alex.

"How lovely. I'm sure we'll see each other around the resort, then. We'll have to meet up for dinner or drinks," he told them politely, but Alex was only looking at Taylor as she spoke. She noticed, and she knew Dean noticed, because she could practically feel him tensing next to her and his body temperature rise in anger.

"That sounds great. It was nice to meet you," she told him politely, and he returned her sentiments before taking his bag and heading off down the hall. As soon as he was gone, and the paparazzi was no longer hanging out on the driveway through the window, she grabbed Dean by the arm and dragged him aside.

"What the fuck, Dean?!" She snapped at him, pushing him against the wall. His eyes widened and she could tell he was debating if he should play dumb, which she hated. Dean never played dumb with her.

"What!?"

"Don't *what* me. I'm surprised you didn't start mauling me in front of him to stake your claim over me."

"Taylor, I would never do that!" He hissed back, and she rolled her eyes. He was acting like a child, and this was highly unlike him.

"Come *on* Dean."

"Listen, I just...I don't like his vibe," he insisted, and this time she was the one rolling her eyes. She scoffed and crossed her arms as she looked at him.

"You literally said five minutes ago that you remember him being a nice guy at school."

"That's what everyone *said,* but that doesn't mean it's true!" He clarified quickly, and she blinked at him, wondering if she should be insulted that he thought she'd truly buy that explanation.

"We're supposed to be trying to *not* let people know we're...*us* and then you go and do that!" She snapped at him. He paused and blushed, biting his lip. It seemed like she had finally cracked through whatever fog was currently clouding his judgment.

"I'm sorry, I just..."

"Don't worry about it. We'll worry about it next time I see Alex and we can do damage control," she insisted. Taylor hated that phrase - damage control. She'd uttered it far too many times this morning for her liking. She could feel Dean tense again near her and he blinked in surprise.

"What do you mean when we see him again?"

"Well, I'm going to need some shots of us hanging out if we want to convince the world I'm hooking up with him!"

She hadn't meant to just blurt out her plan like that, and she could see that she'd hurt Dean when she said it. She didn't know why - he agreed that they should do something to take the heat off of them, but he was looking at her like he couldn't believe she would do this.

"You can't be serious."

"Dean, think about it. All I have to do is have a few pictures taken with him, maybe a few pictures of us kissing, and you're off the hook," she reminded him. She wasn't the only one with stakes in this. His reputation was on the line too, if he ever wanted to look for another job and get into management at a public relations firm. Sleeping with your former boss wasn't exactly a good look for anyone, even if you were a handsome man like Dean.

He looked at her and his next words strung. "You mean without me around."

"It would be kind of hard to do this *with* you around, yes" she admitted softly.

He paused, nodding as he processed it all. He was annoyingly silent. Yet at the same time, Taylor felt bile rising up her throat. She hated that she had to do this to him. It felt wrong. This whole scenario was wrong. But part of her brain was screaming at her that something was off with Dean. He shouldn't be this...*upset* about this. About this plan of hers. She didn't intend to go fall in love with Alex. He surely knew that. She just wanted to use him and his notoriety, which sounded awful as she thought it back in her head, but what choice did she have? Really?

"I'm going for a walk," he grumbled, pushing himself off the pillar he was leaning against and starting to walk away.

She blinked, not expecting his abrupt departure. "Oh, ok."

"I'll meet you back at the room later," he told her, not bothering to look back at her as he started on down the hall. She nodded and sighed.

"Ok, that's a good idea - I'll probably go change and then head down to the beach," she called after him. Dean held up a hand to indicate that he had heard her, but that was it. She felt her heart sinking, suddenly wishing she could go after him instead of heading back up to the room.

No, that would do her no good right now and she knew it. He needed a second to be alone with his thoughts, as did she. Going to the beach would be better for her and allow her some time to reflect on her morning. That had been her original plan, and she wasn't co-dependent on Dean.

She could go have fun without him.

CHAPTER SEVENTEEN

DEAN

Five months ago

Thank God Dean had a key to Taylor's condo, or she would have never heard the doorbell over the music was she blasting.

To say he was confused as he entered the place would be an understatement. He headed into the living room, where she usually had her laptop and planner and all her random notebooks full of writing ideas scattered around her and found her laying on the floor, crying into a bottle of merlot as she was splayed out like a starfish on her back. It might have been comical, had he not found it incredibly alarming.

It looked like a tornado had hit the room, even for her, with ripped-out pieces of notebook paper all along the floor and her laptop open on her manuscript. She was wearing yoga pants and an old sorority shirt, her hair up in a messy bun, as tears streamed down her face from her puffy eyes. Music was blasting, and it sounded like some sort of musical soundtrack. He paused, unsure of what exactly was happening, let alone how to proceed. She'd had anxiety attacks before, but nothing like this. This was on a whole different level.

"What the *fuck* is going on?" He asked, mostly to himself, as Taylor hadn't seemed to notice he was there yet. She kept crying and he walked over to her phone, turning off the song that was currently blasting on her Spotify.

"No, put it back on!" She cried, and he shook his head and knelt down, taking her hand and pulling her up to sit. She flopped up like a rag doll, letting herself be pulled without protest.

"Jesus Christ, Tay, it's 9:30 in the morning, why are you drinking?!" He chastised her, taking the wine bottle from her without much of a fight from her end. Thank God it had been over a month since he last had a drink, so he felt no temptation taking the wine away from her, but the more pressing issue was trying to figure out *why* she felt the need to drown her sorrows in wine before it had even hit noon on a Tuesday. He also noted the bottle was only about half empty, which was hopefully a good thing.

"The entire last half of my book, they hate it!" She wailed dramatically, and he paused. He raised an eyebrow and sat down next to her, trying to comfort her as he took her hand in his.

"I thought you said the editors loved it!" He countered, trying to think back to how she'd boasted about her manuscript when he first started working for her. It was the second in her trilogy, and she always talked about how she felt it was ions better than the first book. About how it was showing that she was really coming into her own as a writer and honing her craft. Taylor hiccuped and he found himself rubbing her arm as she tried to calm herself, to no avail. She reached over and hit the play button, blasting the musical number once more as she began to cry all over again, trying to lay back down, but he stopped her and kept her sitting up.

"I have to redo the big reveal at the warehouse in the end. I made a major plot hole in chapter four, and I can't believe I missed it in my notes when I went through the storyline and made sure all the pieces fit...so it makes no sense they'd even *be* there let alone..."

"Ok, shush, shush, it's ok. It's ok. Calm down and then we can talk about it, ok?" He suggested, thinking that was best rather than letting her continue to ramble on and spiral into a rabbit hole of despair. The fact that she was trying to find a plot hole at least explained the mess of notes around her in the living room.

"What the hell are you listening to, anyways?" Dean asked as he reached over and turned the music off once again. He couldn't hear himself talk, let alone think, with that racket in his ear.

She bit her lip and wiped her eyes. "It's '30/90' from the *Tick Tick Boom!* soundtrack," she explained. He could tell that he must have looked very confused, because she hiccuped again and elaborated further. "Andrew Garfield was in it. It's about a playwright who is dealing with a quarter-life crisis and his impending death while trying to write a musical and get his big break."

At first, Dean wasn't sure what any of that had to do with Taylor or why she was listening to it on repeat and crying, but then he remembered what she'd told him about her journey into the publishing industry. 62 agents had rejected her before she even got her first partial request, and that had turned into an offer from Caroline. That number had been ingrained in her brain for years since she first started querying her debut. She rattled it off like people rattled off their birthdays. He could see why she might relate to a musical about a struggling musician who felt like he was running out of time to be successful.

"Tay, listen to me, it's going to be ok. No one hates your book. *Everyone* has to make edits to their books. You know this," he assured her, using a calm and collected tone as she continued to sniffle in front of him.

"But what if…"

"Taylor," he said forcefully, cutting her off. He gave her a stern look, and he saw her blue eyes searching him, almost like she was wondering what he was doing. He also noticed that her eyes seemed faded - she was there, but at the same time she was far away, lost in her own mind. He didn't think it was just the wine doing that.

"You're having a panic attack, Tay. It's ok. You're going to be fine," he repeated. She looked like she might argue, but she stopped and wiped her eyes.

"Breathe," he told her, and she did so, nodding and taking a deep breath in and letting it out. Slowly, the fog that was clouding her eyes started to lift. He could see her returning to Earth, slowly but surely.

"You said the scene in the warehouse needs to be fixed, right?" He asked quietly. She opened her mouth and instantly started to argue.

"It's not just that, chapter four is…"

"OK, *two* chapters need to be fixed. Now, is that the

entire last half of your book?" He asked, tilting his head and reminding her of what she'd claimed just a few moments ago.

She hiccuped. "No."

"Ok, good. Two chapters is manageable. In fact you can probably finish it by the weekend, right?" He continued softly, taking her hand in his. He rubbed circles with his thumb along her knuckles, watching her face as he watched her visible anxiety start to fade away.

"When did you last eat?" He asked next, and she blinked at him, evidently startled by the change in topic.

"What?"

"Eat. Food. When did you last eat, Tay?" He asked again, more sternly this time. As terrifying as it was to watch her spiral like this, he knew he had to remain forceful with her to keep her grounded back here on Earth. He'd learned throughout his life that dealing with anxiety was different for everyone, and Taylor needed someone to be strong for her to keep her tethered to sanity.

She opened her mouth and then shrugged and he nodded.

"Ok, sit down, breathe, pet Trevor and I'm going to order us coffee and bagels," he said, pointing at the dog who had just wandered in, evidently brave enough now to venture into the room and investigate what was going on now that things had quieted down. "And no Andrew Garfield while I'm gone!"

Standing up, Dean grabbed his phone and headed into the hall to place an order for delivery. Returning to the living room, he found her seated on the floor beside the couch, her eyes closed as she gently petted Trevor between his ears. Though still a bit pale, he noticed that she seemed to be calming down. He fetched a glass of water form the kitchen and sat down beside her, handing it over.

"Better?" He asked. She nodded.

"I think if I rework the scene in the coffee shop and have Jill..."

He clamped his hand over her mouth, surprising her as she looked at him with wide eyes. He found himself smiling softly at her and chuckling before he pulled his hand away.

"Sorry, I just...don't talk about the book right now. Just be here. With me. And Trevor," he added with a chuckle, gesturing to the dog who looked like he might fall asleep next to her as she scratched him.

She smiled at him, resting her head on his shoulder and muttering a small thank you. He informed her that coffee and bagels were on the way, before sitting in silence for a while. He could feel her breathing evening out as she lay on him, and suddenly a thought occurred to him.

"Hold on. Don't you have that tattooed on you? 30/90?" He asked.

Taylor sat up and looked at him almost as if she couldn't believe he'd ever noticed that. He had, of course. She had a small tattoo of the seemingly random fraction on the inside of her ankle. Now, it was all making sense to him. She nodded and held up her ankle for him to see. He smiled, taking her foot and pushing the leg of her yoga pants up slightly so he could examine it, his heart racing slightly at the soft skin of her leg in his palm.

"Huh. Well. That explains that then," he said simply as he put her foot down, and she chuckled softly next to him before laying back down on his shoulder, her other hand snaking out to grab his arm. "We can unpack why you feel such a deep connection to a song about a midlife crisis once you've eaten something," he added with a small smirk, and to his delight, he saw her smile back at him.

"Do I need to put on *Clueless?*" He asked quietly, and she snorted softly next to him before she grabbed his hand and squeezed.

"I'd like that, yes," she whispered, and she closed her eyes as she continued to rest her head on his.

As they sat there, Dean had a startling realization. He wanted to reach over and kiss her, to let her know that everything was ok, and he understood. That he didn't judge her for her panic attack. To let her know that he was going to stay here with her as long as she needed. In fact, he'd almost leaned in, before he remembered that it would be highly inappropriate for him to kiss her like this. Sure, they kissed a lot. But it was always leading to sex. Not because they were sharing a tender moment together.

Just sex. That was what they said. Even though it was just a kiss...no. It wouldn't be *just* a kiss and he knew it. It would be so much more.

Dean pushed aside the desire, and then he pushed away the feelings stirring in his stomach entirely as his phone buzzed, alerting him that coffee and bagels were waiting at the door.

CHAPTER EIGHTEEN

DEAN

Dean had hoped that this walk around the resort would help him cool off, but all it did was make him angry. Especially when he saw Alex hanging out by the beach - thankfully Taylor didn't seem to have followed through with her plan to head down there - and Alex gave him a wave as he walked by.

Dean returned the smile and wave, but he didn't mean it and would have much rather thrown an obscene hand gesture at him instead. Stupid prick, standing there looking amazing with his tan skin and slicked-back hair. He hated him. He wanted to shove his head in the sand and leave him there like an ostrich.

Finally, after about an hour of aimlessly wandering the resort sipping on a to-go cup of coffee, he headed back to the room, wondering if Taylor was still there. He needed to talk to her. He knew that his feelings towards the situation were rooted in jealousy, but there had to be *something* else they could do to get rid of this whole blind item problem. He still had a hard time thinking that people would care that much, but the fact that Alex had actually known who Taylor was made him pause.

Perhaps her star power was growing more than they had ever expected. Perhaps people *would* pay handsomely for juicy shots or inside deets about an alleged love affair with her assistant, or an Italian monarch...shit, did he need to start looking into hiring her a bodyguard? Maybe he should think about that...

He entered the room, kicked off his flip-flops, and took off his glasses before he headed out to their secluded balcony. He wasn't surprised to see Taylor hard at work, typing away furiously on her MacBook out by their private pool. She looked like she had been getting ready to go for a swim, and had gotten distracted by something, abandoning her plans to attend to it immediately. It was probably an idea she'd had for her book, and knowing her, she had to get it onto her computer *now* or she was afraid the idea would leave her brain forever.

She was wearing her pink tie-dyed string bikini, which on any other day would have made him want to do many naughty things to her at the sight. Today, though, after her little show with Alex down in the lobby...nothing.

Well, not *nothing*. He was still a man, after all. But he was too pissed off right now to think of much else.

"What are you doing?" He asked her as he approached, frowning in her direction.

"Working," she answered, using those one-word sentences she usually did when she was deep in thought and plowing away at an idea in her book. She knew that wasn't what he was asking, though. He could tell from the way her eyes briefly darted towards him as he approached, her jaw clenching as she turned away from him.

"This is a bad idea," Dean said simply, crossing his arms as he looked at her. She raised her eyebrows and peered at him from over her laptop, trying to pretend she didn't know what he was talking about.

"What is?" She asked nonchalantly, but he could tell by the slight way her shoulders had tensed that she knew exactly what he was referring to.

"This Alex thing. You don't have to do this, it's too risky and could fuck with his feelings" he called her out for her dastardly plan, and she rolled her eyes in annoyance. That only made *him* more annoyed. Did she care at *all* about who she would hurt in this ridiculous scheme? He'd obviously left the bit unsaid about how this plan was going to fuck with *his* feelings as well, but he was sure she knew it.

Even though he wasn't supposed to have feelings at all. A fact he knew damn well.

"It's stupid," he told her plainly, and she scuffed.

"How is it stupid? You saw the blind item. People think *we're* sleeping together, and not only would they completely tarnish my image but...it's the right thing and you know it, Dean," she insisted, and he rolled his eyes with a grunt of disapproval. There was a lot to unpack there, namely, the fact that she thought their relationship becoming public would tarnish her image, as she so delicately put it. He knew she'd hate the idea of people thinking she only had an assistant so she could sleep with him, but to hear just how *much* she'd hate it...that was a kick in the gut he hadn't expected.

She was probably right, though. Taylor was usually right about these things. She navigated the social aspect of this world well, even though he knew it caused her a lot of stress. He knew deep down she was just as upset about having to do this as he was, but she was doing what she was supposed to do. She was putting on a mask, trying to act like she didn't care.

Dean really *could* read her like a book. Right now, he hated that fact.

He tried to take solace in the fact that she hadn't said anything indicating that they needed to put their own arrangement on hold, or that she really intended on sleeping with this Alex fellow. As a matter of fact, she'd flirted with *tons* of guys since they'd started their little hook-up. Went on a few dates too.

She had insisted they never went all the way, which he'd appreciated, but why was *this* man getting under his skin so much? Is it because he feared that maybe, she'd grow to genuinely care for this guy?

Who wouldn't want to be with someone like that? An Italian socialite with ties to the royal family? Taylor was successful and rich on her own, but snagging a man like Alexander Campano would have her set for life. She'd control the damn paparazzi herself.

Dean shouldn't care if she *did* care for him, though. If so, good for her. They didn't have anything between *them* that she needed to worry about - they were just friends with benefits. That was it. No feelings to be found anywhere.

"There's got to be something else we can do," he countered, and she shrugged, her eyes never leaving the computer.

"You're probably right, so why don't you come up with it? You're my assistant, after all," she reminded him.

Ouch.

That had stung, and it had been on purpose. Taylor

didn't usually fight with her words - she reserved that for her books - but when she did, they were lethal. She had rendered him speechless, and he huffed again and then glanced at the pool nearby. Normally, he would go to the pool and swim laps to burn off his frustration. It was what he had been doing to deal with his stress ever since his teen years.

That was a little hard to do, though, when the person you were angry at was seated ten feet away, and the pool was a private pool in your ritzy hotel suite. He couldn't escape her even if he wanted to, which was precisely his predicament at the moment.

Yet...as he gazed at the clear blue water, his eyes staring at the sea turtle mosaic etched into the tiles at the bottom, he got an idea. What he really needed to do was remind her of what she had right in front of her. Literally.

He knew what he was doing was immature and ridiculous and might not even work, considering how annoyed she seemed to be right now. Still, he couldn't stop himself from walking over to the side of the pool and stripping off his shirt. He very pointedly looked at her as he did so, taking the light white t-shirt and throwing it away on a nearby lounge chair, making his frustration with her known on his face.

Taylor looked up from her computer, her blue eyes narrowing as she stared at him. He followed her line of sight as she looked at his chest before moving her eyes down to his abdomen.

"What are you doing?" She spat at him, venom dripping from her voice even though her eyes were still burning into his muscles. He could feel himself blushing slightly but maintained his composure. He continued to glare at her.

"Nothing," he snapped back. "I'm going for a swim,"

he said as he took his belt buckle and began to undo it.

"No, I *know* what you're doing," she replied, crossing her arms and leaning back in her chair. Her gaze never wavered from his body, though, and he knew that meant he was winning. The thought was exhilarating. His whole world seemed to exist to please Taylor, and while he usually never minded it, today felt different. Alex's arrival had his emotions all over the place. "I meant...what are you *doing?*"

She knew he was toying with her, trying to tempt her and make her forget about this stupid fake relationship with Alex. Judging by the gaze she had on his body, it was working.

"I told you...going for a swim," he grumbled, undoing the top button on his jeans and unzipping them. He pushed them down his legs and kicked them aside. He was just clad in his boxer briefs now, but he didn't hesitate at all as he slipped them down his legs and added them to the pile of clothing, completely bare to her.

She raised an eyebrow at him, obviously not expecting him to get completely naked. Honestly, up until five seconds ago he hadn't intended on doing that, but now he'd caught her attention. She couldn't stop herself from staring at his dick as it hung limp between his legs, but he knew if he didn't get in the pool within the next few seconds, that would quickly change. It wouldn't take long for her hot gaze to get his blood pumping, and then he'd lose the upper hand in whatever game this was that they were playing.

He turned on his heel and walked into the pool, jumping straight in and reveling in the cold water. It helped him to refocus his energy on what he was doing here. Dean needed to make Taylor pay for what she was doing with this scruffy socialite. He needed her in this pool *begging* for him to take her, because, at the end of the day, he knew that no man could touch her the way that he could. He needed to remind her of that.

He surfaced and shook his head, using his hands to slick back his blond hair as he looked back at where she sat at the table. She'd closed her laptop and was glaring at him with her arms crossed moodily.

"I'm not stupid, Dean. I know what you're doing," she informed him. He resisted the urge to smile. The victory was *so* close he could practically taste it.

"I never said you were stupid," he reminded her, allowing himself to give her the *tiniest* of smirks in response as he watched his words grate on her patience.

She stood up and walked over to the edge of the pool, kicking off her flip-flops as she approached. She sat down and dangled her legs in the water, and to his immense surprise, *she* was smirking at him now.

"I think someone is a little *jealous* of Alex," she cooed at him. She was trying to take back control by letting him know she was on to him. He swam up to her at the edge of the pool, running his hands up her legs and resting them on her knees as he looked up at her, tilting his head as if he was confused.

"Jealous? Me? I think you're mistaken," he replied. "There's nothing between us to get jealous of," he reminded her. He knew he was lying through his teeth, though. He *was* jealous, and he hated to admit it even to himself. He sure as hell was not going to give her the upper hand and let her know what he was feeling.

"Really? So you're just out here, letting your dick hang out and going skinny dipping just because you're in the mood for a swim?" she countered, and his hands ran up to her thighs, leaving wet water droplets on her tan skin.

"You know us Brits aren't built for this kind of heat, so I have to cool off *somehow*" He retorted, his fingers moving to play with the ties on her bikini bottom. She wasn't stopping him, letting him know he was one step closer to victory.

"Doesn't seem like you're thinking of *cooling off*," she replied, but he could tell by the way she was watching his hands intently that he was breaking her down. Once again, she'd clocked him correctly - he was thinking of doing a lot of particularly *hot* things to her right now, despite what he claimed.

"I thought you had to work," he said, changing the topic and instead bringing up the point she'd told him earlier when he'd first walked in the room.

"I am working. I'm talking to my assistant," she answered. Once again...*ouch*. Dean knew that had been a jab at him, reminding him of his place in all of this. She was the star, and he was the assistant. He was meant to do whatever was asked of him. The sex was just a bonus, not anything he was entitled to.

It was that unspoken hierarchy that she never usually reminded him of, almost always treating him as her equal. Today, though, she was using it as a weapon. He wondered briefly if it was to protect herself and her own feelings, or if it was purely just to take him down a peg.

Well, fuck that. He was so much more than her assistant.

"I'm on break," he replied, his finger looping through one of the knots on her bikini bottoms. He pulled slightly, releasing the tie she'd had keeping the bottoms secured to her waist, and he heard her breath hitch. The sound made goosebumps erupt on his skin, and he felt himself getting excited as he watched her breathing get heavier.

"You're never on break from being my assistant," she countered, and he just smiled up at her, his other hand going to the other bow she had tied on her bikini bottom.

"I suppose that's true…because I know I'm truly the only one who can please you," he whispered. That did it - he'd won. He could tell from the way her eyes darkened and her lips puckered as he untied her swimsuit, tugging on the bottoms impatiently and pulling them out from under her. She didn't fight as he pulled her towards him, taking his hands to her hips and pulling her into the water with him.

He propped her up against the wall of the pool, pressing his forehead against hers as he slowly slid into her. She groaned, and he could tell she was trying hard not to let on just how good he felt. The smug satisfaction of seeing her bite her lip as she tried to hold back her moaning was so exhilarating - and Dean also viewed it as a challenge. Perhaps he hadn't won this battle quite yet.

He had to coax it out of her. He slid out of her and thrust in harder, moaning loudly into the crook of her neck as he did so. She whimpered, her nails digging into his skin as he kissed her neck softly. He did it again, his hands squeezing her bum as he did so, and she wiggled underneath him, a small gasp escaping her lips. It was working, but not fast enough for him.

He pulled his lips from her neck and nuzzled his nose against hers, keeping his lips deliberately from hers as he increased his rhythm. "You know it's true…I'm the only one who can make you feel this good," he whispered.

Her eyes clamped shut, gasping softly at his words. Even *he* surprised himself as he spoke. True, he'd been a bit more *amped up* this trip than normal, but dirty talk still wasn't exactly his strong suit unless it was via text - although she did have a way of pulling some downright filthy innuendos from him in the heat of the moment.

A fire had been lit inside him right now. Later he might be embarrassed to think about how he was essentially trying to stake his claim over her, a claim that he knew he had no right to, but that wasn't something to think about right now. All he could think about was her wet body pressed against his, her legs wrapped around him, as she squirmed and desperately tried to pretend she wasn't enjoying this.

She bucked her hips and tried to kiss him but he kept his lips away from hers. "I know your body. I know what touches drive you crazy," he muttered. He closed his eyes and ran his hand up her thigh and in between her legs, stroking her as he moved.

"Dean..." she groaned, and he moaned loudly as he heard his name fall from her lips. He was starting to lose control now but he was so close to winning this. Whatever *this* was. He had to focus, even though he felt like he was on the edge of spiraling out of control.

"That's right, say my name," he egged her on as he ran his tongue lightly along her bottom lip. She was clinging to him like he was a tree, her hands scratching along his back desperately. She moaned his name again and he moved faster, allowing himself to give in now that he had her right where he wanted her. She barely lasted more than a couple more thrusts before she crumbled apart and he followed her right off the edge.

After he felt the waves of bliss slowly subside, he slowed himself to a stop, keeping her propped up against the wall of the pool as he stayed settled inside her. Both of them were breathing like they'd just run a marathon. He looked at her and finally relented, kissing her softly as she shuddered underneath him. Both of them stared at each other, neither of them saying a word, yet having an entire conversation at the same time.

She knew exactly why he was upset.

He knew that she would still move forward with her plan, no matter what the cost to Dean's feelings.

Feelings he shouldn't have.

Yet all of it hung in the air, unsaid.

Instead, she closed her eyes and buried her hands in his hair, trying to catch her breath before she let out a soft chuckle. "I hate you," she muttered with a laugh, and he laughed back, knowing she wasn't being serious. He rested his forehead against hers, panting before lightly pecking her lips.

"Yeah, I hate you too," he joked in return.

CHAPTER NINETEEN

DEAN

Reluctantly, Dean agreed to help her with this plan. Despite the fact that he made it very clear to her that he thought this was a colossal mistake. He figured the sooner they got whatever paparazzi fodder they needed, the sooner they could go back to enjoying this vacation. He intended on keeping her locked in the room for the rest of the trip after this whole mess was behind them, having sex with her on every surface of their suite. That daydream was the only thing keeping him from completely breaking down over this whole mess.

Whenever he got annoyed with what Taylor had been planning to do, he just thought of taking her on the coffee table of the room...or in the shower...or in the pool again, that had been really nice...

He also kept a close eye on Alex whenever he spotted him the next day. For being a five-star resort, it was shockingly small so it was easy to keep tabs on him. He was doing a little *too* good of a job at it, though, and accidentally walked into a pillar in the lobby when he'd been trying to listen in on a conversation Alex had been having on his phone. Thank God no paparazzi had been around to witness *that*.

He promised himself he'd be good around him. He knew getting jealous of this situation was bordering on the edge of insanity, and most of the day he did well, saying a cordial hello every time they passed, until they ran into Alex while working out one morning.

It was their fourth full day there, and Taylor and Dean had been slacking on their fitness routine. Despite having multiple workouts in the bedroom throughout the day, their meals had easily been three times the size of their normal portions back home - and they'd gladly eaten every bite. Normally, both of them took their workout regime seriously, so they agreed to force themselves to head to the gym that morning after breakfast. Just as Taylor was getting off the treadmill next to Dean, he heard a familiar voice approach them.

"Well, look who it is, the famous author herself," Alex said, his posh accent absolutely grating against Dean's ears as he approached.

Never mind the fact that *his* accent was essentially the same.

"Alex! How has your time been at the resort so far?" Taylor asked conversationally. Dean had been delighted that they had only seen Alex in passing the previous day, giving him little waves since he always seemed to be on his phone or chatting with the hotel workers whenever they saw him. The man was annoyingly good at making friends.

Taylor had *not* been as thrilled, naturally, since she couldn't put her plan into play if she wasn't actually *talking* to him. She tilted her head and smiled at Alex, and Dean noticed her pop her hip out slightly. He could feel bile rising in his throat as he continued his walk on the treadmill and tried not to intervene. He had to behave. He'd promised Taylor.

"Sensational," Alex replied, and Dean rolled his eyes before he could help it. Who described something with that word? Sensational? *Gag.*

"Are you done with this treadmill?" He asked, and Taylor nodded.

"Yeah, I'm going to head over and do some weights," she explained. Dean felt a small bit of relief at the fact that Alex apparently wasn't going to follow her, but then that relief faded when he realized that meant he was going to be working out next to *him* instead.

"Lovely, I might join you in a bit," he replied before hopping on the treadmill and giving Dean a little nod in greeting. Dean plastered on a smile, deciding to focus on the belt as it ran under his feet, avoiding his gaze.

After a few moments of silence, Alex looked at him. "So what's going on with you two?" He asked. Well, damn, he cut straight to the point, didn't he? Dean's jaw tensed and he looked straight ahead, composing himself before he turned to Alex and shook his head.

"Nothing, mate. Honest," he answered, giving him a small smile to try and sell it. Alex chuckled a little as he leisurely walked, eyeing him up.

"Doesn't seem like nothing. You look like you want to punch me in the face."

"That's just...my face," Dean insisted, clearing his throat and trying to focus on the buttons of the treadmill in front of him.

"Well, that's good to hear that nothing is going on with you two," Alex continued. Dean dared to look over at him, and he could tell by the way that he held his shoulders straighter and focused on the TV in front of them that Alex knew exactly what he was doing. He was taunting him. Baiting him.

"Because I'm certainly going to try and get a piece of that while I'm here," he grumbled under his breath, and Dean felt himself swallow down a lump in his throat. Alex had officially made his intentions known - which shouldn't be a surprise to him, but hearing him *say* he wanted to get with Taylor was far different than just speculating it. This was making it too real.

He had to remind himself that Taylor had a say in this too. Just because Alex *tried* to sleep with her didn't mean she would, right?

"Have at it, then," was all Dean replied, taking his sweatshirt off now that he was warmed up and placing it on the side of the treadmill. He kicked up the speed and began a leisurely jog, hoping Alex dropped the conversation so he could focus on his run and try not to think about what he'd just told him.

Of course, Dean couldn't be that lucky. Alex just smirked at him, and he could feel the socialite's eyes burning into him as he stared straight ahead. Why hadn't he brought his AirPods down?!

"Appreciate the permission, mate. I'd hate to think I'd complete with you...although, to be frank, I don't think there'd be much competition," he added with a sly grin that Dean caught out of the corner of his eye. He tried to ignore him and then realized that Alex had bumped up the speed on his treadmill - to 0.1 more than Dean was currently running at.

He paused and looked at Alex, who had a smarmy grin on his face that was daring him, challenging him. Was he serious right now? Was he really trying to show off and puff his chest *that* much right now that he was challenging him on a treadmill, of all things?

Dean told himself that he was not going to fall for it. Nope.

Except he absolutely did.

He reached down and turned his speed up a few notches. He looked ahead, trying to act casual, like he hadn't just done that to spite Alex, but then he heard Alex increase *his* speed a bit more.

Dean tried not to smile with smug satisfaction, because he knew he could easily go a lot faster than this, and he could see Alex starting to struggle out of the corner of his eye. Apparently those muscles were all show and nothing else. He was doing a good job of hiding it, but as Dean upped his speed more, and Alex followed suit, he could see him starting to crack. Dean focused only on the belt and the buttons in front of him, upping his speed again so he was going in an all-out sprint...

Alex tried to match his pace, and promptly stumbled and fell comically off the treadmill. Unfortunately, he grabbed the emergency stop chord as he tumbled, so he didn't go flying off the belt like Dean had hoped - and he knew it was rude of him to even wish that upon him, but really, the man had brought it on himself.

Dean couldn't help it. He stopped the treadmill and laughed to himself, a snort escaping as he tried desperately to keep it locked inside, but that laugh quickly faded as he heard Taylor run up to Alex and help him to his feet.

"Oh my god! Alex! Are you ok?" She asked, and then she turned to Dean and shot him a dirty look. He had hoped she hadn't seen anything that they'd just done, but he could tell from the expression on her face that she'd seen it all.

"Yeah, yeah, I'm fine, just tripped is all," Alex insisted, but Dean took smug satisfaction in the fact that he was wincing as he got to his feet and he had a nasty abrasion on his knee now. Served him right for being a twat.

"Both of you, come here, right now," she grumbled, grabbing them by the shirts and tugging them off to the side of the gym. Dean hadn't realized until now that the handful of resort guests in the gym were staring at them, and he'd completely forgotten that there were other people here who saw what went down. *Oops.*

"Do you both think I'm stupid?" She hissed at them, and both of the men opened their mouths to protest. She held up at hand, letting them know she wasn't finished.

"You don't have to *compete* for my attention. It's immature and childish and one of you could have gotten hurt!" She exclaimed. "You think I don't know what this is? Enough of this fucking pissing contest you two have going on, or I'm not talking to either one of you for the rest of the trip."

Dean knew Taylor well enough to know she was one hundred percent serious, so he nodded. She looked at Alex expectedly, who also nodded with a small sigh.

"You're right, that was stupid of us. It won't happen again," he assured her.

Dean didn't want to make such a promise, but he had no choice, so he looked at her and nodded. "Agreed. Won't happen again."

She sighed and looked at them, her eyes lingering on Dean for a moment longer, before she announced that she was done with her workout for the day. He decided to follow her, leaving Alex to do whatever it was he had come down here to do, and even though Taylor insisted she was no longer mad, he couldn't help but feel there was some tension still hanging in the air.

Dean knew deep down that he should have never agreed to go along with this stupid plan. Someone was going to get hurt, and he had a gut feeling it wasn't going to be Alex Campano.

CHAPTER TWENTY

TAYLOR

Four Months Ago

Growing up with a single dad, Taylor had developed a healthy love for sports. Particularly baseball.

While she herself had never been blessed with the skills needed to be a successful softball player, her dad had instilled a love of baseball in her from a young age. Dodgers games were one of her favorite pastimes, and aside from the pandemic she had gone to at least one game every season since...well since she was born. She had the pictures to prove it.

This year, she was bringing Dean. She had insisted upon it. How was it that he had lived in the States for over a decade now and had never been to a Dodgers game?! Or any baseball game, for that matter.

Going to a baseball game was also the perfect opportunity to get out in an area where she likely wouldn't be recognized. She'd braided her hair in two long French braids, and with her trusty Dodgers cap hiding most of her face, she could be just another girl in the stands and not worry about being recognized for a day. Hell, they could probably put her on the Jumbotron and no one would bat an eye!

She'd gotten Dean to borrow one of her dad's Kershaw jerseys, as well as his Dodgers cap, so the Brit blended in seamlessly with the crowd. She had tried to brief Dean on the rules before they got to the game but it was becoming increasingly evident that he'd forgotten basically everything she'd taught him.

It was so freaking adorable.

"Ok, so even though that guy got out because he hit the ball over there, the other guy can still advance?" He asked, pointing at the Astros player who was currently on second base after tagging up and advancing on a fly ball that almost went out of the park.

"Yes, because he tagged up first," she explained. He nodded thoughtfully and took a bite of his hotdog.

"And that means..."

Taylor giggled. "It means he touched the base with his foot, and then he ran. If he didn't touch the base and had started to move off the bag *before* the ball was caught, it doesn't count and he's considered off base and can get thrown out," she explained carefully, grinning all the while. She could tell he was trying *so* hard to understand the game, but she had to admit - for an outsider who didn't grow up around the game like she did, it could be confusing. Hell, every season they were changing the rules and even *she* got tripped up on the new changes they made.

"There sure are a lot of rules to this game," he chuckled, finishing off his hotdog and wiping his hands on a napkin. "Seems like it should be exceedingly simple, just hit the ball and run around the bags."

"You say that like any of *your* sports are 'simple'" she teased with a grin, using air quotes to make her point. "Go on, tell me again how you determine the rank order for soccer. Sorry, football."

"Point taken," he conceded with a chuckle, nudging her playfully. He took a sip of his soda and leaned back in his seat with a sigh. "I don't want to know how much mystery meat was in those hotdogs I just ate," he said with a grin, folding his hands on his stomach. She giggled, unsure if he was trying to act like he was super full and bloated because as per usual, his stomach was as flat as a washboard.

"Yeah, best not to think of that while you're eating them," she agreed.

The next Astros player took to the plate, and immediately everyone began to boo the player incessantly - Taylor included. Dean raised an eyebrow and looked around before looking at Taylor with a frown.

"I'm sorry, *why* are we booing him?" He asked. Taylor smirked at him as a chorus of 'Cheater! Cheater!' started from the crowd and Dean looked even more confused.

"The Astros got caught stealing signs one season," she told him. He looked at her like she'd just spoken in Pig Latin, so she elaborated. "Basically, you're not allowed to study the hand signals other team catchers use to signal what they want the pitcher to do. Like what type of ball to throw and stuff. They were doing that and then creating a system of banging noises from the dugout to alert the player which pitch was coming."

He blinked. "Whoa. That's...elaborate."

"Yup, they went on to win the World Series that year, even though they admitted to cheating," she continued, unable to keep the bitterness out of her voice. Sure, the Dodgers had won recently, but the idea that a team had won without playing by the rules and still got to keep their rings? It didn't sit right with her.

"So they won the World Series even though they cheated? And they just let that happen?" Dean asked, and she just nodded and shrugged. Dean snorted and then joined the chorus of booing around her, making her giggle.

"That's bloody unfair! We *should* be booing them, then!"

"I knew you'd like baseball, Dean Coffey," she teased him, taking his arm and giving it a soft squeeze. He turned to her and grinned, biting his lip playfully as she watched his glance fall to her own lips. She blushed and pulled away, still aware that they were in public. Sure, people might not recognize her - but grabbing his arm like that wasn't a great idea. Even if his bicep felt *so* good under her grip...

The game was a pretty exciting one, with each team keeping the other one on their toes each inning. A run or two for the Dodgers, and the Astros would match it the next inning. The Dodgers were slowly getting a more comfortable lead, though, so by the time the seventh inning stretch came around, some of the fans were leaving, sick of sitting in the hot sun and convinced they'd walk away with the win now that they were up by five runs.

Dean looked mildly horrified when Taylor explained what the seventh inning stretch was - he'd reminded her that she had mentioned approximately *zero* singing being involved in this outing - but by the end of the stretch, he was sitting along with 'Take Me Out to the Ballgame' even though his tune was a little off, and Taylor couldn't stop grinning at him.

He looked so damn *handsome* with his blond hair stuffed under that baseball cap. The Dodgers jersey he'd worn over a plain grey t-shirt made him look like every other American guy here, but she knew part of it was the fact that he was trying so hard for her. He had gotten dressed up, tried to study up on the rules of baseball, and was intently watching the entire thing just for *her*. Because he knew that she enjoyed it. It was important to her so, by extension, it was important to him, and damnit, that made her heart positive swell with admiration for him.

She heard a mixture of groans and cheers go out around the stadium, and she turned to the scoreboard and saw that they'd thrown up the kiss cam. She laughed and shook her head as Dean looked at her in confusion.

"What's the kiss cam?" He asked.

She chuckled and pointed to the screen as the camera zeroed in on a married couple holding hands, and the crowd cheered as they politely pecked each other on the lips. "If the camera lands on you, you have to kiss," she explained.

"Really?" He blinked and sounded hesitant. "What if they land on people who *aren't* together? Seems like that blurs some lines of consent..." he muttered.

"You don't *have* to do it but it's fun," she insisted. "Plus, I'm pretty sure they are better now about making sure the people they pick are *clearly* together and not just a man and woman who happen to be sitting near each other."

Sure enough, the crowd began to laugh as it landed on another couple who were also both obviously together, since they had matching shirts on, but neither one of them was looking at the board. Someone behind them nudged them to try and get their attention, and the guy who had been staring off into space looked at the scoreboard and chuckled just in time for the camera to move to another couple.

"I have to admit I'm surprised they even have this in a post-Covid world," she added as an afterthought. He nodded in agreement, just as the camera panned to another couple.

Not just any couple. The camera panned towards *them*.

Of course it did. Why *wouldn't* they end up on the kiss cam? She laughed, thankful she was still hiding behind her hair, braids, and sunglasses, as Dean looked at her in shock.

"What do we do, Tay?!" He asked quickly, and she grinned and stood on her tiptoes, wrapping her hand around the back of his neck.

"You kiss me, dumbass," she joked, standing up and kissing him softly as the crowd erupted into cheers. She pulled away after just a few seconds, and the crowd had already turned their attention to the next couple on the cam as she stared up at Dean with a small smile. She knew he couldn't see her eyes through the sunglasses, but he was still beaming down at her, a look on his face that told her he couldn't believe they'd just done that.

"That was….um…fun," Dean stuttered, and she felt her heart race as she nodded in agreement. Perhaps kissing him like that was a little out of line. They didn't usually kiss unless they were alone, and unless it was leading to something else…

Taylor realized with a start that she'd *wanted* to kiss him in front of everyone here, to let everyone know that this smoke-show man next to her with the gorgeous accent was *hers*. Which was so wrong and so against everything they'd agreed upon…

"Definitely fun," she agreed quietly before taking a seat, and he quickly sat down next to her, neither of them saying anything else about the kiss as the game resumed. Why did she suddenly feel like she'd made a mistake? It hadn't occurred to her that maybe kissing him in public had been too much for him.

She looked over at him and was about to utter an apology when she realized that he was grinning like an absolute idiot. She blushed and looked back at the game, a small smirk forming on her lips as she realized what that meant.

She'd kissed Dean in front of everyone, and he'd liked it. He liked it so much that he couldn't stop smiling, even though he was trying to face away from her and pretend he didn't like it.

It was a thought that made her heart race, and it absolutely should *not* have made her that happy. But it did, and she couldn't deny it to herself. She was very, *very* happy.

The Dodgers ended up winning that day, and Dean declared it was the best baseball game he'd ever seen. In addition to being the only one.

CHAPTER TWENTY-ONE

TAYLOR

"Dean, what is all this?" Taylor giggled as she walked into the living room of the suite. He'd lit a bunch of candles in the entryway and ordered room service so they could skip dinner and have a private night alone, just the two of them. He'd been very secretive about the whole thing, telling her to go to her room and put on a cute dress before the meal came.

Now, he was standing here in his khakis and a light blue button-down shirt, looking more handsome than ever. If he hadn't gone through the trouble of ordering them food she might have peeled all those clothes off him right then and there. He'd snuck out of the room at some point and gotten her roses as well, giving them to her with a quick peck on the cheek. Her skin burned where his lips had touched her and her stomach fluttered with anticipation.

"An apology," he told her with a small smile as he pulled away. "For being an arse."

"Which time? Be more specific," she teased, but she

knew he was talking about this whole mess with Alex. She hated having to tip-toe this line between the two men currently in her life, and part of her felt awful about possibly leading Alex on as the week went on. She felt weird letting him know about her plan, though. It almost seemed easier to seduce him on the pretense that she actually liked him, rather than let him know how insecure she was about blind items and paparazzi.

"The most recent time," he told her, taking her hand and leading her over to the table.

"Oh, so the time Alex nearly broke his leg racing you on the treadmill," she replied, and he rolled his eyes and pretended to scuff at her.

"He started it, I've already explained myself!" He said with a smile.

She smiled back at him and put her arms around his neck, nuzzling her nose playfully to his. "Well, I'm sorry for being a bitch at the pool," she added, biting her lip. "I was kind of mean."

Fuck, the *pool*. She'd been on edge, taking out her emotions on her writing when he'd interrupted her. She could practically felt the irritation radiating off of him as he had come storming in, trying to talk her out of this Alex thing.

But then he'd started tempting her, stripping naked and luring her into the pool, where they'd had some of the best sex they'd had in a while. Not that *every* time wasn't downright amazing. She'd been snippy with him, rougher than she needed to be - but so had he, and damnit, it had been the sexiest thing she'd ever seen.

"Yeah, I deserved it though," he admitted, nudging her playfully. She blushed and pressed her forehead to his.

"Admitting you're right is going to do nothing but stroke your massive ego," she teased.

He smirked back at her. "I think I prefer you stroking something else of mine," he said softly, and she laughed and playfully smacked his chest.

"Dean!" She giggled. He had been on another level this whole trip, and quite frankly, she was a big fan of it. It was almost as if being here made him feel more carefree. True, it was possible they got a bit carried away and took risks they shouldn't have - like with the beach shack - but it was like she was really seeing his playful, flirty side for the first time. She could see what it would be like to be in a relationship with him.

A relationship she could never have. Which was fine. She didn't want one. She didn't want a relationship with anyone, least of all...

"What? It's true...what I had in mind is *also* massive, by the way," he joked, and she rolled her eyes playfully and buried her face in his neck as he brought her back to the conversation with another steamy innuendo.

"It is," she conceded with a smirk, and this time it was him who was blushing.

"You have a dirty mind, Dean Coffey," she prodded him with a giggle, poking his bicep. She couldn't stop admiring how good his arms looked in this shirt.

"You bring it out in me!" He laughed. "Seriously, you...*do* things to me, Taylor Mullins," he whispered softly.

She pulled back and smiled at him before he cleared his throat and pulled the chair out for her at the table. They joked more over dinner and it was almost - *almost* - like things were back to normal.

As normal as things could be between two people having casual sex.

After they finished eating, he stood up and headed to his phone, clicking on Spotify and playing a song. She recognized the opening chords to "Lucky" by Jason Mraz, one of her favorites, which she knew *he* knew. She smiled and stood up, and he took her hand in his and pulled her close to him.

They had never had the opportunity to dance with one another. Not since that night at the club all those months ago...and that hadn't been sweet and tender like this. That had been passionate, lust taking over their thoughts of reason and sending them down the path that had led them right here. His hand snaked around her waist and he led with his other hand, and she could feel her heart racing in a way that she'd never felt before.

"I really am sorry, Tay," he muttered in her ear. She smiled at him, trying to ignore the goosebumps all along her neck that popped up as his warm breath tickled her ear, and he grinned softly back down at her.

"I know you are," she assured him. She had asked him never to lie to her, and so far he'd kept his word on that end.

"You know that you just have to tell me what to do, and I'll do it in a heartbeat. Even if that means helping you seduce some snobby rich Italian socialite," he jested, but she could also see a tinge of hurt behind his eyes. He was trying his best to hide it, but she could see it written all over his face. He didn't want this for them. He didn't want to help her with Alex, and truthfully, she didn't want Alex either. He was a good-looking man to be sure, but he wasn't...

Shit. She'd almost thought that he wasn't *Dean*.

Emotions were creeping up in the back of her mind. This was getting all too...comfortable. That look in his eyes was back. The one she saw so often she had it ingrained in her memory, but she kept forcing herself to believe it meant nothing. It was just a look, nothing more.

Yet Taylor knew as she looked up at him, that she had that same look in her eyes. She wondered if he could tell. If he could somehow read her heart through her gaze and hear all the unsaid words that she had never uttered - *would* never utter - because it would be wrong.

Dean swallowed softly and looked away from her, pressing his cheek gently against hers. "Sometimes I wonder how the hell I ever got through life without you," he whispered.

Her breath hitched. He was saying things he absolutely shouldn't. She should stop him and remind him of the line that they dared not cross. Yet she felt her heart fluttering, excitement blossoming in the pit of her stomach. His words made her want to grab him and kiss him and never let go of him. Instead, she found herself chuckling a little and smiling up at him playfully.

"I've always been here. There was just a huge freaking ocean separating us for a while," she teased, trying to lighten the mood a little, and he laughed, his nerves clearly settling. He nodded and smiled down at her as they continued to sway.

"That's the last time I ever let the ocean get between us," he said playfully, and she rested her head on his shoulder with a soft sigh. She felt him pull her closer, and try as she might, she knew there were thoughts swirling through her brain that she shouldn't be thinking.

They knew what they were doing when they got into

this mess. This was a consequence of their actions. They couldn't tumble further off this cliff than they already had, or it would cause an avalanche they couldn't escape from.

Pulling away from him felt like the hardest thing she had ever done, but she knew she needed to. This was too much, and it was breaking her heart. She willed herself not to show her fears on her face as she smiled at him, cupping the back of his neck with her hand and rubbing the skin softly.

"I think…I'm tired. I'm turning in for the night," she announced softly. He nodded and gave her a look of understanding. He tucked a piece of hair tenderly behind her ear and smiled at her.

"Ok…goodnight, Taylor," he whispered.

"Goodnight Dean," she said softly, leaving the room just as the music ended.

CHAPTER TWENTY-TWO

TAYLOR

The next morning, the pair headed out to the beach like absolutely nothing had happened the night before. Like they hadn't slowed dance to an incredibly romantic song, or stared at each other with unspoken words hanging in the air around them before they both ran away to their bedrooms.

The flags were green again today, so Taylor suggested they head out to the beach. They swam in the ocean for a bit, took a break for lunch, and then headed back down as the waves picked up, just watching the horizon and relaxing in each other's company.

They had brought their respective books down with them after lunch, camped out, and just enjoyed the sounds of the waves and the gusts of wind whipping their hair in front of their faces for about an hour before she recognized someone nearby. Alex was lying on a beach chair about ten feet away, but it didn't look like he had noticed them. He was just lying there with his eyes closed, soaking in the sun.

Taylor hesitated for the briefest moment since neither of the men next to her seemed to notice the other one, before finally taking the leap and clearing her throat.

"Alex! Over here!" She called out, and Alex turned with a grin when he realized who it was and joined them. She could feel Dean tense next to her, and she noticed his right hand move - she would bet good money that he was starting to pick at the skin on his thumb again.

"Hello you two. Beautiful day, isn't it?" Alex asked as he settled down on the towel next to her.

"Yes, it's generally beautiful out on the beach in Cancun," Dean replied, and she discretely reached over and pinched his thigh *hard*. He let out a little yelp and she tried to hide her delighted smirk as she turned back to Alex.

"What have you been up to today?" She asked politely. Alex smiled and leaned back, closing his eyes and tilting his head back in the sun.

"Did some boogey-boarding this morning," he replied, and she could practically feel Dean rolling his eyes next to her. She took a deep breath and felt her hand digging into the towel, smashing it into the sand underneath. He'd agreed to be civil about this. He knew that she didn't care about Alex in the slightest, so why was he still acting like such a jerk?

"Sounds like fun," she replied conversationally. Dean remained silent next to her, and she took a moment to glance at him quickly. His jaw was tense, his gaze fixed out at the ocean. His brow was furrowed - did he know he had super expressive eyebrows? It was nearly impossible for him to hide what he was feeling. In fact, he...

Her thoughts were cut off as Alex nudged her playfully, pointing at the nearby beach volleyball net the hotel had set up a few feet away.

"Would you like to play some volleyball? No one seems to be using that net over there," he pointed out. "I'll happily be a single-man team and take on the both of you," he added with a teasing grin.

Alex had just the perfect amount of flirty undertone to his question, which thrilled Taylor. She didn't need a whole romantic affair with this man to make her problem with the blind items go away. She needed exactly that - just a small bit of flirting. Photos of Alex, Taylor, and Dean playing volleyball on the beach? If paparazzi were nearby, they would eat it up.

"Sure, we'd love to - right Dean?" She asked, turning to her assistant. She tried to give him that look that told him that he wouldn't have a choice in the matter, and he sighed and put on a smile.

"Yeah, sure."

* * * *

Taylor was *not* a good volleyball player, and it turned out that Dean was also not particularly skilled at it.

Still, it didn't matter, as she was having a fantastic time playing against Alex. Even Dean cracked a few smiles and joked around with him, and she thought maybe for a second he was starting to warm up to the whole Alex thing. It was hard not to be charmed by him as he valiantly tried to defend his entire side of the net by himself, but seeing as how both Taylor and Dean only got about 30% of their shots *over* the net, he wasn't working *that* hard.

They played for about an hour, even stopping to grab some nachos together, and she felt like she finally had everyone exactly where she wanted them.

Alex was flirting with her. Dean was accepting it and even being nice to Alex. Everything was falling into place. Her plan was actually going to work!

Until it all blew up with one very ill-timed spike of the volleyball.

After their snack, Dean and Taylor were trying to improve their skills a bit more, with Dean setting up shots for her to try and spike across the net. She wasn't doing very well - apparently, you had to be sort of tall for that to work, and with her barely cresting five feet tall, that was a challenge. Yet, she'd been ecstatic when it set the ball up for her to hit, and she managed to hit it over the net.

For a second it looked as if she might have actually outsmarted Alex with her spike, but then he was there in a flash. He leaped up, his hand expertly placed at the net to block the shot, and he spiked it with everything he had.

The volleyball shot towards the ground at lightning speed, and unfortunately collided right with Dean's face. Dean let out a yell and tumbled backward into the sand as the ball hit him with a loud THUNK.

Taylor let out a yell of surprise and ran to him, and Alex slid under the net and into the sand to help Dean up. Her heart was racing as she collapsed on her knees in the sand next to him.

Dean was moaning and holding his nose, and for a second she thought maybe his nose was broken, but there was no blood. It was certainly red, and he would probably be *very* sore, but overall he seemed relatively ok. Although the way he was hollering on, one might have thought he'd been stabbed.

"What the hell?" He snapped, and Alex immediately started apologizing. Judging by his red face, Taylor felt like this genuinely had been an accident. What did he have to gain from hitting Dean in the face?

"I am so so sorry, mate, I misjudged the angle of my spike, I truly didn't mean for that to happen..."

"Fucking prick," Dean grumbled, and Taylor smacked his arm, and he let out another yelp. She *had* hit him a bit harder than intended but - he deserved it!

"Dean! It was an accident," she insisted, and she knew what he was thinking - he didn't believe Alex. Alex nodded at him, attempting to get closer to him so he could inspect the damage, and Dean kept trying to move away from him.

"Should I go to the first aid tent? Get you an ice pack?" He asked him, and she saw Dean shoot him a nasty look. She had to stop herself from groaning in annoyance. All that progress they'd made this afternoon was gone in an instant.

"I think he's fine. Right?" She asked, glaring at Dean. He returned her glare, gingerly touching his face. He sighed, signaling defeat and nodded.

"Yeah, I think I'll survive. Barely," he said, making a weak attempt at humor as he looked at Alex with a small smile. A very fake smile, but a smile nonetheless. She was pretty sure Alex could tell it was fake too.

"No, I'm getting you an ice pack. Stay right here," Alex insisted. He hopped up and started jogging to the first aid tent. Once his back was turned, Dean stared at him and then threw up the middle finger at his back, and Taylor smacked his chest.

"Ow!"

"*Dean!* Are you kidding me?!"

"He did it on purpose!" He hissed at her, and she had

to physically stop herself from rolling her eyes. This was so unlike Dean. It was like an alien had taken over his body. Men flirted with her all the time, and he never so much as blinked over it. Now, he looked like he was ready to tackle Alex to the ground over her.

It was…kind of hot, but she had to focus on the problem at hand, which was convincing the world that she liked Alex Campano.

"Bloody hell, it hurts," Dean moaned, touching his face gingerly with a frown. She sighed and crossed her arms as he continued to groan dramatically over his nose, which was hardly even red.

"Dean, you got a volleyball to the face, you weren't shot. Stop acting like you're dying," she grumbled. Had this happened any other time - and he hadn't been acting like such a juvenile moron - she would have comforted him and fussed over him far more than she needed to. But he ruined it by acting like a twat, and he glared at her.

"Let's hit *you* in the face with a volleyball and see how you like it," he retorted grumpily.

"I know what this is *really* about, Dean."

"Oh yeah?"

"Yeah. You're acting *jealous* and you have no right to be," she snapped. "I don't know who this Dean is, but whoever he is, I don't really like him all that much."

That had done it. Taylor hated that she'd had to throw such a low blow, but it had the desired effect. They didn't say anything as they sat in silence, but Dean did allow her to inspect his nose a bit more closely. It was red and might get a bit swollen, but overall he'd lucked out and Alex hadn't actually hit him that hard.

Alex approached a few moments later with an ice pack, insisting that Dean use it or the swelling would be worse as the wound set it. He grumbled a reluctant thank you and laid down on his towel, his eyes closed as he kept the ice pack on his face.

Alex apologized again and then looked at her, as if waiting for her to make the next move on what they were going to do now. As much as she hated leaving Dean here - he was going to be fine. His nose certainly wasn't about to fall off any time soon. As much as he'd hate it, she had to take this opportunity to be with Alex. *Alone.* She cleared her throat and stood up straighter, putting on an air of confidence.

She turned to Alex and flashed him a grin. "Walk with me? Dean, you'll watch our things, right?" she asked.

Dean looked up at her and blinked, looking like he might argue for a moment. But then his mouth closed and she could see that he knew he was being difficult. He nodded and resumed icing his face as she stood up, brushing the sand off of her legs as Alex held out his hand for her. After a moment of hesitation, she took it, trying to ignore the burning glare that Dean gave her back as she walked away.

"It really was an accident, you know," Alex insisted again, and she smiled at him and gently nudged him.

"It's ok, I know. I think Dean does too, deep down," she assured him.

"He seems to like you. He seems nice," Alex continued as soon as they were out of earshot, and she had to stop herself from rolling her eyes. Men were *so* transparent sometimes. One thing she had learned over time was that any time someone said someone was *nice,* they didn't usually mean it.

"He really is. He does a lot for me, I never would have been able to survive this past year without him," she said, coming to his defense. He nodded, and she could tell in his face that he knew not to bring up Dean again.

"That must have been exciting. The book tour, and the impending TV show," he grinned at her, and she nodded. She appreciated the fact that he knew all these things about her - maybe he'd researched her, or maybe he really *had* known all that before she met him. Either way, it was nice to hear someone other than Dean and Caroline appreciate her hard work.

"It is! Once I head home, I'll have all the time in the world to finish up the last book. It's almost done, I just need to polish up some things," she assured him. He grinned at her, and she felt herself blush.

"Your book is very good, by the way. You're very talented," he continued, and she felt herself look at him in shock.

"Wait, you've read my book?" she asked, standing still in her tracks as she stared at him. Alex laughed and nodded, acting surprised that *she* was so surprised by this revelation.

"Of course! Well, I will admit - I only bought it on my Kindle after I met you the other day," he told with a smile. Ok, so he *had* just researched on her once he'd met her. That didn't matter in the grand scheme of things, though. He'd read her book! It was a thrill that never got old for Taylor when she learned that someone had read her work.

"But I'm almost done with the first one. Jill is a strong character yet still has her flaws. I always look for that in a good book. No one wants to read about someone perfect," he elaborated.

Taylor felt her heart rate start to pick up. Who the hell *was* this man? Alexander Campano was either the best actor in the world, or a genuinely thoughtful human being.

And she was about to fuck around with his heart. All her excitement fizzled away suddenly, but she kept her smile plastered on her face.

"Thank you very much for the kind words," she replied. She looked back for a second at Dean, who stayed seated at the place where she'd left him. He was pretending to read, the ice pack abandoned, but she would bet good money that he wasn't *actually* reading and was instead pretending he wasn't keeping a close eye on them.

They continued to stroll for a bit, making small talk about their various upbringings and what they did in their spare time, and they ended up sitting down on some free beach chairs and watching the waves. Dean was still within eyesight, but Taylor knew she had to keep her eyes trained away from her assistant in order to give off the appearance that she didn't care at all about him.

Eventually, Alex reached out and took her hand, and she let him. It felt foreign to have someone who wasn't Dean holding her hand. His hands weren't nearly as defined as Dean's, and far rougher and tanner than his as well. She wondered if Alex played lots of sports. His hands seemed calloused in a way that told her he was active, but she knew it certainly wasn't from menial labor.

It all felt wrong, and she wanted to jump up and run back down the beach to where Dean still sat. She couldn't, though, and she knew it. She had a mission to complete.

Making such a bold move meant that Alex was

opening flirting with her. And she was openly flirting back, even though she would have a man ready for her in her bed when she got back to the suite.

At least, Taylor sure *hoped* she would when all of this was done.

"You're doing ok with all of it? The fame and everything?" Alex asked suddenly. She blinked at him and blushed a little.

"I'll admit it's...new for me," she told him with a small sigh. "I was never the most popular kid in school. Never had a ton of friends. I joined a sorority in college to make friends, figuring if they were forced to hang out with me..." she trailed off, suddenly realizing she was bearing her soul to this man that she'd just met. She'd never told anyone else about the thing with the sorority, and how she'd been lonely as a kid after her mom left.

There was only one person who knew about that, and he was down at the other end of the beach.

Alex was good at making her feel comfortable around him, and she also knew that *he* knew what it felt like to be in the spotlight. Sure, he had been the subject of public scrutiny since birth, but he still was one of the only people here who understood what she was going through. Even if she wasn't attracted to him in that way...it was nice to know she had someone she could talk to about this stuff. As much as she appreciated Dean and knew he would always be there to listen to her rant, he wouldn't truly understand how she felt, even with his name appearing in the blind items.

Alex sat up and stood, taking her hands in his and pulling her to her feet. "You're taking it like a champ," he assured her, and she chuckled and looked at her feet, buried in the hot sand.

"I don't know about that…you barely even know me," she pointed out. He smiled and bit his lip and then gave her hands a playful squeeze.

"Is it entirely cliche for me to say right now that I feel like I *do* know you?" he asked softly.

That was when Taylor saw them. Paparazzi. They were about twenty feet away near the dock at one of the neighboring resorts, whose beach area they had wandered into. She wasn't sure if Alex knew they were there or not - if he *did*, bravo, and well played - but this was her chance. She couldn't squander it.

She shut off her brain. The more she thought about it, the more she knew she would chicken out at the last second. She couldn't afford to do that - she had to just *do* it, like diving into a cold pool that you knew was going to be freezing. She had to take a deep breath, not think about what was to come in the next few seconds, and take the plunge.

Taylor stood up on her tiptoes, wrapped her arms around his neck, and kissed him. He paused and then hugged her closer to him as he realized what had happened, kissing her back. He tasted a little bitter, like he'd just had coffee, and he was certainly skilled with his tongue. Yet it wasn't pleasant to her in the slightest - in fact, she was counting down the seconds until she could yank her lips away from his. All of it felt *wrong*. It felt foreign to her, and she knew it was because she was carefully constructing the entire thing for the sake of her image. If she actually *liked* Alex, she knew it would have been far different. She probably would have enjoyed it.

Alex was not the man on her mind in that moment, though. All she could think about was the fact that somewhere deep in her gut, she felt like she was making a huge mistake.

The cameras were too far for her to hear the clicks but she was certain they could get some fantastic shots from that angle. Maybe this would be it. One photo op. One opportunity for the gossip sites to get off her back about Dean, and then she could be done.

She pulled away after a moment and smiled up at him. "I should probably get back to my room and get ready for dinner," she said softly, trying to act coy and playful even though she really wanted to just dart down the beach and run back to Dean. She wanted to collapse to her knees in front of him and beg him to take them home to L.A. so she could run from Alex and run from the look he was giving her as he held her in his arms right now. His brown eyes were sparkling playfully as he looked down at her, his lips plump from the kiss. It made her stomach sick.

"Yes, shouldn't keep Dean waiting," he teased, and she wondered if he had his suspicions about them. If he did, he didn't seem to care at all. She chuckled and rolled her eyes at him like he was *oh* so hilarious to insinuate that.

"I'll see you later though, yes?" He asked, raising a dark eyebrow, and she nodded. She felt like she had no other choice. Truthfully, she wasn't sure she wanted to see him again - she wouldn't know for sure if she would *have* to until the photos were published, which could be anywhere from a few hours to a few weeks.

"Yes. That would be really nice," she replied with another coy smile. If she did see him again, she wanted it to be as a friend only - but Taylor knew he wasn't thinking along those lines.

Alex bid her farewell, and she took a deep breath as she started back down the beach, her eyes looking for Dean amongst the tourists who had camped out in the sand. She looked for his familiar mop of blond hair, but he didn't seem to be there anymore. She wandered back to their spot and found her things abandoned by him, and an empty spot of beach where his things had been.

She didn't realize it until then, but the moment Dean saw them kiss, he packed up his towel, put on his shirt, grabbed his book, and headed back to the hotel in a rage.

CHAPTER TWENTY-THREE

DEAN

It was like someone else had taken over his brain. He had fully intended on staying in the room once he dropped off his things, but everything in the suite reminded him of Taylor. It made him sick to his stomach. Dean couldn't think, he could barely breathe…all he could think about was what he could do to get rid of the pain radiating from his chest.

It was like a fog had descended over him, and he had no clue how he got there, but he found himself at the hotel bar. It was around dinner time now, which meant a crowd of twenty-somethings who were looking to mix and mingle had formed in the area, and he pushed his way to the bar with a determined look on his face.

He ordered a Negroni before he had a chance to second-guess himself and what he was doing. He sipped it down quickly, drinking it much faster than someone should, reveling in the familiar taste and the instant buzz he felt as the alcohol started to seep into his system.

He couldn't get the picture of them out of his mind.

He couldn't stop picturing them kissing…

It didn't help that his face still had a dull ache where the volleyball had hit him. Fuck Alex. Seriously. Fuck that guy.

He ordered another drink and downed that one just as quick as the first. By the time he finished his third drink, he was deep in conversation with a duo of young women nearby. They were probably around his age, maybe a bit younger, and he could tell that they started talking to him in the hopes that he might go to bed with one of them.

Boy, were they in for a rude awakening. Dean appreciated their interest, but neither one of them had anything on Taylor.

He asked for their names and promptly forgot them. He recognized that they had accents - he was pretty sure they were German tourists - but once again, he forgot where they were from the second they told him. He quickly took over the conversation and focused it all on himself, and had he been sober he would have wondered why they were even bothering with him after it became clear that he wasn't interested in them. He was obviously drunk out of his mind and each drink loosened his tongue a little more. Maybe they were taking pity on him until they found someone more interesting.

Over the course of the next hour, Dean laid bare his soul to these random women. He told them all about Taylor. Every detail of her, every little thing about her that made him love her. Like the way she tapped pens against her knee when she was nervous. Or how she would sneak into his Amazon cart on his phone and order whatever he had saved in there if she knew he was having a bad day. Every single thing she did made his day better, even if she didn't realize that he was watching her funny little quirks or noticing the nice things she did for the people she cared about.

He told them all how she had the most adorable voice when she was baby talking her dog, Trevor, when she thought no one was around. He recounted how she'd gotten her dad to help her plan a surprise birthday dinner for him this past year because she knew he wouldn't do anything about it otherwise. She had even started stocking the K-Cup brand he liked in her condo simply because he mentioned it one time, even though she didn't drink it herself, because she wanted him to feel at home there. He hadn't even realized that he'd barely let the other girls get a word in edgewise the entire time.

As far as Dean was concerned, there *were* no other people in the world that mattered besides Taylor. He could care less that he was making a fool of himself over all of this. He even started to cry a little bit, mumbling on and on about how he'd fucked it all up and she was going to be with some other guy now. It was clear as day that Alex Campano was the better choice for her - and that kiss on the beach had just proven it. They may have been down the shoreline, but Dean could see how passionate it had been between the two of them. There was no way they both could be such stellar actors.

"Wow, it really sounds like you like this girl a lot," one of the women said, sarcasm dripping all over her voice, and her friend smirked at her and nudged her with a giggle. Dean was oblivious to all of it, of course, and he shook his head. He was amazed they were still entertaining him. He thought for sure they would have told him to fuck off by now, but apparently, they were taking pleasure in his pain. He was entertaining them with his sorrows. Just when he thought he couldn't sink any lower.

"No, no, I don't just like her. I *love* her," he insisted,

his words slurring. "I love her more than I've ever loved anyone else."

The enormity of the words he'd just spoken hit him suddenly like a freight train. He *loved* Taylor. He loved Taylor Elizabeth Mullins with every cell in his being. Hell, he'd loved her for a long time - there was no point in denying it anymore. It wouldn't matter in the grand scheme of things, though. They couldn't actually be together, not in the way that Dean so desperately wanted. Even with the alcohol swirling through his blood, he knew that much to be true.

Dean loved her. But he couldn't have her.

"Yeah, but you work for her. Seems a bit pathetic if you ask me," the bartender said with a grunt, and Dean shot him a dirty look. The man just smirked and laughed, like he was the most hilarious guy in the room. Great. Now he had *three* people taking pleasure in his misery.

"Aww, poor baby," the German woman said, reaching out and rubbing his arm, perhaps making a last-ditch effort to get him to remember they were there. Normally, if he were single and a woman was rubbing his bicep tenderly like this, he'd have flirted back right away. Not now, though. Nothing could light a fire in his soul the way Taylor's hands on him did.

He completely ignored her blatant advances, taking another sip of his drink. He would be lucky if he ever felt Taylor's touch on his skin again. Would it feel the same, though? Knowing how deep his emotions for her were and knowing they could never be reciprocated? The thought made him sick, and he was certain it had little to do with the liquor.

"I don't want any other girls, no offense ladies, I'm sure you're lovely…and forgive me for being blunt but you're both sexy as fuck but...you're not Taylor," he informed them, not caring if he came off rude or crass. Had he not had three - or maybe four - Negroni's in his system currently, he never would have been that bold.

They both laughed at that, like he was the most hilarious man they'd ever met. The bartender, on the other hand, glared at him and shook his head.

"Alright pal, I'm cutting you off," he informed him, but Dean didn't get angry. He'd had more than enough to drink and even *he* was aware of that. He downed the rest of his drink and threw a twenty on the bar as he stood from his stool.

"You're a good man, looking out for me, I appreciate it, good chap," he muttered back before burping softly. One of the German girls giggled and suddenly they were both holding his arms, one on each side. It was probably a good thing they'd grabbed him, actually - the room was spinning now that he was standing, and he might have toppled over otherwise.

"We could probably make you forget about this girl, this...Tracy," the one said, and he shook his head. They were persistent, he'd give them that. If he'd been back at school, back when he'd been a stupid teenager, he might have taken one - or both - of them back to his room. Thank God he wasn't that young and naive anymore.

"Taylor, it's Taylor...and no one could ever make me forget her," he insisted. He knew that he should probably be looking for her, actually. Taylor would be wondering where he'd gone off to. Or maybe she was with Alex and didn't care at all... the thought caused tears to prickle in his eyes. The other girl on his side tugged on his arm, pulling him to a group of men nearby who were sitting around one of the tables in the corner of the club, talking amongst themselves.

"Then forget your feelings about her for a bit," she offered, gesturing to the men at the table. They were all drinking, and two of them were currently measuring out lines of white powder on the table in front of them. Dean paused, hearing that voice in the back of his head telling him to back away now, and this was a terrible idea. These were bad people, he shouldn't be heading down this path...but it was hard to focus on his conscience when he was dizzy and felt like he might throw up if he kept walking.

"Come on, our friends will let you have a line if you want, right fellas?" She asked, and the men looked up at her, clearly recognizing her as they started speaking in German with each other. They nodded and gestured for him to come sit between them. Dean was grateful to finally be sitting again and plopped down in the chair unceremoniously.

"They say you're heartbroken," one of the men said, and Dean nodded as he wiped away the unshed tears from his eyes. He *was* heartbroken, there was no denying that. Every time he closed his eyes, he saw the image of Taylor and Alex kissing. It was on replay in his brain, and he needed to find something to stop it. The alcohol wasn't helping, so maybe he needed something else.

"Our treat," another one of the men said, handing him a rolled-up dollar bill. As soon as the bill was in his hand, the memories all came back to him. He remembered how much relief he felt when he could simply black out for a few hours and not have to worry about his problems. It would feel *so* good to just forget for a while. To drown his sorrows until the morning and forget about Taylor, just for the night.

Not thinking anymore, Dean smiled at them and took

the rolled-up bill. "Danke," he chuckled, and the men let out a laugh and clapped him on the back before Dean dipped his head down and snorted the line.

CHAPTER TWENTY-FOUR

TAYLOR

Dean wasn't in the room when she returned, and she tried not to think about that. Alex messaged her on Instagram right when she got back to the room, asking if he could meet her for dinner. She felt her heart drop to her stomach as she realized that she would likely have to commit to this bit for just a while longer. Just in case they had somehow *not* been noticed on the beach this afternoon.

She replied back that she would love to and they agreed to meet up in the lobby. She put on some music and tried to ignore her nagging worry about Dean as she prepared herself for dinner. Twenty minutes later she was dressed in her black cocktail dress with flashy heels - a bit dressier than she would have liked, but she figured Alex would like a girl who put a bit more effort into her appearance - and was ready to head out to meet him.

After meeting in the lobby - and earning a few clicks from the nearby paparazzi after Alex gently kissed her cheek in greeting - he took her up to the hotel restaurant where he had reserved a table for them away from the prying eyes of other guests.

Taylor sucked in a breath as she looked at the private dinner he'd had arranged. It was super sweet - it was *too* sweet - and she felt awful that the only thing she could think of right now was Dean and the dinner he'd had for her in their room a few nights ago. Alex took her arm and led her to the table, and she felt her heart start to race nervously.

"You look beautiful tonight," Alex muttered in her ear as he pulled the chair out for her. She blushed and pretended to be bashful and smiled at him, muttering a small thank you. This was…a lot. *Too* much if she was being honest for herself, but she was here now.

Damnit Taylor, she mentally scolded herself, *what have you gotten yourself into?*

They had a lovely three-course meal and somehow he seemed to know exactly what type of food would win her over - Italian. Or maybe it was just because *he* was Italian. Somehow he'd gotten them to prepare special meals for them, and she appreciated all the effort he'd gone through for this evening. Either way, she had no qualms about eating her fill, and he seemed pleased that she wasn't one of those girls who didn't eat on dates. They talked about their lives and their childhoods - which were very different, of course - and then he invited her back into the room for a drink after dessert.

Things were getting far too *real* now. A man inviting her back to his room had only one thing on his mind. She was in dangerous waters now.

Taylor hesitated at first, and she was positive he had

noticed. She checked her phone quickly, hoping that she would find a text from Dean. Nothing. Where was he? Nothing from Caroline either. She hoped she'd find a missed call from her best friend, or an elated text stating that the paparazzi had published a photo of her and Alex on the beach, and she could finally end this charade. With no news from either of them, she had only two options - cut her night short with Alex and go back to the room, worrying all night, or accept his invitation and try to take her mind off of things.

She reluctantly agreed to go back to his room, but she did her best to act like it was no big deal and she was excited to do so. Not *too* excited, though, since she didn't want him to think she was heading back there because she expected to sleep with him. She knew it was stupid to be this calculating about simply going back for a glass of wine, but she knew how men worked. Especially *rich* men.

She shouldn't feel guilty about possibly sleeping with another guy, after all. She and Dean were not exclusive in any sense of the word. Just friends. Who had sex. It was what they had agreed on, so if she did end up sleeping with him, Dean would never have any right to be upset.

Of course, Taylor wasn't planning on doing anything with Alex anymore. Not only did she feel the guilt taking over every time she caught him smiling at her, but she couldn't stop thinking of how Dean smiled at her and lit up every time she entered the room.

God, she was a mess. An absolute mess. How had she managed to fuck up this vacation *so* badly over the course of just a few days?

She tried, without success, to turn her brain off as she

followed Alex to his suite. His was smaller than their room, having gotten a much more modest suite that still had a full kitchen and bath, along with a private deck and pool. It was out there that he'd brought her when they first arrived, bringing out two glasses of some fancy Merlot he claimed was the best that Paris had to offer.

She hardly touched it. She wanted to stay totally sober if she was going to do this tonight. Especially as he moved closer to her, causing her to freeze up in a slight panic. The closer they got, the more her anxiety skyrocketed. It was like the less space there was between them, the more her brain started to think of Dean. He was her comfort, and who she would usually turn to when she felt this level of anxiety start to creep up on her. She couldn't go to him for obvious reasons, but she so desperately wished it was *him* sitting across from her. She didn't want a romantic evening with Alex. She wanted a romantic evening with Dean, she wanted...

Damnit, he was getting closer now. Their knees were touching.

She should give in to this. A gorgeous, rich socialite was attracted to her, and she wasn't attached to Dean in any sense of the word. She should allow herself to explore another man, and she had the perfect specimen right in front of her. Maybe it was possible that she could start something *real* with Alex, and she was better off just being friends with Dean, no strings attached...

Her thoughts were interrupted as Alex finally hie his move, bringing her inner turmoil to a complete halt. In the blink of an eye, he was leaning in, and then he closed the gap between them and kissed her. He tasted like the wine they were drinking, and he opened his mouth and ran his tongue along the bottom of her lip. She opened her mouth the slightest amount out of instinct and he moaned softly, his hands moving to her waist and trying to pull her into his lap.

She should have thought that this was a phenomenal kiss. She should have thought that he was handsome and charming and he wanted her, that much she could tell as she allowed herself to be pulled into his lap, but there was just something off about all of this. She didn't enjoy it at all. Her heart wasn't in it, and she just felt uncomfortable and stiff and as his kisses became more passionate, she knew he could sense it as well and was trying to coax more emotion out of her. She knew what thought kept plaguing her brain, refusing to allow her to give this a fair shot.

All she kept thinking about was that he wasn't *Dean*.

He never was Dean, and he never would be Dean. There was no more denying that. She couldn't do this anymore - not to Dean, and especially not to Alex. He didn't deserve it. Dean didn't deserve it. It wasn't worth the hurt.

She pulled away, her face flushed. "I'm so sorry, I..." she looked down at him in fear, blinking wildly as she gazed into his eyes. He looked at her in confusion, his hands lightly running up and down her back.

"Are you ok?" He asked. God, he was so kind and caring and thoughtful. There were millions of women who would kill to be in this position right now.

Taylor couldn't think. She couldn't breathe. She was on the verge of an attack, but Dean was nowhere to be found. He wasn't here, holding her hand and turning on *Clueless* and rocking her back and forth in his arms...

"No, no I'm not ok. I'm sorry, this is all...it's too much," she whimpered. She jumped off his lap and settled her skirt, and she saw him open his mouth to protest, but she didn't wait to hear what he said before running out the door.

CHAPTER TWENTY-FIVE

TAYLOR

Taylor blinked away tears and wandered around aimlessly on the beach, her heels dangling off of her fingertips as she tried to keep herself from crying. The sun hadn't set completely, casting an orange glow over the beach as a few tourists tried to get a last minute swim in before it became too dark. Normally, she would have taken out her phone and snapped a picture for her Instagram, but her emotions were all over the place right now. She needed to find someone to comfort her. She'd debated texting Caroline, Penelope, or Betsy, but she wasn't sure how she could explain the situation she was in without coming off as a horrible person or revealing the entire sexual relationship she had with Dean.

She *was* a horrible person. How could she have done this? How could she have actually thought it was a good idea to pursue things with Alex just to save her reputation? What sort of person did that? She had to be seriously fucked up in the head to even come *up* with the idea in the first place.

Taylor knew there was only one person she wanted to talk to right now, and that was Dean. But how could she talk to him? He probably hated her because of all of this. It was what she deserved. Still, she was worried. It was highly unlike him to go completely dark, even if he was upset with her. She hadn't seen him since she left Alex on the beach earlier that day. It was like he had disappeared off the face of the Earth.

She picked up her phone and tried to call him, but it just rang and rang and went to his voicemail. She hated that she listened to it just so she could hear his voice. Where *was* he? She was seriously regretting never setting up that 'Find Your Friends' feature on her phone. It would come in ridiculously handy right now. He hadn't *left,* had he? No, his things had still been in the room when she'd gone to check a few minutes ago, heading straight there after she left Alex's suite. He had to be around here somewhere, but he was likely avoiding her.

She didn't blame him.

She sat down in the sand, staring out at the dark waves as she thought over what had just happened. How was it that she had been in those very waters a few days ago, playfully splashing Dean and having the time of her life? Not worrying about any fucking blind items or the battle of the British boys - she had just been enjoying herself. Relaxing and letting loose, just like he'd wanted her to. They had just been Taylor and Dean, not Taylor Mullins and her assistant. She'd just been spending time with her best friend. With the man she...

No. She had to stop. This was all getting too out of hand. Her thoughts were a complete mess.

How had she let her life suddenly get so complicated?

Dean had been right. This whole thing with Alex was

wrong, and it wasn't fair to him that she using him. She was wrong to take advantage of him like this, especially since he seemed to think there was something else going on. That was her own damn fault. She was leading him on, and she knew it.

Wasn't she also leading Dean on, though? A little bit. She should have just kept her legs closed around him and never succumbed to temptation. She wouldn't be in this situation if she had just walked away and not led him out of the club in London six months ago.

Fuck. She hated this. Maybe she should go to a therapist when they got back to Los Angeles and she could unpack all the things that were wrong with her. Dean always said she had imposter syndrome, and she was slowly accepting the fact that he was probably right.

What would happen when she finally found Dean? She'd apologize for this mess with Alex, of course, but that would also mean acknowledging that he was clearly upset by her staging a romance with her. He shouldn't be upset with her about that, and she shouldn't be worrying about him being upset about it…

Was it too much to hope that maybe, just maybe, they could act like nothing happened? That nothing had changed between them, and this whole friends-with-benefits situation could keep existing? They'd been doing so well the last six months. Things had been great. Just sex, nothing else.

Except…that wasn't the truth. Deep down, she knew it.

Hell, who was she kidding? Trying to act like this was still *just sex* was clearly doing no one any favors. There were things they had to face head-on, and even though she wasn't sure she was quite ready to do so - they had to figure it out soon. Otherwise things were going to explode, and Taylor didn't think either of them would come on the other end unscathed.

She groaned loudly, lying down on the sand and staring up at the darkening night sky. She sniffled and tried to keep the tears at bay, especially since she still had her fake eyelashes on. She should be having the time of her life right now in paradise with her best friend, and instead all she could think about was how royally she was fucking up her life.

For what? A few paparazzi pics? A new blind item about her and Alex?

The fact that she even had to *think* about things like that was so sick and twisted. Why did anyone care what she did with her life? She was just an author. An author who just wanted to share her character with the world.

Yeah, but you wanted this. You wanted to be noticed. Well, you dumb bitch, you got it, and then some. Her thoughts nagged at her, reminding her that if she was ten years younger and a lot stupider, she'd be on cloud nine knowing paparazzi wanted pictures of *her.*

Thinking about it made her sick. It sounded so dumb and trivial when she thought about it like that. This whole thing *was* dumb.

And the only person she had to blame was herself.

Taylor was the one who let Dean into her bed.

Taylor was the one who kept at it, when she knew she should stop.

Taylor was the one who was leading Alex on.

Taylor had driven Dean to…wherever the fuck he was right now.

She sighed and stood up after a few minutes, brushing the sand off herself and trying to get as much of it out of her hair as she could - in hindsight, lying down in the sand wasn't the best idea. Maybe she should just head to the bar, get a drink, and let herself loosen up a bit. Then she'd be able to regain some of her confidence and apologize to Dean.

She would just wait in the room for him and eventually, he'd have to return. Maybe they could put this whole thing behind them. After all, she'd gotten the pictures she needed with Alex down by the beach today, she was sure of it. The paparazzi wouldn't have missed out on such a tremendous opportunity that was literally right in front of them. There had been that moment in the lobby when he first greeted her that evening as well, and he'd kissed her on the cheek. Even something as simple as that had to do the trick. If, somehow, they *hadn't* gotten a picture, well - she'd figure out something else. She couldn't use Alex anymore. It wasn't right.

Taylor could apologize to Alex and offer to be friends. He *was* a very kind man, and he could be the person she turned to if she needed help navigating the world of being in the public eye. Plus, her friend Betsy was always begging her to set her up with someone, maybe he liked high school teachers from Beverly Hills...

Taking her heels in her hands and trudging her way through the sand, she headed back to the resort. She had a plan now. A newfound confidence began to set in as she rolled her shoulders back and gently pressed her eyelashes back into place.

First the bar, then find Dean.

She could make this right. She was sure of it.

She was Taylor fucking Mullins, she could do anything she set her mind to.

CHAPTER TWENTY-SIX

TAYLOR

Three months ago

Dean wasn't answering his phone, and Taylor was worried. He was over an hour late for work, and usually, he was running no more than five minutes late, tops, if the line at Starbucks was extra long that day. Yes, she was worried. So much so, that she finally headed over to his apartment, abandoning her plans for the day.

Something was terribly wrong, she could feel it deep in her gut. The day before, he'd gotten a call while they were eating lunch from someone back home. It was a heavy conversation because he'd stepped outside to take it, and when he came back in half an hour later, his eyes were red like he'd been crying.

He wouldn't tell her what happened, but she could tell he had gotten bad news about something. Hopefully not a death in the family or anything that serious - but whatever it was, it had been weighing on him. Something about him dimmed after he'd gotten the call. He'd left as soon as it hit 5 PM sharp, and now it was radio silence from him. Even his Instagram hadn't been updated, which was unusual, because she knew he scrolled late into the night and often ended up sharing funny posts or reels to his stories.

Taylor pulled up to his apartment building and parked in the guest parking spots, quickly hurrying to the front door and buzzing his apartment. There was no response, so she waited a minute before she went ahead and rang it again. This time, after a few seconds, the door buzzed. She let out a sigh of relief she hadn't realized she'd been holding in. At least he was alive - or someone in that apartment was.

She took the stairs two at a time to his door, knocking impatiently. After a moment, Dean opened the door, and she was shocked to find him looking like absolute death. His blond hair hung limp around his face, and he had large dark bags under his eyes. The usual bright joy behind his brown eyes was completely gone. He was pale, and she wondered for a second if maybe he was sick with the flu or a terrible head cold. He was wearing his pajamas - a Led Zeppelin t-shirt that she borrowed a lot when she stayed over, and a pair of red flannel pajama pants that were wrinkled, and she wondered if he'd thrown them on just to answer the door.

She barged in uninvited, and he allowed her entry without a word, promptly heading to the bathroom. Pausing in the doorway, she wondered what was going on and was about to open her mouth and ask exactly that when she sensed something was off about the place.

That was when she noticed that it smelled heavily of alcohol in the apartment - it downright *reeked*. Like there had been a frat party in here, even though the apartment itself didn't look like a mess at all.

Heart pounding, she hurried after him to the bathroom. He sat down on the floor next to the toilet, looking like he might be sick again, and sure enough after a second, he threw up into the bowl. She could tell now that he must have been getting sick all morning, as he hardly seemed to have anything left in his stomach. She sat down next to him on the floor, rubbing his back gently, not saying a word until he wiped his mouth on a piece of toilet paper and flushed it down, leaning back against the wall.

She waited for a moment, studying him as he closed his eyes and tried to avoid her gaze. He was ashamed. She gently rested her hand on his thigh, rubbing his knee comfortingly with her thumb as she looked at him.

"What happened?" She asked quietly. He glanced at her and she saw him swallow, and he didn't say anything for a moment. He took a deep breath, then finally opened his eyes and looked at her.

"My mum, she uh...her cancer came back," he explained, his voice barely more than a whisper. Taylor inhaled sharply and bit her lip. She hadn't even know nhis mother *had* cancer. She had met the woman only one time and she had been so bright and vibrant and full of life. Florence Coffey was the picture of health - when they'd met her in London, she'd talked at great length about running a marathon last year! To think that she had once had to deal with such a debilitating disease, but had come out the other side of it...until now, apparently...it was hard to comprehend. He'd never mentioned it once.

"They have high hopes, it's *less* than last time, I just... fuck," he grumbled, running a hand through his greasy hair. She realized suddenly that a tear had dripped down his face, and she found herself reaching out to brush it off without realizing it.

Dean paused and looked at her, almost like he was shocked that she would do something so tender and gentle for him, and the next thing she knew, he buried his face in her shoulder, and she was pulling him close to her and cradling him in her arms.

She wasn't sure how long he cried for. It was probably only a few minutes, but it felt like forever, and honestly - she *wanted* him to keep crying, to get all of his emotions out so he could get back up and put this behind him. She felt herself shed a few tears of her own as she held him, listening to his muffled cries in her shirt as he clung to her. She found herself wishing there was a way for them to switch places, and she could somehow take this pain from him.

Dean was the best guy she'd ever known, and for something like this to happen to him was almost too much for her to bear. It wasn't fair, to him, to his mum, or to his family, who had welcomed them with open arms when they came to visit.

For some reason, holding him as he cried made her feel closer to him. He was comfortable enough to be his most vulnerable self around her. Dean was a crier, she knew this about him - they'd watched *Marley and Me* together which, to be fair, would make anyone cry - but he was soft and sensitive. It was one of the things she liked best about him, and he wasn't afraid to let her see that part of him. It was endearing as hell.

"You must think I'm an absolute fuck up," he whispered, finally pulling away and wiping his eyes. Taylor bit her lip and looked at him sadly. She'd almost forgotten about the real reason she was here - to check up on him because he clearly wasn't doing well. The stench of alcohol in the air made that plain as day. She shook her head and pushed his hair gently out of his eyes, running her finger down his face and tilting his chin up to look at her.

"I don't, Dean," she assured him quietly. "People slip up and make mistakes. It's called being fucking human," she reminded him. She herself had never dealt with addiction, but he'd seen her on the verge of a mental breakdown - and in the midst of one too - so he had to know that she had *some* idea of what it was like to feel out of control.

"I was doing so well," he muttered, avoiding her gaze again. She nodded, knowing how hard he had worked to get here. She'd seen the last time he had a drink - it had been the night they first slept together almost three months ago.

"So now you recover, get back up, and start over again," she told him firmly. "Today is the new Day One. And lucky for you, I brought my laptop so I can work here," she added with a small grin. She didn't intend to sit here and babysit him, but keep him company? That was definitely something she could do.

He chuckled a little at that, and her heart swelled to finally see him smiling again. "What, are you gonna force-feed me soda crackers and ginger ale?" He teased, his voice still quiet and a little shaky, but she grinned to see him finally starting to come back to his old self.

"No, because I didn't know you were hungover so I came ill-prepared," she reminded him with a laugh as she stood up. She held out a hand, and with a small grimace he took it, pulling himself to his feet. He swayed for a moment but didn't look like he was going to be sick again, thankfully.

"So don't worry, you don't have to get nervous that

I'm about to act all domesticated and shit around you," she added, and he cracked another small smile at her. Part of her knew that was a lie, though. If he needed her to clean his apartment, get him food, change his sheets...whatever it was he needed today, *she* would be the one assisting *him* for a change.

Taylor ushered him to his bed, and he collapsed on top of the sheets, passing out within minutes as she set up shop in his living room. She went to check on him once, bringing a blanket and covering him with it gently. She watched him for just a moment - she didn't want to be that creepy girl who watched a guy sleep - but fuck, he was gorgeous. His high cheekbones and soft lips...even hungover, his blond hair dirty and pushed up at odd angles as he slept, she couldn't stop admiring him.

Dean did so much for her on a daily basis. She hoped he'd stop and remember to take care of himself too, especially with all this happening now in his life.

She ordered herself some coffee and got lunch for them delivered to the apartment, putting the food his in the fridge for whenever he felt like a human again and needed to eat. She then headed into his living room, opened her Spotify playlist, and began to pound away at her keys and work through her massive to-do list. He didn't emerge from his room until almost 3 PM.

When he finally shuffled out of his bedroom, he came and sat down next to her on the floor. He was wearing the light green blanket she'd covered him with like a cape, hugging it around his body as he settled next to her. She'd long ago moved from the sofa to the floor, pressed up against the couch as she typed away on her laptop. Her MacBook was propped against her knees and she realized as she set it aside for him that she had indents on her skin where the vent of her computer had sat. She must have been sitting there for hours - probably since she'd had lunch around noon.

"Well, look who's alive," she joked with him as he came and sat down next to her, and she was relieved when he let out a small little chuckle as he sat down.

"Barely. How about you? Did you survive the day without an assistant?" He asked with a small smile. The color was finally returning to his face and she could smell his toothpaste and face wash, meaning he'd felt well enough to try and clean himself up a bit. She grinned playfully at him.

"Calm down mister, you still have...two more hours where you might be useful to me," she pointed out as she nudged him with her elbow. She was pleased to see him laugh, his face lighting up with that beautiful smile of his.

"I'm afraid I'll probably be out of commission until tomorrow," he informed her with a sigh. He bit his lip and paused before he reached over and took her hand, giving it a soft squeeze. Her heart began to race, not just because he was holding her hand, and she loved when he did that. It was something else. Something she couldn't quite place.

"Thank you," he said quietly. She smiled at him, her face blushing ever so slightly as she nodded. She wasn't sure why. He would have done the same for her if the roles had been reversed. She was sure of it.

"Of course," she retorted, waving her hand in the air as if it was no big deal. Because it really wasn't. "And I'm sorry about your mum," she added quietly. He tensed and nodded, and she squeezed his hand again. She wished she could leech some of the burden from his shoulders by holding his hand like this.

"Is there anything I can do?" She asked, hoping he caught her meaning. She felt weird saying outright that she'd happily donate money to her treatment, but he shook his head.

"No, no, it's fine, really. They've got a good team working with her and a therapy plan in place. The only reason I'm not on a plane right now is because my dad talked me off a ledge," he clarified. "The last time she was sick, it tore him apart, so…to hear him sound put together and calm on the phone…I know they aren't lying and they really *are* optimistic."

"That's good!" She encouraged him, and he smiled gingerly at her and nodded in agreement before he looked back down at his blanket. He was thinking about something hard as he studied the light green fibers, she could tell by his furrowed brow.

After a moment, he looked in the direction of the kitchen and then looked back at her. "I need you to do something for me, Tay," he told her softly. He let go of her hand, and she saw him beginning to pick at the skin on his right thumb nervously.

"Anything," she replied instantly, and he closed his eyes as if what he was about to say caused him physical pain as he spoke.

"There's two bottles of wine in the fridge and the remnants of a six-pack in there. Get rid of them for me, please," he whispered. She was going to ask why but then realized why he was asking *her* to do it. He didn't trust himself to get rid of the alcohol. He didn't trust himself in front of temptation.

Taylor nodded and stood up, leaving him on the floor where he made no effort to move. She went to the fridge and saw the alcohol that he had mentioned - she wondered how she hadn't seen it when she put his food away - and then paused. She trusted Dean and trusted him to do the right thing, but…

She started looking through the cabinets, just in case. She didn't want to take any chances that maybe he forgot something. She didn't want to think that he might have intentionally lied to her about all the alcohol he had, but she knew how addicts were. She'd been in a sorority and known enough frat boys in her life to spot the signs. To her immense relief, there was nothing else, and she even checked the bedroom for good measure.

She knew Dean could hear her going through all his drawers and cabinets, but he made no move to come to assure her that she got it all. He knew why she was doing it, and hopefully, he appreciated it.

Once she was sure she'd done a clean sweep of the house, she headed to the trash and took the bag out. She could hear the clinking of already discarded bottles - she peeked inside, horrified to see at least two empty vodka bottles that she hoped had been close to empty before he started his bender last night. She threw the other bottles she'd confiscated from the fridge into the bag before she walked out to the trash and threw it all in the dumpster, taking it and pouring it out on the sidewalk first.

That might have been overkill, and she could have just taken it home and given it to Caroline or her dad without wasting it, but she wasn't taking any chances. Not that she really expected Dean to crawl down here and go dumpster diving but... again. Addicts.

She walked back upstairs after disposing of the alcohol to find him where she'd left him on the floor. She walked over and sat down, pulling him in for a hug again, and he mumbled a soft thank you into her shoulder.

"You're not weak, Dean," she reminded him softly. He closed his eyes, another tear escaping as she held him.

"I know," he mumbled quietly, so quiet she almost didn't hear him. "It feels like it, though."

She nodded. "I know. It'll get easier though," she assured him.

"How do you know?" he questioned, looking up at her with skepticism. She could almost see the thoughts swirling around that pretty blond head of his. He was worried about staying sober again. He was worried about his mother. She wondered for a moment if he was worried about letting her down, and almost told him that he couldn't do anything to disappoint her, ever. He could confess to murders and she'd probably still find a way to justify it for him.

She didn't do that, though. Instead, Taylor smirked at him.

"Because this time you have me to help you."

CHAPTER TWENTY-SEVEN

TAYLOR

Taylor sat down at the bar and looked around, wondering if Dean was nearby. She doubted he would be down here at the bar, but she couldn't help but hope. It was a good thing he wasn't, of course, as she knew what a trigger alcohol was for him, but she was disappointed nonetheless.

"Hello pretty lady, what can I get for you?" The bartender asked, and she ordered her usual vodka cranberry. She waited impatiently, and a man with a heavy Eastern European accent approached her and tried to make conversation. After about five minutes, she politely turned him down and, undeterred, he walked away and approached the next girl at the bar. A pair of blonde girls next to her giggled quietly.

"Oof. That was rough to watch. For him, I mean," the first girl said as her friend nodded in agreement. Taylor just shrugged.

"He was nice enough, I'm just not interested," she explained. In another life, she might have entertained the idea. He was nice enough, but there was only one man on Taylor's mind at the moment.

"You're gorgeous, girl, I'm sure you'll find someone better," the second one assured her, as if that was the reason she was turning him down. Taylor just smiled and gave her a small smile before turning back to the bartender, waiting for her order. She tried not to come off too cold, but she *really* wasn't in the mood for casual small talk right now. Not when she couldn't stop thinking about Dean and where he might be.

"No shortage of single guys here looking for hookups," the bartender chimed in as he started shaking up her drink. She had a feeling from the look he was giving her that he was including himself in that. Gross. No thank you.

"Yeah, pretty much every guy here! Well, almost every guy here," the first girl chimed in, and the three of them laughed as if they had an inside joke that Taylor was not privy to. She became even more anxious now, tapping her nails impatiently on the bar as she waited for her drink. Best to just get out of there and go back to the room, where Dean was hopefully waiting for her.

"Good point. That man who was down here before was absolutely pathetic," the second girl laughed. Taylor detected a hint of an accent in her voice that she hadn't noticed before, but she couldn't quite place it. Maybe Dutch? Or German? She never was good with accents. The bartender nodded and handed Taylor her drink, rolling his eyes.

"A real mess," he said in agreement. Taylor had no idea who they were talking about, and really had no interest in finding out more about this unfortunate gentleman they were gossiping about. "Going on and on about how in love he was with some girl who didn't love him back."

Taylor just shrugged. That seemed like the normal sort of thing a bartender would encounter on a day-to-day basis, so she wasn't sure why he found this particular guy so hilarious. She took a long sip of her drink, hoping the alcohol would bring her some liquid courage, and fast. She needed it if she was going to approach Dean in the room.

The two girls giggled and nodded in agreement at the bartender's statement.

"He was so cute too, with that bright blond hair, and such a yummy accent, it's such a shame he's...what's the term? What do the kids say now? 'Down bad' for this girl?" She asked Taylor with a grin, and even she had to admit that was funny and chuckled, nodding.

"I think so, yeah," she conceded with a small smile, still trying to avoid the conversation.

"Not just a girl," the bartender reminded them. "His boss, that's what makes it so much worse."

Taylor paused and tilted her head, raising an eyebrow at him. "Wait, his boss?" She asked. Her heart started to race. It was very possible that they might have been talking about another random blond man who happened to be hung up on his boss. Another random blond, with an accent. True, it was a small resort but they entertained people from all over the world. There was no way they could possibly be talking about...

"Yup. He said he was her assistant. What sort of pussy works for a woman?" The bartender asked with a chuckle, shaking his head as if it was the most ridiculous thing he'd ever heard. She felt a surge of anger rising up in her throat as he made fun of him for that. *Misogynistic prick*. "And even worse, cries about her at the bar at a hotel? When he has all these other lovely ladies here to choose from?" He asked, shooting a grin at the two girls, who giggled playfully as he poured them another round.

Taylor suddenly felt like she couldn't breathe. The air seemed to get heavy around her as she blinked down at her drink. They had to be talking about Dean. There was no one else who could possibly could fit the description. She started to put the pieces together of what had happened after he left the beach earlier. He came to the bar. He got drunk. *Very* drunk, apparently. He had to have been wasted if he had poured out his soul to total strangers at the bar.

He was in love with her.

Dean Coffey was in love with her.

And, even worse…he was drinking.

"Fuck. Do you know where he went?" She asked the girls. They both looked at her in confusion and shrugged, and the bartender had moved on to another group of girls. Not that he would have cared enough to know where he went, she was sure of it.

"He disappeared after he did the coke," one of the girls informed her. Taylor blinked, her heart dropping into the pit of her stomach. She had to have misheard her.

"After he did the *what?*"

"Oh! Are you Taylor?!" The other girl screeched, and the other one let out a loud 'awwww!' as they drunkenly reached over to hug her. All of a sudden, they were best friends. Under normal circumstances, Taylor would have been all for some random drunken girl power camaraderie, but there were far more important things at stake right now.

"He cares about you sooo much!" The first one exclaimed, hanging on to her and looking like she might cry. As if this was all the plot of a Hallmark Christmas movie that she was watching and not someone's actual life.

"Go back to the part about the coke," Taylor insisted, trying to keep her on track. The other one pointed to a group of men who were screaming loudly, watching a soccer game on the TV and drinking beer.

"Our friends over there let him have a line for free. To feel better," she informed her. Taylor swallowed loudly. "Then some of them went off together down to the pool bar."

Fuck, this was bad.

Really *really* bad.

"Thank you for telling me...have a good night," she said quietly, and the girls bid her goodnight before she ran off, eager to try and find Dean.

CHAPTER TWENTY-EIGHT

TAYLOR

Taylor's head was spinning and she'd barely had more than a few sips of her drink. She walked around the resort at least three times, looking for that familiar head of blond hair, but she couldn't find him anywhere. She wondered if he was back in the room, but if he was...she wasn't sure she was ready to face him yet, knowing what she now knew.

No, Dean was drunk and high and *not* dealing with his emotions well. She owed it to him as a friend to find him and make sure he was alright, even if it felt uncomfortable to her.

She finally ripped the band-aid off and headed to the room, looking for him in his part of the suite. *Nothing.* The room had obviously not been stepped in since she'd come up here an hour earlier looking for him Good lord, she hoped he hadn't done something monumentally stupid and ended up in the ocean or something. If he got hurt, or drank too much and ended up at the hospital, or overdosed...her brain couldn't stop thinking about the worst-case scenarios. It would be all her fault, because she'd driven him to this point with her stupid mind games with Alex.

Dean consumed her every thought. She realized that she had been shaking this whole time as she marched forward in her search for him, and tears were threatening to spill from her eyes as she finished her third lap of the resort to no avail.

He loved her. The implications of it were making her heart race in a way she had never experienced before. Even knowing that he was stumbling around blackout drunk somewhere, she still had a desire to find him and kiss him hard and…well, she didn't know what else. But she knew that the fact that he loved her was making her heart do all sorts of crazy gymnastics in her chest.

She had always suspected he cared deeply for her, but she never allowed herself to actually believe he was *in* love with her. That all felt like a fantasy to her - like something that happened to characters in a romance novel. Not to people like her. Hell, she'd only ever had two real boyfriends before and those had both ended in disaster.

Neither of them had ever looked at her the way Dean did, though. That look. She should have known from the start…

She sat at one of the chairs by the pool bar, staring back out at the dark waves of the ocean. This whole day had turned into a disaster. How was it that yesterday they were dancing in the living room of their suite, joking around and laughing as if they didn't have a care in the world? It felt like centuries ago now. Hell, it felt like years since she'd been in Alex's room, drinking wine with him.

Speak of the devil.

Taylor heard someone approach her from behind and she found herself hoping it was Dean - but it wasn't. She looked up and saw Alex, who looked…timid as he approached. Like she might bolt and run away if he made any sudden movements.

"Hey…are you ok?" He asked quietly, sitting down in the chair next to her.

She swallowed, shaking her head. "No…I don't think so," she admitted. The way she was feeling now, she didn't know if she'd ever be ok after this.

Alex paused and then slowly reached over and took her hand, squeezing it gently and reminding her so much of Dean. He did the same thing all the time, especially when he sensed she had a panic attack going on. It wasn't the same when Alex held her hand, though. She looked at his hands. They were *very* nice hands, and she had no doubt he knew how to use them well, but they didn't evoke the same feelings of protection that she felt when she looked at Dean's hands.

"I'm sorry I panicked and left you earlier," she added. She wasn't usually one to get up and run from her problems, but this whole thing was getting too complicated for her. Her anxiety was creeping in and taking hold and she didn't know what else to do. She knew full well that it was all her own doing, but her desire to keep running from the situation was overwhelming. Alex smiled a little and shook his head.

"Don't worry about it. I didn't mean to scare you," he whispered. Of course the charming prat would think *he* was somehow to blame for it. "We've only known each other a few days, that might have been…a lot."

She shook her head. "No, it was absolutely lovely and sweet and I don't deserve that at all."

Alex paused and tilted his head at her. "I don't think that's true. I think you deserve people to be sweet to you, Taylor."

She could feel her heart starting to crumble as he spoke. All Dean was ever doing was sweet things for her - bringing her coffee, cleaning her dishes when she got sucked into a meeting, ordering her soup from his apartment when she told him to stay home because she was sick…

Dean Coffey was the greatest man she'd ever known, whether they were just friends or something more, and she'd let her reputation get in the way. She'd cared more about what random strangers had said on the internet about her, than the man who had been through her side through it all. She had been so busy trying to keep her career from possibly spiraling, that she hadn't thought about the one thing that meant far more to her than anything else in the world.

Once she found Dean, she needed to talk to him about this. They couldn't act like things hadn't progressed between them any longer.

Dean had asked her once to consider making their relationship public. He had seemed so terrified to bring up the subject, even though he had been doing his best to put on a brave face. She bit her lip, not realizing *why* he had been so nervous at the time, and firmly told him it wasn't going to happen.

Caroline had warned her of another up and coming author, Veronica Leslie, who had been in a similar situation and started dating her agent. She didn't think Caroline had *suspected* anything between her and Dean, and was instead just trying to spread a cautionary tale, but it stuck with her nonetheless. The industry began to whisper and spread rumors about them, talking about how they were unprofessional and she was using him only to get a foot in the door in the publishing industry. No one ended up picking up her book, despite may promising leads from major publishing houses. While it wasn't a complete mirror to their situation, Taylor had used it as a shield at the time.

Dean had never asked her about it again.

Perhaps that was her way to trying to shield herself from his obvious feelings for her. Or maybe she was using it as a convenient excuse so she could continue to ignore the truth that was so plainly in front of her.

Taylor felt hopeless. Bile was rising her throat and she blinked back more tears. She couldn't find Dean anywhere, and now that she knew how he felt about her - she couldn't help but feel like she'd monumentally screwed things up. True, the resort itself wasn't that large, but he could have wandered off property...her chances of finding him were slim to none. She'd even looked out on the beach - or started to until she heard a loud group of German men down the way, and she'd promptly turned around. The beach was deserted otherwise, and she had a feeling that she was continuously missing him and they kept passing right by each other without realizing.

What she needed right now was a friend, and Dean was nowhere to be found. Taylor wiped her eyes and looked at Alex, who was still sitting next to her, silently watching her with interest. She knew she hadn't spoken in a few minutes, and he was probably concerned about her as she mentally tried to work out this whole problem in front of him.

"What are you doing right now?" She asked him quietly. Alex looked at her and tilted his head in confusion.

"Nothing, why?"

"Can I come up to your room?"

CHAPTER TWENTY-NINE

DEAN

Six weeks ago

"Happy Birthday!"

Dean was taken aback as they entered Taylor's condo and flicked on the lights. Taylor was bouncing excitedly next to him as she gestured to the wrapped present on the table, sitting next to a small cupcake with a candle in it.

"What is all this?" He asked with a soft laugh as her dad followed them in, closing the door behind him.

"She insisted we wouldn't get you out for your birthday unless we tricked you and acted like we weren't celebrating something," he explained with a small smirk. Erik Mullins was a quiet man, very soft spoken especially when compared to his daughter, but he was also one of the nicest guys Dean had ever met. He'd paid for their expensive sushi dinner tonight - which, now that Dean knew it was a secret celebratory birthday dinner, he felt awkward about immediately - but he knew if he tried to pay him back Erik would insist it was no big deal. It wasn't hard to see where Taylor got her generosity from.

Their plan *had* worked. Erik had offered to take them out, under the guise that he just wanted to catch up while they had a break from promoting her book. Dean had made a point not to remind Taylor it was his birthday - he never got excited for his birthday, and this one was no different, despite being a *big* birthday to some people, and had been relieved when she hadn't questioned it.

He had been a fool to think that she would just forget that easily.

"Thanks for helping with the bamboozle, Dad," Taylor grinned at Erik and gave him a hug. Before he knew it, Dean was being hugged by him as well, and he patted him back and chuckled awkwardly. This made him feel like part of their little family, and as much as it excited him, it was also setting off alarm bells.

They were getting dangerously close to crossing a line again, but before he could think about it further, Erik handed him a card.

"Happy birthday, kiddo. Now, I'll leave you to open your present from Taylor alone," he announced, bidding them both a goodnight before letting himself out. Dean paused and found himself flushing with embarrassment. Did Erik know what was going on between them? Or was he just afraid that he'd be intruding on a sweet moment between two friends?

"What did he get you?" Taylor asked, wrapping her arms around him from behind as he heard Erik's car start up and pull out of the driveway.

Biting his lip, he opened the card - it was a nice, friendly birthday card, something generic from Hallmark - and a Visa gift card fell out. He chuckled and blushed and Taylor gave a little 'aww' from behind him as he shook his head.

"You two are really spoiling me," he muttered softly, and she bit her lip as she turned to him, and Dean suddenly worried that maybe he had said the wrong thing.

"Is it too much?" She asked quietly, and he quickly shook his head.

"No, no!" He insisted. "It's lovely, really, I just...don't know what I did to deserve it," he admitted, biting his lip. She looked at him in confusion and then smiled at him playfully.

"Dean...you just...*exist*. That's reason enough for me," she told him, her hand reaching out to gently run along his chest and his light purple button-down shirt. He smiled and cupped his hand over hers, holding it to his chest as he looked down at her and her blue eyes tilted up to meet his.

"Thank you, Taylor," he whispered.

"You're welcome...and you haven't even opened your present yet!" She reminded him, leaning back and bouncing over to the table and handing him a small blue box. It was tiny, about the size of his hand, and he had absolutely *zero* clue what could be inside.

"Are you proposing, Taylor Mullins?" He asked playfully, and she rolled her eyes and nudged him.

"That box is way too big to be a ring box, you goof," she teased him back as he pulled the top off of it.

"Who wrapped this? Definitely not you."

"Penelope did. She's amazing at gift wrapping."

"And she didn't spoil the surprise? Wow. I'm impressed with her."

All joking aside, when he saw what was in the box he swore his heart stopped for the briefest of seconds.

"Taylor...this is too much!"

"No, it's not! You keep saying you want to go on a vacation, so we're going on vacation," she said with a grin, grabbing his arm excitedly as he looked down at the two plane tickets she'd gone through the trouble of wrapping up.

"Cancun?" He questioned, and she nodded as she bit her lip, barely able to contain her excitement.

"It's going to be so much fun! Just the two of us, all week, at an all-inclusive resort!"

Dean was certain he was going to pass out. Taylor was officially the best woman - no, the best *person* on the planet. She had just gifted him an *entire* vacation and acted like it was no big deal.

"This is really too much," he insisted again and she rolled her eyes.

"Stop being such a Cancer and take the gift," she teased him, and he snorted.

"If you weren't such a Sagittarius who acted on her every impulse, maybe I wouldn't be so reluctant to accept it," he joked back, and she just smiled and kissed his cheek.

"Well, I am, so tough luck!"

He laughed again and bit his lip before he muttered a soft thank you and pulled her close to him for a kiss. It wasn't just the thoughtfulness of the gift that was making his whole body light up with excitement. It was the fact that he was going to have Taylor to himself for a whole week. Just the two of them. In a secluded resort, away from prying eyes, where no one knew them...where they could be together, and he could touch her and kiss her and fulfill every naughty fantasy he'd ever had about her...

He might not live to see it. He might die of anticipation before they even got there. Once again, Taylor seemed determined to kill him and she didn't even realize it!

"Ok, now the cupcake," she said softly, pulling away and whispering against his lips before hurrying back to her kitchen table. He'd completely forgotten she had a cupcake for him too. She took the lighter she'd set aside and lit the candle, holding it out in her hands as she walked towards him with a grin.

"I promise I won't sing to you, but you're not getting out of making a wish on your *thirtieth* birthday, old man," she jested with a giggle. He smirked and rolled his eyes.

"Taylor, you're literally a year older than me."

"Oh, whatever."

He smiled at her and pushed a piece of hair behind her ear before looking back at the cupcake. It was a simple dessert - just a regular cupcake with vanilla frosting and one lone candle in the middle. Yet the gesture felt like Taylor had moved mountains for him.

A feeling he couldn't quite describe was growing in his stomach as he realized how happy he was at this moment. It was easy, almost *too* easy for him to forget what their lives were like outside this little condo. Outside this one perfect moment, with the perfect little cupcake, being held by the perfect woman.

He closed his eyes and blew out the candle, and she grinned and pulled it out of the cupcake before peeling back the wrapper and holding it up to him.

"Open up!" She teased, and he laughed and allowed her to feed him a bite of the cupcake, and then he insisted she finish the other half of it. He wanted to share it with her, because they shared so much of their lives already.

"What did you wish for?" She asked, and he looked at her in

shock.

"Taylor! I figured you would know better than anyone that you're not supposed to reveal that! It won't come true otherwise," he reminded her playfully as he wiped a piece of frosting off the corner of her mouth. He noticed her inhale sharply and he grinned, licking the frosting off his finger as he smiled down at her.

Now this…*this* was going to be the fun part of his birthday. He could tell.

"Oh, fine. But when it comes true, you better tell me," she said, taking his hand in hers and pulling him over to the living room couch. She playfully pushed him down, and his heart started to race as she loomed over him.

"I promise, once the magical birthday powers that be grant me my wish, I'll tell you what it was," he assured her, his voice growing low and husky as she reached down and pulled her dress off and over her head, tossing it aside.

He knew, though, that his wish could never come true. Feeling like he was part of her family, part of her inner circle with her dad this evening - he hadn't realized until their impromptu birthday celebration that he actually liked that feeling. He liked feeling like he was just another important part of her life. Someone that even her dad cared about enough to get him a gift card for his birthday. Someone whose birthday she would remember even if he tried to not act like it was a big deal.

He wished he could be that part of her life forever. He wished that they could just be together - just them, doing normal things that two people did when they cared about each other.

And that would never happen. He knew that. He'd always known that. To wish for anything else was stupid, but at least he'd be spared the embarrassment of admitting it to her.

"Now, sit back birthday boy - I'm not done celebrating you this evening," she announced as she leaned down and kissed him deeply. She tasted like the vanilla frosting of the cupcake, but it was hard for him to focus on that as her hands anxiously worked on the buttons of his shirt.

Once his skin was bare to her, he groaned softly into the kiss as her hands ran down his chest to his stomach, playing with the belt buckle of his pants. She made quick work of unzipping them and pulling them down, taking his briefs with them. He tensed and his head began to spin, butterflies of anticipation fluttering in his stomach as she gripped his thighs with her hands and kneeled in front of him.

Yup. Definitely trying to kill him, she was. Death by extreme horniness.

"Happy birthday, Dean," she whispered before she bent down and began to kiss up his thighs. He watched her as he bit his lip, trying and failing to stifle a loud groan as his excitement skyrocketed with each touch of her lips against him. A few simple kisses and he was already a complete goner, his body a complete slave to her every touch.

So what if he didn't get his wish? At least he had *this,* and as she took him in her mouth and he moaned her name loudly, all other thoughts completely vanished from his mind as his thoughts were consumed only with her. Happy birthday to him, indeed.

CHAPTER THIRTY

TAYLOR

Taylor had made it perfectly clear to Alex that she did *not* want to go to his room to have sex with him. She didn't want to make out. She didn't even want to cuddle. She just couldn't stand the thought of going back to her empty room without Dean there.

Alex, being the gentleman that he was, had agreed without any further questions. He'd thrown on Netflix in the background, flipping to some British show she'd never heard of, and made her a cup of tea. It didn't do much to take her mind off of Dean.

She could only think of him wandering around, drunk and high and alone in a foreign country. She tried not to keep glancing at her phone, hoping to see it light up with a call from him. Alex was trying to make small talk, asking her about her family and life in America, clearly as an attempt to distract her. She appreciated him greatly for that, and tried to tell herself that at least one good thing was coming out of this debacle.

Apparently, she'd made a new friend.

After about half an hour, she sighed and ran a hand through her messy blonde hair. "I'm sorry I'm such terrible company, Alex," she grumbled. Alex paused and set down his tea, shaking his head.

"You have nothing to apologize for, Taylor. I can tell that this whole thing is eating away at you," he observed, and she nodded, unable to deny it. That was when she found herself realizing that she didn't *want* to deny it. Now that she was certain she wasn't going to be using Alex anymore for her own personal gain, she *wanted* him to know how special Dean was to her. Not because she wanted to make him jealous, but because it was important to her.

God, she was an awful person, trying to *use* Alex like that. She'd hurt Dean. She'd probably hurt Alex too, in some way. A few tears fell down her cheeks and he moved from his spot on the opposite love seat and sat next to her, putting his arm around her. She took a deep breath, burying her head in his shoulder. His cologne was nice. Nothing like Dean's natural scent, mixed with ocean spray body wash but...it was still comforting.

"You have feelings for him, don't you?" He asked quietly. She looked up at him in shock, and he gave her a sad smile.

"I'm not stupid, Taylor. It's clear you two care about each other a lot," he admitted. Well, shit. She knew they were probably a bit too flirty out here for their own good, but apparently they weren't nearly as conspicuous as they thought.

"Its complicated," she muttered, and he gently kissed the top of her head. Just like Dean did after they had sex...she was in the arms of another man and all she could think about was

Dean. Sure, it meant nothing in the romantic sense, but she couldn't help feeling guilty. If she hadn't done any of this, she would be curled up in Dean's arms right now, enjoying their vacation.

It was consuming her. The worry and pain of this entire situation were wrapping so tightly around her heart that she was certain it would just break in half from the pressure.

"I imagine so, him being your assistant and all," he nodded in agreement. She appreciated that Alex was being so understanding about all of this. He could very well just be saying what she wanted to hear to keep up the act of being the nice guy, but she didn't care if he was. He was saying all the exact right words in this moment.

"I need to talk to him. I'm afraid I've really hurt him, and caused him to go on a bender. I'm really worried about him not answering his phone when he's drunk like this," she whispered. Alex squeezed her hand comfortingly.

"I could call room service and talk to one of the maids, see if they can keep an eye out for him. Or the front desk. They can alert me if they see him."

She bit her lip and tried not to look too desperate when she answered. "Oh, would you?! That would be so great, Alex. Thank you. You can give them my number too," she insisted. That was a brilliant idea and she couldn't believe she hadn't thought of that earlier. She pulled his phone towards her so she could send herself a text and then handed it back. "Now you have my number," she said with a smile.

Taylor realized a second too late what that might be implying to him, but if he thought along those lines, he didn't say anything. No, it seemed to have gotten through to Alex that things were not going to progress with them any further, and he seemed to accept it. For once today, something had gone right.

"You should rest. Feel free to sleep here tonight if you want, if it's...too much for you to go back to your room," he offered. "I promise I will be the perfect gentleman," he added, blushing a little when he seemed to realize what his offer might look like to her.

She let out a sigh and smiled at him. "Thank you so much, Alex. You're great, really," she whispered. Even if she wasn't attracted to him, he was a kind soul. Dean had been wrong about him. His dislike of him was truly out of jealousy, nothing else. She watched as he grabbed his room key and his phone, heading out the door, and announcing that he would be back in a bit.

She watched him go and then sighed, kicking off her shoes and crawling into his bed. A bit presumptuous of her maybe, but he *had* offered to let her sleep here. After today, she was completely drained, but now that she knew Alex was going to help locate Dean, she felt a bit better. She checked her phone one last time and decided to try calling him again - still nothing. But it also hadn't gone straight to voicemail, so at least his phone was *on* and not dead at the bottom of the ocean. It was somewhat comforting.

Before she knew it, her eyelids started getting heavy, and she felt herself drifting off to sleep.

****

Alex had been heading down to the lobby, not to alert the front desk for a drunken blond British man on the loose, but to get a drink. For all he cared, Dean could stumble into the jungle and never return. He didn't really remember the guy from school, but from what he had seen on this trip, it was clear that he was desperately in love with Taylor. He was acting like a jealous, possessive prick, but Alex couldn't exactly *say* that without coming off like a bad guy.

He didn't necessarily have *that* much interest in Taylor, but he liked her enough to know she deserved the best. She was sweet, worrying about him this much. Did Dean deserve that level of worry from her? In his opinion, no - but it was clear he was interfering with something that was far more complex and complicated than they were letting on.

After he finished his cocktail and as he headed back to the elevator, he spotted Dean getting on and riding it up. What a weird stroke of luck. He hadn't actually been *trying* to find him, yet here he was. He paused and waited in the lobby, watching the number above the elevator change, and when it hit three and it paused, he took the stairs two at a time and hurried up to the third floor.

He emerged just in time to see Dean stumble his way down the hallway, take out a key card, and head into the suite at the end of the hall. That must be their room. So evidently, Taylor had nothing to worry about. Dean had seen himself home, although he was very obviously drunk as she had suspected. Good. The idiot could sleep it off and deal with the fact that she'd spent the night in Alex's room in the morning.

Alex headed up a floor to his own suite, heading back to his room to find Taylor asleep under the covers. She was asleep on her stomach, half of her face buried in his pillow and she breathed deeply in her sleep. She looked peaceful, and she must have been exhausted from everything that had happened that day.

It *had* been a long evening, and he hadn't even been chasing a drunk man around the resort for most of it like she had.

Smirking to himself, he took out his phone and snapped a photo of her underneath his covers. She looked so serene, her hair billowed out behind her on the pillow like that. And not to toot his own horn, but this was a great picture he'd taken. It looked like one of those artsy photos that someone would title 'My Sleeping Lover' or something sappy like that. You couldn't even tell who it was in the picture, it was just a nameless, beautiful woman in his bed.

Suddenly, a lightbulb went off in his head. He felt a twinge of guilt for the briefest of moments, but he quickly pushed it aside. After all, had she not started this whole thing with him to achieve the exact same purpose? She didn't have to tell him her master plan - he figured it out the second she approached him, her blue eyes glancing every so often at the paparazzi that constantly followed him. It had been so painfully obvious.

She had been navigating this world well for a rookie, but he'd dealt with this his whole life. He was a professional, and there would be no outsmarting him.

This idea had been brewing in his mind for a while, but in an instant, he had all the materials to make it a reality. The best part was, he hadn't even had to reveal his plan to Taylor to put it into motion. She'd unknowingly given him the perfect ammo.

As she slept he headed into the other room quietly and opened his email on his phone. He had a hot tip he needed to call in...

CHAPTER THIRTY-ONE

DEAN

Dean woke up the next morning feeling like he'd jumped off a cliff and landed face first into the ocean.

He had fallen off the wagon last night, and he'd fallen off it *hard*. He wasn't sure how much he'd had to drink, but he did remember doing some coke with a group of men at the bar as well, which was a *huge* issue. It's not like it was the first time he'd done cocaine, but it was the first time in a long time, and that usually led to worse things down the line. He had blacked out, and he just prayed that he hadn't done anything too stupid last night that would come back to bite him in the ass later.

Damnit, his nose still hurt from the volleyball incident too.

He had to snap out of this funk he was in. He was a complete train wreck, and trying to drown his sorrows in alcohol had only made things worse. Just like it always did. He knew it would make things worse, but he had no self-control. He was *weak,* no matter what Taylor said.

Damnit, *Taylor.*

Gingerly he sat up in bed and realized his arm hurt terribly, and he looked down and saw a big bruise on his shoulder. The memory flashed in his brain like a photograph. He remembered stumbling into the room and tripping, crashing into the corner of the TV stand. He crawled out of bed and walked to the door, looking around and listening for any sign of Taylor from her room.

It was radio silent. He dared himself to push through the nerves and go across the living room to Taylor's door, and he peeked inside. Nothing. The bathroom was empty too.

She wasn't in the room.

He panicked a little and looked at the clock on the wall. It was 11 AM, and she very well may have gotten up earlier than him and left him to sleep. Just because she wasn't here didn't mean she was in someone else's bed…

It didn't mean she was in *Alex's* bed…

Groaning to himself, he walked back to the bed and took his phone out. Shit, it was dead. He plugged it in and waited for the battery to get some juice so he could turn it on. Once he had it booted up, an onslaught of notifications dinged, and they were all from Taylor. She'd tried to call him last night, many times, but she didn't leave a message. No texts either.

Dean sighed and stumbled his way into the bathroom while his phone charged the rest of the way. He needed to shower and sober up. He examined his face and frowned at his red nose, but overall it wasn't swollen or bruised by some miracle. Perhaps he *had* overreacted a little. He needed to get some food in him and find Taylor and apologize for abandoning her on the beach and then disappearing for hours.

Yet...she hadn't tried to text him. She'd only called him a few times and then given up. No voicemail. And she wasn't in the room, so she was clearly avoiding him. Did that mean she didn't *want* to be found?

She must still be with Alex. There was no other explanation. Her bedroom didn't look lived in since the maid had come in yesterday, which led him to believe she *had* slept somewhere else last night.

He had really screwed this up, hadn't he?

He was going to be sick, and not just from the alcohol.

* * * *

After heaving his guts out into the toilet and showering so he no longer stunk of booze, Dean wandered down to the pool and looked for her. She wasn't there, but he didn't spend much time looking for her since the hot sun was making his head pound and his stomach churn.

He headed inside to the coffee bar and got himself something to try and get some energy flowing through his veins, but he just ended up throwing that up after a few minutes so he ditched the rest of the drink.

He realized shortly after that that he could check his watch and see where he'd gone last night. It would be the first step in trying to piece together is night, like he was in a real life version of *The Hangover*. Nervously, he opened the exercise app on his phone and checked his steps from the day before. His steps tracker said he'd just walked in circles around the resort, apparently.

He let out a little sigh of relief, thankful to know that

he hadn't wandered off the property or gone anywhere outside the resort with strangers. He wondered if he'd run into Taylor at all, but he felt like he would remember if he did. Hopefully, he hadn't run into Alex, because he was sure the smarmy git would use it against him if he'd run into him plastered out of his mind.

This resort was small, but somehow they were doing a great job of avoiding each other. And Dean intended to keep it that way for just a little while longer. Just until he figured out what exactly had happened last night.

Next, he headed to his photos. There were quite a few blurry shots added to his camera roll since yesterday, and he quickly pulled them up and started to scroll through them. He'd taken some pictures - or at least attempted to - with the German men who'd given him the coke. Then he'd apparently followed them out to the pool bar.

There was a picture of one of the men running through the water with his shirt off. Another picture of Dean himself, lying on one of the beach chairs and drinking a Corona. Then more blurry pictures of the lobby. A video of himself doing another line - he deleted that one immediately. Then a photo in the billiards room with the German men and some other guys he didn't recognize. It ended with a picture of a burger that he had apparently thought needed to be captured at that moment, and it was time-stamped at 2:13 AM. He vaguely remembered ordering room service before he passed out last night, and could tell the background of the burger photo was in his bedroom. Trying to create a timeline of the evening, he thought back to the previous day and everything they'd done up until Alex had shown up. He knew he had left Taylor at the beach with Alex a little before dinner, perhaps around 4:00…

So for ten hours, he'd been drunk, belligerent, and

gone on a tour of the resort with a group of German men high out of his mind on cocaine.

Not his best night, but also not his worst. Sixteen-year-old Dean had done some wild things at boarding school, and seeing as how he was *pretty* sure there hadn't been any Molly last night, and he hadn't woken up with his ear pierced like David Bowie, he had to call that a win.

Except for the fact that he couldn't find Taylor. Thankfully she didn't appear to be in any of the photos, which was reassuring. She must have spent all night with Alex and their paths had never crossed. Maybe there was still a way he could salvage this.

His thoughts were rudely interrupted as another wave of nausea hit him, and he hurried to the nearby trash can before he could think over his predicament any further.

CHAPTER THIRTY-TWO

TAYLOR

She hadn't meant to sleep in, and she could tell it was late as she slowly opened her eyes. Something else felt off. The room didn't smell...*familiar* to her, and the wallpaper was different. Taylor picked her head up, looked around, and realized she wasn't in her room. *Fuck*.

She must have fallen asleep after talking to Alex last night. She had intended to wait for him to come back before taking a short nap, but after she'd crawled under the sheets, she'd passed out. She didn't see him anywhere, but she was wearing all her clothes at least. Not that she had been under the impression that she'd *done* anything with him.

She remembered every bit of her night from the day before, despite having been a little tipsy after her downing her vodka cranberry in three minutes at the bar. She rubbed her head, a migraine setting in from the sheer stress of the previous day. She needed to find Dean.

She heard movement at the door and looked up to see

Alex standing there in a plain white t-shirt and gray sweats with two cups of coffee. She couldn't help but think about how there were likely girls out there who would *kill* to wake up to that sight. "Morning," he said with a small smile as he approached the bed, handing her the cup of coffee.

Taylor muttered a small thank you and took the coffee from him, taking a sip. She set the coffee down on the nightstand and grabbed her phone, which Alex apparently had thoughtfully plugged into a spare charger for her. Nothing from Dean. Her heart started to race as she looked up at Alex, who had settled next to her and was drinking his own coffee.

"Did you hear anything about Dean? From the staff?" She asked him, remembering that he had offered to reach out to them and have them contact him if they spotted him. Alex shook his head, taking another sip with a sigh.

"Nothing. I'm sorry, Taylor," he told her, and she felt like he genuinely meant it. "I know last night was hard for you."

She sighed and pulled up her Instagram, and realized with a thrill of delight that Dean had updated his stories since she had last checked. She inhaled sharply and clicked the circular little icon with his profile picture, and let out a sigh of relief when she saw a picture of his bed sheets and duvet.

It looked like it had been taken by accident - probably while he was drunk - as it was blurry and looked like it had snapped a picture while his phone had been tumbling off the bed. Then he'd somehow accidentally added it to Instagram. Still, she knew it was their room and recognized the wallpaper, and the pile of gym clothes he'd left outside the bathroom.

She did some time math and realized he posted it around 3 AM. Instant relief flooded her as she excitedly turned to Alex.

"He's in the room," she revealed with a heavy sigh. She showed Alex the picture and he chuckled a little.

"Well, look at that. You were worried for nothing," he teased. There was just a hint of flirty playfulness in his tone, which reminded her of the mess she'd made with him. She was still 99.9% sure he knew that she wasn't interested in him that way, but Christ's sake, she'd slept in his *bed* last night. She wouldn't be surprised if the man still clung to a bit of hope that something would happen between the two of them. She shook her head and bit her lip, realizing that she needed to put a squash to…whatever this was right now.

"Listen, Alex…"

He sighed and set aside his coffee, evidently already knowing what she was going to say. He looked sad, but also not surprised. He probably knew this was where their little fling had been headed all along.

"Go ahead, Tay," he said softly, tilting his head at her to let her know he was listening.

"It's Taylor, actually,"

He raised an eyebrow. She had no idea why she had said that. For some reason, him calling her Tay was just…wrong. It wasn't right. It wasn't *Dean*. Dean was the only one who ever called her that, and to hear it fall from another man's lips just reminded her of how much everything had gotten out of hand with her assistant. She missed him so much, but she had to take care of this before she went looking for him.

No more fucking around with any British boys or their feelings.

"I'm sorry, I just…I can't do this."

"Do what?" He asked, tilting his head as if he had no

idea what she was talking about. It was one last attempt to get her to stay with him. To keep this going, whatever *this* was. She shook her head.

"Don't do this, please Alex. I'm so sorry, I should have never led you on, I should have never kissed you on the beach, I just…"

"Shush, it's ok…" he reached out and grabbed her hand, squeezing it. It was comforting, but at the same time, she also wanted to throw up. All she could think about was Dean's strong hands doing the same thing for her, and she felt sick to her stomach.

"I would be lying if I said I wasn't….disappointed," he admitted with a frown. "I do genuinely think we'd be good together."

She sighed and smiled at him. "Thank you, Alex. You're very kind. But I just…" she trailed off. It was hard trying to admit to herself what she was feeling and trying to admit it to a stranger was a whole different level of difficulty.

"You don't have to say it. I know," he assured her, giving her a kind smile.

She bit her lip and crawled out of his bed. "Thank you for letting me stay here last night," she mumbled as she unplugged her phone from his charger. Jesus, she was about to do the walk of shame through this hotel - granted, it was just down one floor - and she hadn't even *done* anything with him last night. Not since her college party days had she felt like such a mess.

"Of course. And if you need anything…I'm still here. As a friend," he assured her. She appreciated the gesture, and after everything he had done for her so far, she found that she believed him. Alexander Capano was a good man, and deserved someone far better than her.

"Go find him, Taylor," he encouraged her with a smile, and she thanked him again for the coffee before heading out of the room in a hurry, her heels in her hand as she rushed back to her suite, hoping to find Dean.

He wasn't there when she returned. There was a half-eaten burger on the table that she left outside for the maid before putting the do-not-disturb sign on the door. She walked back and looked around, wondering what her next move was. Maybe he'd gone down to get something for his hangover. She opened her phone and was about to call him, but suddenly found herself pausing with her thumb over the call button.

What would she say to him? Crap. She hadn't thought that far ahead. She wanted desperately to tell him that she knew the truth...but at the same time, she realized that she was a little hurt by the revelation. She'd asked him to never lie to her. It was what their friendship was based on, and yet...he kept insisting this was ok. He knew it was just sex. No feelings attached. Just friends.

What did she say to that? More importantly - what did she *feel* towards him now that she knew?

Shit. Taylor couldn't call him. She couldn't face him. Not yet. She needed to think. She needed to gather her thoughts. She would take a long hot bath and think about what she wanted to say when she finally saw him again. She would head down to the spa and make an afternoon of it - really clear her head while thinking things over so that when he came back...she could talk to him. She could figure this out.

But first, she had to do what she always did when she had too many thoughts in her brain and she couldn't keep track of them. She ran to her laptop, flinging it open and booting it up.

Still in her black dress from the night before, she pulled open a blank Pages document and wrote "Dear Dean" at the top of the page.

She knew one thing for certain - if she planned out what she was going to say to him, it would be infinitely easier to face him later. She needed a roadmap to guide her through the feelings currently constricting her brain and her heart. She paused, staring at the blinking cursor for a moment before she took a deep breath.

And then, she began to write.

CHAPTER THIRTY-THREE

DEAN

After wallowing out by the beach for a bit, Dean began to feel eager about seeing Taylor. Yet he was still afraid. Seeing Taylor would force him to confront the fact that he had a lot of feelings about her, and this Alex situation wasn't helping.

He pulled out his phone, staring at the screen which still didn't show any messages from Taylor. She must be royally pissed at him. He pulled up her Instagram and saw she had shared some reels, nothing too crazy - just some videos of cute dogs, a funny horoscope meme, and then she posted a picture of the beach from their room. So she was in the room. It was posted about 20 minutes ago, so that meant they'd missed each other again. Something he felt very grateful for.

He wasn't ready to face her yet, he realized. He needed to do something else. Just for a little while. He knew he was putting off the inevitable, but he needed just a bit more time to compose himself and gather his thoughts.

After relaxing in the lazy river of the resort for an

hour or so, Dean felt slightly more human. He also stopped by the buffet now that he was able to hold down food, thankful that he wasn't running into Taylor anywhere he went. Maybe she was just having such a great time with Alex that she had forgotten all about him. Oh shit, was Alex in their room with her right now? He hoped not. The thought of them being in her bed together, the same bed they'd shared...

He hated thinking like that - he knew that was dramatic of him, but he couldn't help it. The feelings of jealousy just kept creeping up like some sort of snake ready to bite.

Finally, he headed back to the room, fully intending to run into Taylor and finally face the problem - only she wasn't there this time. The do-not-disturb sign had been put on the door, so no one had come to clean, but she wasn't there. After he changed out of his swimsuit, he looked around the room, noticing her discarded dress from last night crumbled up on the floor, and an empty coffee cup on the nightstand.

They'd missed each other again - maybe this was a sign that he *should* just keep avoiding her. Hell, maybe he should just leave Cancun entirely. What would she do if he'd just disappeared? Would she even care? She still hadn't tried to contact him...

He decided to go for a walk outside of the resort, just down the street to a local market. He highly doubted he'd run into Taylor there, and he could buy himself some time instead of just anxiously sitting in the room waiting for her to get back.

Dean knew he was being dumb. He couldn't just *leave*. He was sure that she was just feeling upset about the day before as well. She was probably doing the same thing as him - avoiding him while she tried to think of what to say to him.

Although she was probably going to ream him out for how he had behaved around Alex. Honestly, he deserved every bit of the verbal lashing she would no doubt give him when he finally got back. He'd fucked up so badly yesterday. He was probably making her worry sick over him.

As he browsed the shops, he thought about what she'd said when they'd first booked the vacation. She wanted to support local shops and artisans, but they hadn't planned when they were going to visit the local markets. Or go visit the Mayan ruins. Things had gotten out of hand with this Alex thing and now he wasn't sure there'd be time left to do any of the things she had been excited for. Great. Another reason for her to be pissed at him.

Dean walked along when one vendor caught his eye, selling jewelry at a relatively reasonable price. It didn't seem to be the cheap kind that every other airport shop sold. He scanned the shelves as he did some light browsing, but then his eyes fell on a small dolphin necklace. He chuckled a little, thinking of an old Lisa Frank folder she kept some of her notes in at home - she explained to him that it was popular when she'd been in elementary school and it made her nostalgic for the good old days, so she bought some when they started to come back in style. It was stupid and silly and one of the many things he loved about her.

He still shouldn't be thinking things like that. But he did anyway. And then he purchased the necklace.

It was perfect. It was small and covered in silver stones - not real diamonds, but still high quality. It glittered in the sun, casting different colors on the nearby counter as he held it to the light - how fitting considering Lisa Frank was all about rainbows. It was small though, and she could fit it under her shirts if she wanted because he knew she didn't usually wear jewelry. Sometimes she wore large earrings, but that was usually it.

He purchased it and then got her some candy as an apology as well. He downright hated that he was having to apologize so often this trip, but it was his own damn fault. He just had to keep his wits about him for a few more days. Then Alex would be gone, they'd be back in L.A, and maybe things could go back to normal.

First things first - he had to buck up and finally talk to Taylor.

CHAPTER THIRTY-FOUR

DEAN

After avoiding her all day, Dean knew it was time to finally return to the room and face Taylor. The sun was starting to set and he'd wasted enough time putting off their reunion. As he walked in to the kitchen of the suite, he immediately saw her sitting on her bed with her phone in hand, and he let out a small sigh of relief. Part of him had worried that she actually got herself another room so she wouldn't have to see him anymore. She hadn't texted him all day, which led him to believe she was angry with him, and he didn't blame her. He *had* been pointedly avoiding her.

As soon as she saw it was him, she wordlessly got up from the bed. Feeling his heart start to race, he wandered over to the living area, trying to brace himself for whatever shit storm was about to come. He sat down on the sofa and rubbed his hands over his face as she sat down across from him on the matching armchair. He had already decided that whatever she was about to unleash on him, he would sit and take it because he deserved it.

"You fell off the wagon last night didn't you?" She asked quietly after a moment of silence. He paused, unsure how she knew that, but he nodded nevertheless, avoiding her gaze. Maybe it was just obvious from his demeanor. Or maybe she'd heard about a drunk British man causing chaos in the bar with a group of German football fans. Either one was possible.

"You need help, Dean," she told him quietly, and he felt his heart plummet into his stomach. He *knew* he needed help, and it was something he was desperately avoiding. It was much easier to focus on all the good days he had in *between* benders that didn't end in disaster. But last night had been awful. He'd done drugs too, and his nose still stung from it. He shuddered to think what might have happened if those men had something stronger on them.

"It won't happen again. I just got...lost in my feelings," he insisted, trying half-heartedly to justify his actions. He knew it was a lost cause the moment the words left his mouth. Even he didn't believe his own excuse.

Taylor tensed and ran her hands over her thighs anxiously, shaking her head. "That's been...three times in the past six months, Dean. That's not *good*. That isn't a sign that you're in recovery..."

"Maybe we should talk about your shit while we're at it," he snapped at her. He instantly regretted bringing it up, and he'd only done so because he felt like he was being chastised like a schoolboy. He knew what she was saying was true, and maybe a good verbal lashing was what he needed, but it slipped out before he could stop it. She paused and looked at him curiously with a frown.

"*My* shit? What are you talking about?" She demanded, and he realized that she truly had no clue what he was referencing. Perhaps this was the wrong time to bring it up, but he'd brought it up and he couldn't undo that.

Dean paused and took a deep breath. Alright, time to lay it all out on the table, then. He was sick of acting like he was the only one capable of worrying the other in this situation.

"Ok, let's start with the fact that you're *obsessed* with your image. You're so focused on getting people to like you, and when they don't, or you think something is going to happen to tarnish your image you…you fucking *spiral*. I can't get that damn sight of you laying on your floor, sobbing into a bottle of merlot out of my mind!" He told her. She paused and he could see the wheels turning, and he wondered if she truly had never made the connection until now. How did she not see that she had some serious trauma related to not being successful? To all the rejection in her life up until she was published? "And I know it's because you feel this need to be accepted, out of fear that people are going to walk away, like your mother…"

"Don't," she snapped, pointing her index finger at him, a look of fire in her eyes. Dean knew he instantly had crossed a line. He felt like shrinking into the sofa as she stared at him, her face turning red. "Don't you fucking *dare* psychoanalyze me right now. Tread very carefully here, Dean Coffey, because I've been worried sick about you all day! You could have been dead in the ocean for all I knew, I've barely been able to eat, or sleep, because I…"

She trailed off, clearly fighting back tears, and he sighed and ran his hand through his hair. All of the anger he felt fizzled out, his heart sinking into the pit of his stomach. Fuck. He was an arse for bringing that up. None of this had anything to do with the real problem at hand and he knew it. He just wanted to get the attention off of him and his drinking.

"I'm sorry, Taylor. That was out of line," he whispered. She glared at him, but he could feel her softening from where he sat. The anger in her eyes was slowly turning and giving way to sadness, which was almost worse for Dean to look at.

"So we both have fucking issues, that isn't the point," she said gruffly, letting him know that she was dropping this topic of conversation. He shook his head and started to walk away. She was right, and he didn't want to fight with her right now. Maybe they both needed to take a minute to breathe and cool down. He thought about the necklace in his pocket and headed to his room, kicking off his flip-flops as he heard her following him. She didn't say anything, but he could feel her behind him, just watching.

"Do you remember what I asked you? When I first hired you?" She asked him quietly, her arms crossed in front of her. She leaned against the door, her blonde hair cascading over her shoulders and coming to rest just above her breasts. She was wearing a black camisole tank top over a red lacy bralette, with a white tennis skirt that made it look like she was ready to go on a midnight run. He was so entranced by how good she looked standing in his doorway that he almost missed her question.

"What?" He asked, blinking at her as he ran the question back in his mind.

"What did I ask of you when I first hired you?" She repeated, slowly, a frown forming on her face.

Dean paused, his heart starting to race as he remembered what she'd said. Taylor had made it very clear to him that she had expectations from him as her assistant. She had only asked one thing of him, and it wasn't sex. It was one thing, one simple thing, and he realized only now in this instant that he'd been breaking his promise to her for months. He hadn't even noticed he had been doing it...

"To never lie to you," he answered quietly. He tried to remain calm. *He* knew now that he had been lying for a very long time to her, but he was positive that couldn't be what she was talking about. How could she know? He had done everything he could to make sure she didn't know. Hell, he'd done everything he could to try and trick *himself* into believing he wasn't lying to her, to himself, to everyone around them...

"I haven't lied to you," he assured her quickly, although he wasn't sure if he even had to defend himself right now. She had that hard look on her face that told him she was upset about something, but she also had a vibe about her that he couldn't quite place. He could usually read her like a book, but tonight, he was at a loss. He had no clue what was going through her head.

"But you *have*, Dean," she replied, biting her lip. Her big blue eyes were glassy and he felt his heart starting to fall into the pit of his stomach. Was she about to *cry?* He was lost, unsure of what to do to try and help the situation, and he knew his face showed his confusion. She shook her head in disappointment. She knew that he wasn't getting the point she was trying to make.

"You've lied to me every time I've asked you if you were ok with this no-strings-attached arrangement we have," she continued. Fear started to squeeze his chest, the realization dawning on him about what was truly happening. His heart sank even further.

She *knew.*

How had she figured it out? He'd always been so

calculated, so *careful* about his feelings. He never let his mask slip around anyone, especially her. He had never even allowed himself to think the words to himself. He shut those thoughts down as soon as they tried to rear their ugly head, refusing to accept it. Refusing to believe it was true, even though he knew deep down he was fooling himself.

There was one word to describe his feelings for Taylor Mullins, and he adamantly denied it and pushed it down, squashing it in the hopes that it would die down and fade away.

He couldn't think of what else to say or what to do. All he could think to do was continue to deny it, like he always had. Like he'd been trying to do to everyone, including himself, for a very, very long time now. He took a deep breath and tried to swallow away the lump in his throat. "I *am* ok with it, Tay."

"No, you're not!" She exclaimed, dropping her arms and marching up to him. He could see the hurt in her face and he felt his own eyes starting to water. He was trapped and he knew it. She had him stuck in a corner and there was no way out of it. No escape.

"Stop lying to me, Dean. I know! I...*know*... everything," she admitted, her voice dropping as she looked up at him. He felt like she was studying his face, looking for some sign that maybe she was wrong. He knew she wouldn't find what she was looking for, though. It was pointless to try and keep it hidden any longer, as much as he wanted to turn and run from it.

"I heard about your night at the bar," she elaborated further, and he blushed. He could barely remember what had happened last night, but he *did* remember having drinks at the hotel bar. "You spilled everything to the people there. All your thoughts and...feelings," she revealed, sighing heavily and staring down at the floor as she allowed him a moment to process what she'd just said.

Well, shit. He really *was* trapped now. The two girls at the bar suddenly flashed into his mind, and the memory came screaming back to him. He had no doubt that he'd laid his heart out on the table for complete strangers, and through some dumb twist of fate, Taylor had coincidently struck up a conversation with those same strangers and heard about his pathetic rant. God, this was the most humiliating moment of his life, and he'd once been stripped down and made to run through the rugby field at school in the pouring rain as a hazing ritual.

There was only one thing to do now - beg for forgiveness. Dean had lied, and done the one thing she'd asked him *not* to do. He was nothing if not a loyal assistant, though. Taylor always told him what to do, and he did it with a smile because he wanted to. He could do that now. She just needed to tell him what he needed to do to fix this with her, and all could be forgiven.

Right?

"Just...tell me what to do, Tay," he whispered, a tear dripping down his face. There had to be *some* way that he could fix this. He found himself thinking that it didn't matter if she loved him back, as long as he had her in his life, he would find a way to be content. He could even do away with the sex if that was what it meant. Hell, he'd even quit being her assistant. Anything to keep her here and keep her from hating him. The thought of them not being friends in *any* capacity...it felt like it was suffocating his heart.

"No, Dean, I can't," she sighed and shook her head, her hair falling in front of her face. She looked up at him, furrowing her bow and frowning sadly at him. "Not this time. I can't tell you what choice to make," she told him sternly.

He paused as she thought over her words in his head. She hadn't told him to get lost and go fuck himself yet, so that was a plus. But she also wasn't going to say anything to help him figure out what the right move was here. He had to choose on his own.

The fact that she was giving him a choice, though... did that mean she *wanted* him to want more? To him, it seemed obvious what his choices were. The first choice, and the most heart-wrenching, would be to turn and walk away, acknowledging that he'd hurt her and run from the pain he'd caused her. Let her deal with it on her own and cut ties with her completely.

The other choice...would be to admit he'd lied. Apologize and tell her he'd never lie to her again, starting right now. That would mean he'd have to face the truth at this moment, not tomorrow or next week when they got back to L.A., but *now.* Lay it all out on the table. She knew what that truth was, and if he finally admitted it, and said the words with his own lips...what would she say in return?

His head was spinning again, and for a moment he thought he might need to sit down. He forced himself to look down at Taylor, though, trying in vain to study her face again. To look for any indication of what she wanted him to do - which choice she wanted him to make.

"And what about you?" He asked her. "What do *you* want?"

She swallowed audibly, her face blushing, and that was all he needed. He knew what she wanted.

He knew in that moment which choice he was making.

"Dean, don't put this on me, don't…"

He didn't get to hear the rest of her sentence because he reached forward, grabbed her by the hips, and pulled her towards him, leaning in and kissing her roughly.

They kissed all the time, but he'd never kissed her like *this* before. To his immense shock - and relief - she leaned into him, throwing her arms around his neck and kissing him back with equal fervor. Even on that first night months ago, when he'd pounced on her in the hotel room and started falling down this rabbit hole, their kisses had never been full of as much passion as this.

His hands pushed her cami and bralette off impatiently, and she was making quick work of the light button-down short-sleeved shirt he was wearing. He ground his hips into hers, grateful that he wearing thinner shorts so she could feel how much he wanted her against her thigh. Those shorts came off quickly as he fumbled with the button and zipper himself, desperate to be close to her.

She pulled her lips from his long enough to push his shirt off over his head, clearly too impatient to finish unbuttoning it. She kissed him again as they stumbled back towards the bed, his hands pushing her tennis skirt off and taking her panties with it. He couldn't get her naked fast enough.

Taylor straddled him, her hands moving down his chest and her finger following the line of light blond hair that ran down his abs. He grunted and bucked his hips, eager for her to continue, but she paused and looked down at him, her blue eyes glassy once more.

"Tell me the truth, Dean," she whispered to him. He

didn't need to ask her to clarify what she meant.

Dean knew exactly what truth she was asking for. His heart raced and he tensed ever so slightly before he sat up and pulled her close to him, settling her in his lap as their legs tangled with each other. He stared at her, his hand moving to tangle in her long hair as he used his other hand to cup her cheek.

"Tell me," she demanded again, even softer this time, hardly more than a whisper, but she looked like she was going to cry. He couldn't deny her - or himself - this any longer.

"I love you, Taylor Mullins," he told her, telling her his true feelings for her for the first time. It was the truth that he had been pushing into the back of his mind day after day for months now. He had known, he had *always* known and been too afraid to truly face his feelings and come to terms with the fact that he'd gone and done exactly what he *shouldn't* have done when it came to Taylor Mullins.

It was like a weight had been lifted from his chest, but time also seemed to stop as he paused and waited for her to respond. There was still a chance, the smallest little chance, that she would turn around and run away, the reality of it all being too much for her to bear.

She bit her lip and smiled at him softly, and he felt all his fears melt away.

"I love you too, Dean Coffey," she replied, and he was quite certain his heart was going to explode right then and there. He had never once envisioned a reality where she actually loved him in return. He had never allowed himself to. He'd convinced himself a long time ago that his feelings were crazy, and that she could never feel that way about him in return. Yet here she was, sitting in his lap, running her hands over his chest and staring at him with pure love in her eyes.

She lifted her hips and settled on him, moaning softly as he filled her and held her in his lap. Neither of them moved, they just stared at each other as they reveled in the moment together. Carefully, almost as if he was afraid he was going to break her, he reached out and brushed a piece of hair out of her face. His fingertips gently ran down her cheek and to her chin, which he tilted towards him so he could lean in and kiss her as she whimpered into his mouth. His name tumbled softly from her lips, and he felt another tear drip down his cheek.

Dean had wanted this for so long, maybe since the moment he'd met her.

Her hands slowly ran down his biceps, just feeling his skin under her gentle touches, and he peppered kisses lightly against her cheeks as he made his way down to her neck. He moved his hips softly, bucking into her as she moaned, her hands moving down his back, her fingertips grazing his skin.

His hand moved down her chest, lightly over her breasts, and then down and around to the small of her back. He pushed against her, pulling her closer and further down on top of him as he moved slowly, agonizingly so, just reveling in the feel of their bodies pressed against each other.

This was it for him. There was never going to be another woman, he knew that with utmost certainty now. And he prayed that she thought the same way, because he didn't think he would be able to bear the idea of her looking at another man the way she was looking at him right now.

He brought his lips back up to her cheek, kissing the corner of her mouth before he pressed his forehead against hers. She shuddered as he moved again, the bed creaking underneath them as he started up a rhythm. She bit her lip and groaned out his name again. Fuck, he always loved the sound of her screaming his name, but this was somehow even better.

He felt her hot breath on his face as he moaned her name, biting her lip gently as his hands ran up and down her back. They'd never done it at this angle before and now he couldn't figure out why, because he was able to touch every bit of her, and he could tell by the way she moved her hips into his that he was hitting every nerve of hers that set her on fire. He moved his hand to the back of her neck and pulled her closer to him, his nose smashed against hers, tears on both their cheeks as he tried to get as close as humanely possible to her.

"I love you, Taylor," he whispered again. He wanted to say it over and over to her. He never wanted to stop saying it.

"I love you, Dean," she whispered back, and a few seconds later she broke apart. She cried out his name and gripped him harder than she ever had before, her nails digging into his shoulders as her head flew back. He gasped as he felt her come undone around him and he followed her, releasing hard into her and pulling her close as they both crumbled. He muttered her name over and over like a prayer as they rode out the wave together before she collapsed into a heap in his arms.

Slowly, he pulled out of her and laid down, tugging her down with him. Neither of them said anything for a while, they just looked at each other, trying to catch their breath and holding each other close.

Sex with Taylor had always been amazing, but to make love to her was otherworldly.

It was obvious to them both that neither of them knew what tomorrow was going to bring. As far as he was concerned, he didn't want to think about tomorrow. He wanted to just stay in this moment forever with her, right now, and just *be.* Just the two of them.

He gave her a small smile, and Taylor smiled back at him before she nuzzled her head into his shoulder. Slowly, they drifted off into sleep, and Dean knew without a doubt that this night had just changed everything.

CHAPTER THIRTY-FIVE

DEAN

The next morning, Dean woke up in a bit of a haze. He wasn't hungover, but he still felt like he could sleep for another day or two at least. It wasn't until he rolled over and saw Taylor asleep next to him that he remembered the night before, and his heart soared in his chest.

He remembered every kiss, every moan, every touch of skin against his from the evening before after they both professed their love to each other. Dean wasn't a sentimental sap by any means - or at least, he hadn't considered himself one until last night. Yet he couldn't stop replaying the words over and over in his head.

I love you too, Dean Coffey.

They were the words he never thought he'd heard her say. He had never dared to hope it could turn into that, even if he sometimes woke from dreams where they threw this whole life behind so they could be together.

It wasn't going to be simple or easy. He knew that.

Things were complicated. He was her assistant, her literal employee. She was in the midst of a whirlwind career to the top and it was only going to get crazier once the book launched next week and the show began production. They were going to have to figure out a way to make this work. There was simply no other option in his mind. Now that he knew she loved him back, he wasn't going to just let them push that aside like they'd been doing all these months.

The familiar feeling of a caffeine headache was starting to creep up on him, and Taylor was still fast asleep. As much as he wanted to curl back into bed with her and hold her in his arms, he knew they'd have to have some sort of talk about their next steps once she woke up. Yet he didn't feel terrified of that fact anymore.

Dean was confident they'd be able to come up with something. He wanted to have a clear head when they did so - and truthfully, he was a little *sore* from last night. They'd had a *lot* of sex this trip and it was catching up to him, probably best to skip a morning session today.

He rolled out of bed slowly and put on a pair of jeans and a T-shirt, grabbing his wallet and his phone. She stirred a little next to him, rolling over and blinking up at him.

"Where are you going?" She asked, still half asleep judging from her voice. He smiled and leaned down to kiss the top of her head.

"Shush, go back to sleep. I'll bring you coffee," he assured her. Not awake enough to argue, she rolled back onto her stomach and nuzzled her head further into the pillow. He smiled to himself and then willed himself to turn away, heading out of the room.

As he passed by her room, he realized that she had left her computer on. It was still lit up, plugged into the charger and lighting up her whole room in the darkness. He'd told her *how* many times to close her laptop? Or at least put it into sleep mode when she wasn't using it. Shaking his head playfully he headed over to close it, until he realized that his name was on the document.

It was a long document, and now that he knew he was mentioned in it, he kept reading it. He couldn't help it. It was a jumbled mess of words, each paragraph beginning with the same two words - 'Dear Dean'.

Dear Dean,

I know you love me, and I wanted you to know that I love you too. So much so that I'd happily throw all this away, the fame and writing and all of it, just to be with you each and every day.

Then it was like her brain switched gears, and she restarted the letter to him.

Dear Dean,

I'm so freaking pissed at you right now. I hope you're hungover as shit and when you get back to the room, I'm going to yell at you for how irresponsible you are and then I'm going to kiss you until you can't breathe.

That one made him chuckle a little, although he felt guilty for worrying her so badly.

Dear Dean,

We might be the two stupidest people on the planet. How did we not know this was going to end up like this? Or...did we always know and we just chose to pretend it wouldn't?

On and on it went, for nine pages, with different variations of the same thing. All of them culminated in the same sentiments they'd eventually shared with each other last night. That they loved each other. They were *in* love with each other. A lump was forming in his throat as he read her words, only instead of sadness, it was formed out of pure happiness.

With a smile, he shut the laptop and wiped away a few tears that were pooling in his eyes. Her words were echoing in his mind and giving him a fresh perspective on the day. With that, he left the room and headed towards the elevator.

He was on cloud nine. He was pretty sure he couldn't stop smiling - and he kind of hoped he ran into Alex so the git could see just how excited and happy he was this morning. He'd be a gentleman and not brag about the details, but he'd let Alex work out that information for himself. Intrigued by his deliciously wicked idea, he boarded the elevator and realized his phone was buzzing in his pocket.

Who could be calling him at - shit, it was almost noon, he hadn't even realized how late they slept in. He was shocked to see a picture of Caroline popping up on his phone as it rang - it was a selfie she'd drunkenly taken with Taylor at her birthday party back in December, and she'd set it as her profile picture when she stole his phone that night. She'd been insisting that she wanted to check for illicit texts between him and Taylor.

The joke was on her, that had been three months before they even started sleeping together.

Dean answered the phone in confusion. Caroline didn't usually call him, but Taylor was probably still passed out in the room. Maybe she wasn't answering her phone. A feeling of dread passed over him as he answered because Taylor had given Caroline explicit instructions not to call unless it was an emergency.

"Caroline?" He hesitantly answered.

"Oh fuck, thank fuck *one* of you answered!" Caroline exclaimed on the other end, so loudly he had to pull the phone away for a second. The feeling of dread grew in his stomach and he gripped the phone tighter against his ear as he stepped off the elevator.

"What's up?" He asked, trying to remain cool and not let on that he was getting nervous.

"Have either of you checked Twitter - or X or whatever the fuck it is now - have any of you checked it today?" She asked quickly. He could tell she was practically dying to blurt something out and was showing restraint as she spoke to him.

He shook his head before realizing she couldn't see him and he had to actually answer her with words. "No, we - I - just woke up," he explained.

"Oh my god, Dean, it's amazing! Paparazzi published pictures of Taylor and Alex at the beach, and a blind item showed up saying they actually slept together. You guys are off the hook!" She exclaimed. Dean felt his heart sink, especially when he heard how gleeful Caroline sounded on the other end.

"What?" He asked, trying to process it all. He knew deep down he shouldn't be so upset. This was what Taylor had wanted, right? Caroline, oblivious to his reaction, continued on excitedly.

"Yeah, he even posted a picture of her in his hotel room! It's really cute actually, she's asleep and nothing torrid. In fact, I wouldn't have even known it was her if he hadn't tagged her in it. He captured the whole 'boy meets girl on vacation and falls desperately head over heels for her' vibe perfectly. He captioned it with some sappy quote from some Italian poet or something...but now that takes the heat off of you! You're a genius for cooking this up," she added. Dean felt himself inhale sharply at her statement. She thought *he* had manufactured this?

And how did Alex have a picture of Taylor in his bed? Unless they actually *had*...

"I...I didn't come up with...is she really sleeping with him?" He asked quietly.

"How should I know? Didn't you come up with this idea? Taylor said she'd ask you what to do when the first blind item came out," she told him.

He shook his head again. "No, I didn't..." he said, unable to keep the hurt from his voice.

Caroline was silent. Almost a minute passed before she said anything, to the point where he thought maybe the call had been dropped, and then he heard a sigh. "Oh, honey."

"What?" He asked quietly.

"Shit. It's true, isn't it?" She questioned him.

He swallowed a lump forming in his throat, deciding the best course of action was to keep being oblivious, even though he had a fairly good idea about what she was alluding to. "What is?"

"Dean, I can hear it in your voice. The two of you... you *are* aren't you...how long?" She asked quietly.

He bit his lip, wondering if it was a good idea to reveal everything to Taylor's agent, but she seemed to have already figured it out. His emotions had given it away. And knowing Caroline, she was not going to let it drop. "A...while."

It was silent again as Caroline processed everything on the other end. She sighed heavily again and he could practically see her playing with her red curls as she thought things through back in L.A.

"I think you need to talk to her, Dean," she

encouraged him.

"I think you're right," he admitted sadly. How was it that two minutes ago, he'd been on top of the world, and now...

"You love her, don't you?"

He was silent, unsure what to say, but his silence was enough of an answer for her.

"You two got yourselves in a real big fucking mess, you know that right?"

He swallowed. "I know."

"Don't do anything stupid."

"I won't," he muttered as he hung up, unsure if he could keep that promise. Already he could feel himself starting to get angry. She'd *slept* with that asshole? And then come to his room as if nothing happened? Told him she loved him?

He probably wouldn't have believed she actually did it, but Alex had a picture of her...

Dean sat down on one of the couches in the lobby and pulled up Instagram, searching for Alex and immediately heading to his profile. His hands were shaking as he waited for the feed to load, hoping and praying with everything he had in him that it wasn't true.

Sure enough, the first picture was a photo of her asleep in his bed. He felt his heart sink into the cushion of the couch as he stared at it. He would know the curves of her back anywhere. Her face was away from him but it was clearly her, with her long blonde hair waved out behind her on the bed.

She was wearing a spaghetti strap dress that he recognized because she'd worn it out to dinner with him before, but to the untrained eye who didn't have every piece of her wardrobe memorized, it looked like skimpy lingerie the way it was cut in the back, which is what was facing the camera. The sheet pulled up over her body just so to make it look like sexy negligee. He swallowed a lump in his throat as he read the caption - it was in Italian, but he could tell by the responses that whatever it said was something romantic. The photo had almost thirty thousand likes.

His eyes started burning. She'd been in Alex's bed. She'd let him take this picture of her and share it all over the internet. Then she'd come to their room and slept with him, telling him she loved him.

Hurt and anger started squeezing his heart, threatening to suffocate him.

His first instinct was to march up to their room and demand an explanation. Perhaps she hadn't actually slept with him - the thought didn't comfort him like he wanted it to, but at least he would know that she'd only used him for her sick game with the media. He stood up, fully intending on marching straight back up to the room, when the elevator dinged, and one Alex Campano emerged, heading to the breakfast buffet with not a care in the world.

Dean's plans immediately changed, and he followed him.

CHAPTER THIRTY-SIX

DEAN

Anger was coursing so strongly through his veins that Dean was certain it would strangle him. He was seeing red. He never let his temper control him like this, but for some reason, this whole situation was making him lose it completely.

To be fair, he'd never been this *angry* before. The roller coaster of emotions he'd experienced over the past two days had tipped him over the edge, and when he saw the shaggy brown hair and tanned skin of Alex Campano in front of him, the rage took over.

"Tell me it isn't fucking true," he demanded as he approached him. Alex turned to him and raised an eyebrow, crossing his arms. Dean hated the way he stood there, proud and confident, aware that they were in a crowded lobby and that he was the clear frontrunner to win whatever fight they were about to engage in. He had a good three or four inches of height on him, and definitely more muscles. Not that Dean was looking to fight the guy, but he was the superior specimen in every regard. Why *shouldn't* he be confident in himself?

"Is what true?" Alex asked, feigning confusion. "That hitting you in the face with that volleyball *wasn't* an accident? Because yes, it's true, I did that on purpose," he taunted him with a grin. "Oh, wait, that's not what you're asking. You're asking if I fucked your girl? I think you should probably ask her. Although I think the picture speaks for itself," he added with a smarmy smirk.

"What the fuck is wrong with you? Did you ask her if you could post that?" He asked, raising an eyebrow. Alex scoffed, as if he couldn't believe Dean had the nerve to ask him that.

"It was her bloody idea, mate. You know she was just using me to get paparazzi off her back. You think you're the only two who know how to twist things to make a story in the blind items?" He asked.

Dean couldn't believe what he was hearing. None of this sounded like Taylor. She was desperate for a good image, yes, but to allow something *that* private to be posted to the internet? That seemed so unlike her. True, she made him take snapshots of her for Instagram all the time, but to post a picture in someone's bed? She didn't even like her *dad* knowing she had sex, let alone the entire world.

"She told you about that?" He asked, wondering what had happened between the two that she felt it was a good idea to let him in on the plan. Alex just shrugged.

"It was pretty obvious. Not like I give a shit. If I can still shag her, does it really matter?" He asked with a raised eyebrow. "I mean, she opened her legs for *you* so I'm assuming she'll screw anyone."

Dean just blinked at him, in shock that he would even

say such a thing. He knew it was meant to be a dig at him - to try and make him feel like he wasn't worthy of her even giving him the time of day - but in his eyes it was far more of an insult to her.

No one insulted Taylor Mullins in front of him. Certainly not rich, entitled, billionaire asshole playboys.

He stared at him, his head bobbing slightly as if he was trying to convince himself that yes, what he was about to do was a good idea, before he curled his hand into a fist and punched Alex square in the jaw.

Dean had never punched anyone. He didn't even think he knew how to do it - and judging from the pain radiating from his knuckles and wrist, he could venture a guess that he definitely hadn't done it right. He let out a yelp and cradled his hand as Alex swore loudly.

A second later, a gruff-looking bodyguard - who had probably always been nearby Alex and he'd just never really noticed - was pulling Dean away from him, and suddenly Taylor was there, having appeared seemingly out of thin air, standing between the two men with her hands up.

"Enough! What the fuck are you two doing?!" She exclaimed. Dean felt that blinding rage deflate out of him, like a balloon that had been popped. *Fuck*. That had been a really, really stupid decision. He stared at her, and Alex wordlessly moved his mouth as if he were trying to find the words to say something. It was too early to see if his punch had had any impact on him, but he did have a red spot on his face where Dean's fist had made contact. It was slightly satisfactory.

"Ask him, he's the one who assaulted me!" Alex snapped at him, and Dean simply glared at him. He wanted to snap at him and tell him he'd do it again in a heartbeat, but even in his anger, he knew that would be a dumb decision.

"What has gotten into you?" Taylor hissed, turning to him, and he had no words for it. He could argue to her that Alex had insulted her in front of him, and he'd…what, come to defend her honor? He knew there was no justifying punching Alex, other than the fact that it made him feel good for just the briefest of moments.

It truly had been just the briefest of moments too, because his hand hurt like a *bitch* now. Could you break your hand by hitting someone incorrectly? He honestly had no idea.

The bodyguard glanced at Alex, wordlessly asking him if he needed to step in further, and suddenly Dean felt himself getting nervous. He'd just punched a very well-protected man in front of his bodyguard, and there could be paparazzi around as well. *That* photo would catch a pretty penny if they submitted it to TMZ, he was sure of it. Fuck fuck *fuck*. This wasn't good. Alex could press charges against him if he really wanted to.

Alex shrugged though and shook his head, waving the bodyguard away. Dean felt a wave of relief wash over him. So far, so good. At least with Alex. Although he would be lying if he said he didn't want to punch that stupid smirk off his face again, because he was looking at Dean as if he'd won.

And Dean figured he was probably right.

"I'll deal with this. I'm sorry, Alex," Taylor said softly to him, who shook his head and insisted it was fine. She glared at Dean and started marching back up to the elevator, and Dean had no choice but to follow. The whole time he felt everyone in the vicinity staring at him, and he could feel the beady little eyes of Alex Campano watching them leave. He didn't have to turn around to know he still had a smug look of satisfaction on his face as he watched them go.

CHAPTER THIRTY-SEVEN

TAYLOR

"What the fuck, Dean?!"

It was all she could think to say as she closed to door behind her. The urge to throw something at his stupid blond head was strong, especially when he looked at her with such a look of hurt on his face. *Shit.* She knew exactly what this was about, and it was all her fault that Dean had been fighting Alex in the lobby. She had really screwed things up this time. Badly.

Caroline had called her as soon as she got off the phone with Dean. She explained everything in a panicked hurry, and Taylor had never gotten dressed faster in her life. She ran after him and had gotten off the elevator just in time to watch Dean land a punch on Alex in front of God and everyone.

As upset as she was with Alex, Dean was out of line to actually *hit* him.

"What is *wrong* with you? You've never...I can't believe what I just saw!" She exclaimed. Even though she knew he was upset over the blind item - and he had every right to be, after last night - the answer wasn't to punch Alex in the face. Dean was so sweet and gentle, and then to physically attack someone...

Ugh, and it had been so *hot* too. Something was *wrong* with her. She needed to focus on the issue at hand, which was that Dean was obviously upset about this whole thing - not the fact that watching him punch someone made her want to pounce on him right now.

"Stop playing dumb, Tay," he whispered, avoiding her gaze as she could see the tears starting to well up in his eyes. She knew then that she was right. This *was* about the blind item. She had been naive to hope it was about anything else. Plus that Instagram post that Alex had made...she'd pulled it up in the elevator, and it was damning. It definitely made it look like something had happened with him in his hotel room. Not only that, but it made her pissed as hell that Alex felt he had the freedom to post something like that without asking her.

One problem at a time, though.

"I'm not playing anything," she informed him and he took a deep breath, steadying himself. Whatever anger had taken over the man who'd punched Alex in the lobby was gone. Now all that remained was the hurt - and she tried to ignore how much it was breaking her heart to see him like this.

"Stop denying it. Please, give me that courtesy at least. I know...I saw the picture, I know about the blind item... you slept with him and then came..." he paused, swallowing hard and he turned away from her.

Taylor desperately wanted to run to him and tell him that he was wrong. This was all a misunderstanding and it looked...well, it made her look terrible, to be honest. She understood completely why he was upset. She could feel tears rising up inside her and she took a deep breath. She needed to just explain herself, remind him what they'd told each other last night...

"Dean, I only went there that night because I couldn't find you anywhere," she began, moving towards him but he cut her off, turning wildly on his heel and pointing at her.

"Don't. Don't you fucking dare turn this into something *I* am responsible for!"

"Just listen to me!" She cried, tears streaming down her face although she couldn't remember when she started to cry. "I didn't sleep with him!"

"Then why did he post a picture of you in bed? Why did an 'anonymous' source say you two are sleeping together?" He asked, using air quotes when he said the word 'anonymous'. She felt like she knew what he was implying, and she felt like a dagger had stabbed her in the heart.

"Are you insinuating I did that? That I sold the story to the press?"

"I wouldn't put it past you to save your image."

"Fuck my image! Is that how little you think of me?"

"No!" He exclaimed, running his hand through his hair as he looked at her with a frown. There was a heavy sadness in his eyes as he looked at her, and she wasn't sure what to make of it as he continued.

"The worst part is, I don't think you'd do that at *all*. Because I know you, I know the real you, and I just...I hate that you have to hide behind this wall all the time, and you feel like you have to calculate your every fucking move to get people to like you. People will like you if you just be yourself, Tay. They'll love you, like I love you!"

She opened her mouth to argue and realized…that she was speechless. She didn't have anything to say to that. In one fell swoop he'd captured everything about her every insecurity, and she saw instantly how much it hurt him to watch her struggle. She knew he meant every word he said. What he had just told her had been so…raw. So real.

And apparently, he wasn't done yet.

"I wish you could see that it doesn't matter if people reject you. *I'll* be here for you, always. You'll never have to worry about that from me. And they won't reject you. You're fucking talented, you're the most talented, creative person I've ever met, and you're doing *amazing* things. You're kind and thoughtful and this big ball of light that people can't help being drawn towards. I know you worry about not being good enough or never accomplishing enough, but look around you, Taylor! What more do you want? You have it all, you have…" he paused and trailed off, and she knew what he was going to say. *You have me.*

She paused, biting her lip. Her face was warm, and her stomach was in knots because she had no idea what to say to something so…*nice.* No one had ever said such kind things about her before. She wasn't sure she deserved such high praise, especially after this whole mess with Alex. A mess that was mostly her fault.

None of this would have ever happened if they hadn't left that club together in London six months ago.

Yet she found herself thinking she wouldn't trade this for anything in the world, even now as they fought. Even after Dean punched Alex in the face. Because at the end of the day, Dean knew her better than anyone else on this planet. He knew every bit and piece of her, even the ugly pieces, and he still loved her with all his heart.

It should have all been so simple. Boy liked girl. Girl liked boy. Who cared if he was her assistant? They should have just confessed their feelings to each other long ago instead of making it complicated, and now things were so tangled up between them that she wasn't sure they could ever undo the knot they'd made.

"What the hell are we doing here, Dean?" She asked quietly.

He balked and looked at her in shock, blinking a few times before he let out a breath. "I...I have no idea."

"This has gotten out of control," she whispered, and he nodded in agreement. She wasn't just talking about this fiasco with Alex. All of it had spiraled out of hand, ending in a collision that they could have completely avoided if they'd just been honest from the start.

"It has."

"We need to talk about...last night," she said finally, frowning as she looked at him with sad eyes. She could see him hurting, and she knew that the only way they could move past this was to talk about the evening before.

He closed his eyes, like it was almost painful for him to recall the memory.

He didn't think it was a mistake, did he? She felt a twinge of panic setting in deep in her chest. Perhaps something had changed. Maybe he didn't really love her, and seeing what she'd done with Alex, seeing the blind item had made him realize that none of it had been real between them.

Panic and horror set in as she thought for the briefest of moments that she might actually be losing him.

"Nothing has changed, other than the fact that I

screwed this up completely," he said softly as he looked back up at her again. She blinked at him, confused, and she shook her head. If anyone messed this up, it was her. She was the one who'd been so afraid of anyone finding out the truth about them, about tarnishing her image, that she'd embarked on this ridiculous crusade with Alex in the first place.

"What are you saying?" She asked in confusion.

"I'm saying that I freaking punched Alex in the face. In public! I'm sure paparazzi saw it since they've been following us the entire time, and I'm sure I'll probably be a fucking meme by the end of the day!" He exclaimed. She took a deep breath. She hadn't thought about that. He had just taken out his frustrations in a very public way, and now the blind items that Alex had set in motion would be useless. Everyone would see them for what they truly were. Dean the jilted lover, taking out his frustrations on Alex, the *other* man. All anyone would see now would be a twisted love triangle.

"I should just leave," he said finally, and she shook her head.

"I don't want you to leave. We can talk to Alex and then just go back to -"

He cut her off and shook his head. "What if I don't *want* to go back to before? To before...last night?" He asked quietly.

The implications in his words nearly knocked the wind out of her. He didn't want to go back to hiding their relationship. To sneaking around, having sex on the down low, and insisting it meant absolutely nothing. He wanted her, all of her, and she'd be lying if she said she didn't want all of him too. But could they truly do that after all of this? Could they have everything they wanted, and somehow do damage control to fix things?

Taylor had no idea if that was even possible. She had no clue how to fix what had happened. It was out there now, in the world and on the internet. It was true that the internet was forever. She had to sit and think, because there had to be some way out of this. There just *had* to be.

"This has done nothing but complicate things, Tay," he insisted, looking back at her with tears in his eyes. "*I* have done nothing but complicate things."

"It's not just your fault, Dean, I was the one who…"

"No, but it is, Taylor!" He insisted. "I…I've loved you…maybe since I first walked in that conference room a year ago," he admitted, his face turning red as he looked at her.

She felt her breath catch in her throat. After he confessed his love to her last night, she'd wondered if feelings had been simmering there for months. Even before their first hook-up. Hadn't she always known, though? Every time his brown eyes met her blue ones, and she saw that look. The look that told her everything she needed to know about what was in his heart, that she had tried to ignore, that she'd tried to convince herself wasn't real…

It was the look he was giving her now. Which is why she didn't truly believe what he had to say next.

"I should have walked away a long time ago. And I definitely shouldn't have…" his voice trailed off, but she knew where he had been going with it. He shouldn't have slept with her.

"You regret it," she said simply. He looked physically pained and took a deep breath.

"I…" he trailed off. She shook her head. She still

didn't believe it. If he'd regretted it, he wouldn't have come back to her time and time again. He wouldn't be this upset right now. Dean was lying again, but this time she didn't blame him, because she knew he was doing it to try and protect his heart - and hers.

"Well, I don't. I don't regret it at all, Dean," she told him. "You're not the only one who was lying this whole time," she said softly.

He looked at her with a frown, almost like he didn't want her to say what he knew she was going to say next.

"Taylor, please…"

"I've loved you since the day you first helped me through a panic attack. Where you didn't even need to think, you just *knew* what you needed to do to help me," she explained as she walked up to him. "I looked over, and you were watching *Clueless* with me, and I could tell you wanted to walk over and hold me and comfort me, and it was the kindest thing I've ever had someone do for me," she whispered. He was trying desperately to look away from her, but she took his face in her hands and forced him to look down at her.

"I don't think I realized it at the time. I don't think I did until very recently. So don't you fucking *dare* say you regret this because I don't. We can fix this. We can figure out a way to get past this," she insisted.

Dean took her hands in his and gently pried them from her face, and she suddenly felt her heart dropping. He was stepping away from her now, and with each step he took, she felt like he was slipping through her fingers.

"What if we can't?" he asked quietly.

She stared at him. Then, she wiped her eyes, took a deep breath, and grabbed her key card from the table.

No. She refused. There was simply not going to be any outcome here where they *didn't* make it. She didn't know how she was going to do it, or how long it was going to take, but she was going to find a way to make Dean see reason. They could do anything together as long as they put their mind to it.

Taylor would fix this unbelievable mess, and even if people thought she slept around and had hired her assistant just because she wanted to bang him - she didn't give a shit anymore. Let them talk, let them judge her. It didn't matter, as long as she fixed what had broken between her and Dean. That was all that mattered.

She had a pretty good idea of where to start.

"Where are you going?" He asked as he watched her turn on her heel, heading towards the door.

"I have to go find Alex and hopefully I don't have to talk him out of going to the cops," she replied as she flung open the door. Once she got rid of the Alex part of the equation…she was pretty sure she'd be able to keep going and make Dean see that this could work.

She just hoped Alex would be understanding, and wouldn't somehow make this situation even worse.

CHAPTER THIRTY-EIGHT

TAYLOR

She found him sitting at the bar, drinking a beer as if nothing had happened a half hour previously. His face had a bit of a bruise forming near his left eye but overall he looked to be relatively unharmed. He didn't look at her as she sat down next to him, but she took a deep breath and crossed her arms as she settled on the stool.

"How's your face?" she asked quietly. Alex glanced at her and sighed heavily, taking a sip of his drink again.

"A little tender but I think I'll live," he grumbled back. She wondered if he felt any remorse for any of his actions. True, she'd thrown herself at him to try and use him for her own gain. Yet he'd done the same to her. And he'd done it *after* she apologized to him and came clean about how she couldn't pursue anything with him because of Dean.

"It was really shitty of you to post that picture on Instagram, you know. Especially without asking me," she pointed out. He paused, and she wondered if maybe he hadn't expected

291

her to be bold enough to bring that up.

Clearly, he didn't know her very well.

She wasn't going to sit back and let herself be used like that. It may not have been a steamy photo, or even showed her face, but he'd still made a huge impact in an expert way. He'd come off as someone who was enamored with their new love interest, but still wanted to be coy about showing them off. The type of thing that *tons* of Hollywood A-listers did all the time.

"You knew how that would look. And don't think I don't realize how coincidental the timing of this whole blind item thing is either," she added, referencing the other part of all this. The blind item was likely going to be seared in her brain for all eternity after that.

The A-list author has dropped her assistant in favor of the higher-on-the-list Italian socialite. Apparently, she has a thing for British boys.

"What are you implying?" He asked cooly, glaring at her, and she stood her ground, sitting up straighter.

"Did you leak the story, Alex?"

He paused, and she knew he was trying to figure out the appropriate response to this. Did he deny it or tell the truth? Which move would be better for his image? Perhaps he was still trying to figure out a way to get her into bed after all of this. All she knew was that he had a very calculated look on his face - she could tell he was thinking over all the implications of his next sentence, yet his stone face gave nothing away. He really *was* good at navigating this world.

Taylor knew deep down she was right about the blind item, but she wanted to give him a chance to do the right thing here.

"Yes," he said simply, his jaw tensing as he spoke before he took another sip of his drink, not looking at her and staring up at the rugby game on the TV. "You're not the only one who could benefit from a PR boost."

She wasn't entirely sure what to make of that. Judging by the blind item - and the many blind items she'd read about him after she learned his name, scrolling her phone after their first meeting when Dean had been stomping around the resort in a huff - Alex didn't *need* a boost.

Everyone seemed to love him. Hell, even the blind items about him were generally boosting about how thoughtful he was and the nice charitable things he did for others. Sprinkle in a few items about the girls in his life - actresses, singers, fellow billionaires - and it was no surprise that they'd named him a 'higher on the list' socialite in the blind item concerning her.

She was just a *little* bitter about that.

She looked at him in confusion, wrinkling her eyebrows and tilting her head in interest. He looked at her and sighed at her obvious confusion before dropping his voice, even though they were alone at the bar.

"I recently told my family I'm…bisexual," he admitted, and her eyes widened. She hadn't expected that to come from his mouth and wondered what the heck any of this had to do with her, so she was thankful that he kept explaining. "They weren't exactly pleased. They're basically trying to squash the idea that I might be attracted to men, forcing me to go on dates with lovely women across the country - which, don't get me wrong, I do enjoy but…" he trailed off, and suddenly she felt herself feeling sorry for him.

"But you want them to accept that you *might* date a

guy someday, if given the chance," she finished for him. He paused and looked at her, nodding slowly.

"So by hanging out with me, you keep the charade going just a little bit longer," she elaborated, and he nodded again. All the pieces of the puzzle fell into place.

The PR boost wasn't for his image or his fanbase. It was for his family.

She didn't say anything for a second. She stared at her hands, thinking over everything he'd just told her. It was a lot to process, and it certainly didn't excuse his behavior. He wasn't looking at her, his eyes still glued to the screen even though she could tell he wasn't processing anything happening in the game. Finally, after a moment of thought, she took a deep breath and stood up.

"Well, I just wanted to say that I'm sorry Dean punched you in the face. I hope you weren't thinking of..."

He shook his head, chuckling a little. "No, he didn't do enough damage for me to care that much," he smirked, looking at her mischievously, but she felt a great sense of relief to know that he wasn't going to make a big deal about the hit. "And I'll...take down the Instagram post. I'll post on my story that people misconstrued my words and it was in poor form to use such a...*romantic* caption," he added. "I've got a whole week left of this trip, I'm sure I can find another woman to help me out around here."

Taylor felt her heart soaring. She knew, she *knew* that Alex had a good heart deep down. She grinned and reached over to hug him, which clearly took him by surprise as it took him a minute to hug back.

"I'm...sorry, Taylor."

"Thank you, Alex. I really do wish you the best of luck. With the whole...everything," she told him as she pulled away. He smiled at her - he knew what she meant. She appreciated his apology, and she truly believed him when he said he'd set things right. Hopefully, she wouldn't be accosting him before they left tomorrow, reminding him to take down the post like he'd promised...

"Thank you, Taylor. And best of luck with you and your...assistant. If that's still what you want me to refer to him as," he added, raising an eyebrow.

She paused, unsure *what* exactly Dean was to her right now. They hadn't had a chance to talk about the night before, and then this whole blind item fiasco happened. Then they'd gotten in *another* fight before she stomped off to find Alex...even though one problem was taken care of, she had no idea what she was going to walk in to when she got back to their suite.

She said a small thank you before heading back up to her room, preparing herself for another fight - but she hoped against all hope that it wouldn't come to that.

CHAPTER THIRTY-NINE

DEAN

Dean hadn't wasted any time packing his things and booking himself a flight out of Cancun the moment Taylor left the room. He needed to get back to L.A. as soon as possible. He simply couldn't stay here anymore with her, knowing she was so close by and not being able to touch her, or talk to her, or laugh with her...

She kept saying they could figure it out, and find a way to fix this, but he couldn't ask her to do that. This was a public relations nightmare, and the easiest thing for everyone involved would be if he just removed himself from the equation. Taylor was the most amazing woman he had ever met, and even if he never met another woman like her, she could find someone else easily.

He wouldn't put her through any more trouble, because her career and her writing were the most important thing. He wasn't going to allow himself to screw this up for her just because he'd been stupid and went ahead and caught feelings for his boss.

He had been hoping he could sneak out of the room undetected, and he'd almost made it before she returned to the room - but they ran into each other in the entryway. It was pretty obvious what he was doing, considering he had his suitcase in his hand and his carry-on bag slung over his shoulder. She paused at the door and then closed it slowly behind her, not looking at him as she pushed past.

"I saw Alex downstairs," she told him, evidently ignoring the fact that he was clearly packed and ready to leave. His jaw tensed and he didn't move, watching her as she walked across the room, tossing the room key on the coffee table.

"Good to know he is still up and walking around after I punched him," he grumbled. Not that he had any delusions about his punching abilities - he knew he'd probably barely scratched the man. Dean's fist had taken the brunt of the blow. Taylor didn't say anything in regards to that. She stood near the table and stared at him, and finally, through sheer force of will, he turned to look at her.

"So we had an interesting conversation. It ended well, actually," she continued. Damnit. She'd hooked him and she knew it. He swallowed, gesturing at her slightly to let her know she could continue.

"Alex is the one who submitted the blind item," she told him softly. He let out a sigh, shaking his head and rubbing his eyes under his glasses. He'd had his suspicions, but she must have gotten him to admit the truth. Still, it didn't make a difference. It didn't matter who submitted the blind item. The damage was done and he'd only made it worse.

"Not surprised," he muttered, hoisting his bag higher over his shoulder. He took a deep breath and looked at her, surprised to see her eyes watering as she stared at him. She still looked angry at him, but he wondered - or maybe he just dared to hope - that she was sad to see him standing there with his things. His intentions were very clear, and he couldn't let himself get sidetracked by her face. He looked down at his bags.

"He said he's going to clarify that we're just friends, and find a way to take the heat off of me," she continued. Dean just looked at the floor and nodded. He appreciated that Alex was trying to make things right, but he was still a prick in his eyes. He'd believe him when he saw him actually do it, and the proof was on his Instagram forever. Although he wasn't surprised that Taylor had managed to talk him down and convince him to do the right thing. She could convince countries to sign peace treaties, he was sure of it.

"And he's not going to go to the police about the punch," she added, and Dean realized that his heart had been pounding while waiting to hear about that detail. He gulped and nodded, still looking away from her.

They both remained silent for a moment. She was clearly waiting for him to do something, so he took a deep breath and finally cleared his throat to speak.

"I'm leaving," he announced. "And before I leave I just want to say..."

He paused, trying to figure out how to say everything in his heart. She looked at him expectantly, and he tried not to keep eye contact with her. It would hurt too much. She looked like she was angry and sad at the same time, but she made no move to come up to him. He knew it was better this way, and he could tell she knew that too. She might not have liked his decision, but she respected it.

"I'm sorry, Taylor, that I lied to you," he told her

softly, looking up at her and trying to blink back tears. "And I'm sorry that I accused you of leaking the story with Alex. And for punching Alex in the face, and just...all of it," he admitted. It was truly his fault that things had gotten so bad. He let his jealousy get in the way. Maybe if he had just waited until the trip was over - let her have her fun with Alex and then maybe he could have sat her down, told her his feelings...

No, because even though they loved each other, this was still just too complicated. It wasn't meant to be. In some other world, where he didn't work for her, maybe they'd have stood a chance...but not here. Not on this timeline.

"But I'm not sorry that I fell in love with you," he added, and he watched her inhale sharply. "I'm not sorry about what I said - that you don't have to *try* so hard. I know you're scared of people not liking you, or not being successful, but when you let your guard down and finally show people the real you... it's beautiful," he said softly. It was true - even though things had ended in disaster, he wouldn't have traded this past year for anything in the world. She was biting her lip sharply and staring at the floor now, avoiding his gaze.

"Oh, before I forget..." he reached into his pocket and pulled out the box with the necklace in it. He set it down and slid it across the table to her, and she caught it, picking it up and opening it. She sucked in a breath as she looked at the glittering dolphin pendant, then looked back at Dean.

He swallowed. "I got you something small because I know you hate gaudy jewelry," he explained. "I figured this was small enough that you could tuck it away if you wanted to and... yeah."

Dean stopped because he realized he was laying out all his reasons for buying that particular necklace for her, which only proved that he knew her like the back of his hand. He shouldn't have *ever* known her that well. He shouldn't have ever been able to look behind that wall and see the real Taylor. That was their first mistake, and he hated himself for looking behind it without question.

"I read your letters," he added, his voice barely more than a whisper. She paused, looking at him with a sad frown. He knew he had invaded her privacy doing that, but if she cared about that, she didn't let on about it. She nodded and looked down at her feet.

"I meant every word of it," she informed him. Dean felt his heart breaking even more and more. If he didn't leave soon he was going to suffocate from it. He *knew* she'd meant it. And he hated that it made him all warm inside, and he hated that he knew he'd never forget every word she'd written to him on that blank page.

Dean especially hated himself for falling in love with the one woman he couldn't have. He took a deep breath and wiped his eyes, clearing his throat.

"Thank you very much for this opportunity, Ms. Mullins," he said softly. He saw her yank her head up when he said that, and he knew that calling her that had been a little dig - but he wanted to make it clear to her that he was cutting all ties with her. She could go on and continue her career without the mess of a scandal that dating her assistant would make.

"So...you're quitting as my assistant?" She asked quietly. He nodded.

"Yes. Effective immediately," he responded, trying not to think about how his heart was breaking as he spoke. Once he left here, she would never have to think about him again. She'd never have to see him again - it would be like he never existed. She could run off with Alex if that was what she wanted, and the paparazzi would have a field day with it.

"Good," she said simply, and he tried not to think about how much that hurt. Her single word had been like a stab in the chest.

This was his own damn fault. He'd always known he cared for her more than he let on, and he should have never started down this road with her. The only destination had always been heartbreak. What had he *thought* was going to happen? Really?

"I thought you'd see it that way," he replied softly. If he spoke any louder he was sure he'd start to cry. Not only would that show her how much he was hurting, but it would do absolutely nothing for his ego and just make him feel even worse.

Taylor had that determined look on her face, and he figured she was about to lay into him and berate him for everything he had done. He knew he deserved it, and would take whatever verbal lashing she gave him before he left. He owed her that much. She was clearly thinking about her next move, and he wasn't surprised when she dropped her arms and took a deep breath.

"That means I can do this," she continued, and she walked forward to him. He braced himself, wondering if maybe she was going to slap him, but instead, she wrapped her arms around him and pulled him close, kissing him.

He immediately forgot about everything else. All the hurt and pain he'd been feeling vanished in an instant. The only thing he could think about was her lips. He dropped his bag and pulled her to him, kissing her back deeply as he drank in the taste of her. A moment later, however, he remembered what they had been talking about, and he pulled away.

"Taylor, what are you doing?" He asked softly, his hands brushing over her arms as he looked down at her. This wasn't what he had expected at all. He was giving her an out, and yet, here she was. Kissing him with all that same fiery passion they'd had last night. She cupped his face in her hands and he whimpered softly, trying to swallow away the lump in his throat. This couldn't be real. This couldn't be happening…he refused to allow himself to believe it…

"Dean, my feelings towards you haven't changed," she whispered, brushing her thumb along his cheek. He closed his eyes, refusing to look at her as his heart started to race. Her hands felt warm on his face, and he wanted to take her hand in his and squeeze it.

"Everything would be easier if I just left. You know this is going to be a mess for you," he reminded her, a tear dripping down his face as he spoke. He was trying desperately not to get emotional, but he felt like he was at a crossroads in his life right now. The outcome of this conversation was going to change the very trajectory of everything, he knew it without a doubt.

He couldn't allow himself to think, even for a second, that it might be headed in the very direction he desperately wanted it to go. He had already gotten his hopes up before on this trip and look where it had gotten him. Not yet, not until he knew for certain…

"I know it would, but I don't want that. You don't either," she said simply. He opened his eyes and realized she was crying as well. As usual, her voice wasn't shaking or giving any indication that she was emotional, because she was staying strong and she was determined to show him how serious she was. His grip on her arms tightened and he looked down at her nervously.

He took a deep breath, biting his lip so hard he was afraid he might draw blood.

"Don't you dare do this unless you mean it, Tay," he whispered. His voice cracked - he was giving her one last out.

"I mean it," she told him forcefully. He knew from the fierce look in her blue eyes that she did mean it. With every fiber of her being.

"Say it."

"*I love you, Dean,*"

He pulled her close and kissed her hard. He kissed her like it was the last time he would ever kiss her, and he held her tightly as if she'd float away if he let go for even a second. She whimpered into his lips and threw her arms around him, and he picked her up off the ground and she wrapped her legs around him.

"I love you, Taylor," he muttered into her lips as her hands went to his hair.

"I want to be with you, Dean," she uttered, and he groaned, squeezing her thighs as he held her against him. This *was* real. It was really happening.

"I want to be with you too, Taylor," he muttered.

"This is it, ok? The two of us...no more fucking around," she muttered as she kissed him. He nodded in understanding against her lips, groaning softly.

"No more fucking around," he muttered in agreement as he pushed her against the wall, grinding his hips into hers. He kissed down her neck as he peeled clothes off of her, and he felt her hands moving to his jeans and working on the button.

"What about the..."

"I swear to God, if you say blind item right now, I'm

walking away," she growled into his lips, and he felt himself chuckling slightly. He knew for a fact she wouldn't, not when he had her pinned against a wall like this, her hands desperately pushing his jeans down to his knees.

Once she'd exposed him, she wrapped her arms around him as he eagerly pawed at her shorts. "Aren't you afraid people will talk?" He asked as he fumbled with the denim, stepping back and releasing her for a brief moment to slide them down along with her underwear.

"Let them," she panted into his lips as she kissed him again. His heart was soaring. This wasn't a dream, it wasn't a fantasy, or some stupid plan to get the paparazzi to buy a certain story.

This was perfect and it was real and it was all his.

"It's going to be a PR nightmare for a while," he reminded her, and she shook her head.

"I can handle it."

"I punched Alex Campano in the *face*."

"And it was fucking hot as hell."

"I'm unemployed now, you're going to have to take care of me until I get a new job," he added playfully, and she laughed against his lips before she moaned, feeling him line up at her entrance.

"Worth it," she muttered into his lips, and he groaned as he slowly slid into her and he felt her wrap his legs around her.

"Taylor...I love you. I love you so much I think sometimes it's going to eat me alive inside," he whispered softly. She moaned into his lips and they locked eyes. Those beautiful blue eyes twinkled with delight as she smiled at him, cupping his face with her hands.

"Dean, I love you too. You're…fuck, you're my whole world," she muttered, her thumb grazing his cheek. He smiled at her, and she smiled back, and then they kissed again.

"I'll always be your world. I promise," he whispered as he began to move, and she groaned.

"I know you will. You'd never lie to me," she reminded him, and he grinned into her lips before losing himself inside her completely.

EPILOGUE

DEAN

Five Months Later

Taylor was tapping her pen against her knee nervously, as she always did right before she was about to do a reading. Dean couldn't help but smile to himself as he watched her.

It amazed him how she was always able to let anyone read her work and ask for opinions on it all the time, but when it came to reading it out loud, she was on the verge of a breakdown. He knew that wasn't the only reason, though. She was doing the reading from her second book to help promote the TV show - the trailer was dropping tomorrow and her manager, Ryan, insisted it would be good for her to drum up some buzz around the trailer by doing a reading to go along with it. Dean still wasn't sure how you could have a trailer ready for the first season when it was still six months from premiering and hadn't even wrapped shooting, but that was just another thing about Hollywood he was going to have to learn as he continued to navigate his way through this world.

"You ok?" He asked, reaching over to squeeze her hand. He winced slightly as the diamond on her ring dug into his palm - he still constantly forgot about it, because it was so new. Every time he accidentally pinched himself on the diamond, however, he smiled, because it just reminded him that the woman next to him wasn't his boss anymore. She wasn't his girlfriend either.

She was his *fiancé*.

"Yeah, other than feeling like I'm going to throw up," she grumbled. He raised his eyebrow of concern.

"It's not because...?" He paused, glancing at her stomach, which was still very flat and very inconspicuous looking.

She chuckled and shook her head. "No, although that isn't helping," she admitted with a small chuckle. Neither of them had told anyone they were expecting yet aside from their parents. They were going to have a little reveal party next week - just something simple, a small little dinner with their friends, who thought it was a casual get together to celebrate their engagement. While that was *partially* true, they had more big news to share, and Dean was simply ecstatic. He was pretty sure he hadn't stopped smiling since they found out two weeks ago.

"Oh! Alex is bringing his *boyfriend* to the engagement party," Taylor said suddenly, and Dean sighed heavily and pretended to wave his finger in the air like 'whoop-dee-doo' which earned him a good shove from her as she giggled.

"Still not his biggest fan, huh?" She asked, and he shook his head.

"No, he said some really hurtful things about you before I punched him. I'm not going to just forget that," he reminded her. She smiled and kissed his cheek softly.

"Always looking out for me," she mumbled playfully, nuzzling her nose into his skin as he blushed. It was true - Alex still had to earn back his trust. He was getting there, slowly but surely. Once Taylor and Alex had brought him in on Alex's secret about his bisexuality, that had helped a *bit,* but he still had a *long* way to go. Just because you were closeted didn't mean you got to be a dick.

"You probably *should* show him a little grace, though. He never pressed charges following the punch," she reminded him, raising an eyebrow as Dean sighed in defeat. It had cost them a *lot* of their vacation spending money to bribe the paparazzi to throw out the pictures of the infamous punch. Alex had begrudgingly apologized to him about what he'd said and promised he wouldn't go after Dean for assault. He had kept his word, but when it came to Alex, Dean would always be on his guard.

Things definitely could have been complicated when they got back from Mexico regarding Alex. They were both very lucky that it hadn't blown up in their faces - otherwise, their relationship would have been the least of their worries.

"Your mom is still coming, right?" Taylor asked suddenly, and he nodded with a grin.

"Yup, she called me yesterday to let me know she's cleared to take a long trip out here."

"And she's still feeling good?" She added, asking the same question she'd asked hundreds of times ever since they got word that she was back in remission. He chuckled and assured her that yes, she was good, and Taylor went back to anxiously tapping her knee with her pen. He couldn't help but just sit there and watch her, thinking that in that moment she was still just as pretty as ever.

Somehow, he'd gotten everything he ever wanted. A beautiful woman, a baby on the way...and after the news of his relationship with Taylor became public, and people in Hollywood heard he was unemployed, he'd had no shortage of job offers at public relations firms. It had been tough dealing with the fallout of their scandal, and Caroline had chastised them for a good month after they returned from Mexico about all the damage control they had to do.

One of the most mortifying days of his life was when his sister Vicky came to visit, and they'd been chased out of a Starbucks while the paparazzi demanded to know if he was cheating on Taylor with her. His *sister!*

After a few weeks though, the excitement began to die down. Alex had held up his end of the bargain, posting a clarification to his story and then immediately going and flirting with the two German girls (Gabi and Katarina, apparently) and posting them all over his Instagram less than a day later.

To prevent things from getting out of hand in the future, and to deal with her rising star power, Taylor hired a publicist, a manager, and a new assistant - her name was Jodi, a 19-year-old red-headed girl fresh from the Midwest, and she'd nearly fainted when she met them, she was so star-struck. It had been a very weird experience and one he was not looking forward to repeating any time soon.

Her new publicist, Ariana, was the one who got him his new job. She worked at a smaller place, where he could get his feet on the ground and really learn the business. Being an assistant to a high-profile author and being a public relations manager for a Hollywood star were two *very* different things, so he needed to dip his toe in the waters before shooting for bigger, better things. His boss assured him he was doing great, though, and really managing his small client base well.

He was also regularly attending AA meetings. Taylor had set him down when they came back from Mexico all those months ago and told him through tears that she was worried about him. He didn't blame her - he'd fallen off the wagon a few times over the course of a year, so clearly his self-control wasn't as strong as he wanted to believe.

It was nerve-wracking at first, admitting to himself how much of a problem he had, but he went to the first meeting, Taylor in tow, and immediately felt a sense of relief. After a few more meetings, he was able to go alone, and he was able to muster the courage to call his parents and Vicky and tell them what was going on. As he had suspected, they supported him fully in his journey to getting a handle on his drinking problem, and once he got all that off his chest, the rest was easy.

Well, not *easy*. He knew it would never be easy when it came to alcohol with him. But it was manageable now.

Taylor was working on herself too. She'd taken the huge step of going to therapy to deal with her issues. Both of them knew deep down that she had some deeply rooted trauma and fears of abandonment and rejection that she was going to have to seriously work on. Otherwise, she'd be anxious about her writing and her career forever, and would never be able to truly enjoy it.

She'd told him that she hadn't expected to cry or open up the way she did, but five minutes into the session, she started talking about her mother and before she knew it she'd gone through a whole box of tissues. Or maybe that was partially due to the pregnancy hormones. Either way, they were both healing, working on themselves so they could be better for each other.

Caroline was wrapping up her introduction, so they both stood up and he turned to her, taking her hands in his. She squeezed them tightly and looked up at him, smiling softly.

"Hey. You got this. You're gonna kill it, just like you have every book reading before this," he assured her. She took a deep breath and leaned in, standing on her tiptoes - even in her heels she was still shorter than him - and kissing him softly on the lips.

"I know. I have my best friend waiting back here for me, cheering me on," she whispered into his lips. He grinned and playfully bit her lip since they were alone, and she giggled. God, he loved that giggle of hers. It was like magical wind chimes in his ear.

"I love you," he encouraged her before kissing the top of her head.

"I love you, Dean. I don't care what anyone else says, as long as you're here."

"And I'll *always* be here. Now, go out there and kill it."

ACKNOWLEDGMENTS

I can't believe I'm really here, writing an acknowledgments page for my first novel.

Ever since I was little it has been my dream to see my name on a book, and now after over a decade of taking my craft seriously, my dream has become a reality. I'd of course be remiss to not thank my parents and my family for their never ending support. Mom, Dad, Michelle, and Uncle Joe Joe - thank you for always supporting me and my big dreams, which were probably a bit far out of my reach to be realistic at times. Thank you for raising me in an environment where I was able to explore my storytelling talents and for providing me every privilege and opportunity to you could to help further my education. Without you, I wouldn't have been able to build a life where I *can* take time to work on my books and I *do* have disposable income to publish my books on my own.

To my sister, Michelle, in particular - thank you for allowing me to play Barbies and Bratz with you for years as we were growing up. I probably won't ever write a novel about murders and kidnappings at the Bratz ski lodge like we played when we were kids, but playing and creating ridiculous storylines to exercise my imagination has definitely helped me become a better storyteller. Thank you for being my Disney travel partner and for letting me borrow your books (even though you never return the ones *I* lend you).

Actually, scratch that bit about never writing a murder novel starring our Bratz dolls. There might be something there...

To Roger, my love. Thank you for being my cheerleader. You came into my life at the exact right moment and truly made my life complete. Everything I do is to build our dream life for us, and your words of encouragement keep me going. Thank you for being a beta reader and giving actual criticism instead of just mindlessly boosting my ego. You are truly such an amazing man. Dean Coffey has nothing on you.

To all my friends who supported me along the way - Jordie, Kaylea, Katie, and Jess to name a few, as you ladies heard me talk about NaNoWriMo every November in college - thank you for letting me share my dreams with you. Special shout out to my online friends who have role-played with me for almost two decades at this point. By simply making up characters and coming up with elaborate plots with all of you, you have helped my writing improve immensely over the formative years of my life. I can't name each and every one of you or this acknowledgment page would go on forever, so I'd just like to drop special shoutouts to Anna, Kath, Ali, Shan, Dee, Nicole, Felix, Eli, Kimmy, Lauren, Ariana, Chrissy, Ern and Chris for not only helping me with my writing, but also being emotional support for some of the roughest periods of my life. I love and cherish you all more than you could ever know.

Special shout out to my TikTok Vet Med friend Courtney for encouraging me to self-publish my novels. Knowing that someone I knew was able to do this made it feel so much more achievable for me and I probably never would have jumped into the indie publishing waters if it hadn't been for you.

To my co-workers, who are super supportive and humor me as I talk about all my wild dreams and my millions of side projects I always have going on. You guys feed into the delulu of my Sagittarius sun and I am so appreciative of that. I'm so thankful I work in such a great clinic with such a fantastic team so I don't stress about work nearly as much as some people do. Without that burden, I *can* chase my delusional dreams and it's all because of you guys!

Next, I have to shout out the two lovely ladies who made this physical book possible. Thank you so much to Ivanna and Ayesha on Fiverr for helping make this book into an actual *product*. Ivanna, I can't stop gushing over how perfect the cover for this book is, and how you captured the likeness of both Dean and Taylor exactly as I imagined it. Ayesha, thank you for helping edit my novel. Your feedback was honest when it needed to be, and your words of encouragement and highlighting of your favorite parts helped beat the imposter syndrome for me and made me think people might actually enjoy what I have to write. Words cannot express how lucky I am to have found both of you!

Last but not least - to my readers and my followers on social media. Everything I release into the public, whether it's a silly TikTok video, an educational blog post about writing, or my novels - it's all for you. The best thing in the world is knowing that I put smiles on faces across the world, which is not something I ever dreamed would be possible until the last few years. I hope you enjoyed Taylor and Dean's story and love them as much as I do. I hope this book was everything you wanted it to be and more, and I sincerely hope I've convinced you to stick around and see what else I have in store for you. Thank you for all of your support, your kind words, and your honest feedback. You have made this little Melissa's dreams a reality, and words can never express how grateful I am for that.

Love, Melissa

Melissa Gresko has been writing ever since she figured out Microsoft Word was a thing in the dark ages of the 1990's. Her obsession with writing only grew when she discovered the incredibly nerdy world of online roleplaying and fan fiction. A lifelong creative, Melissa began writing novels in college and after years of keeping her writing secret, finally decided to pursue publishing her works. *BLIND ITEMS AND BRITISH BOYS* is her debut novel and certainly will not be her last.

When not writing, Melissa works as a certified veterinary technician in the suburbs of Chicago and currently lives with her boyfriend and their dogs, Shenzi and Nova. In her free time, she likes to play video games (anything from The Sims to Assassins Creed) work out, crochet, diamond paint, make a fool of herself on TikTok, and spend any remaining money she has on Disney vacations.

CAN'T GET ENOUGH OF DEAN AND TAYLOR?

Sign up for my newsletter to receive an exclusive FREE chapter from *BLIND ITEMS AND BRITISH BOYS* that didn't make it into the final cut of the book!Also be sure to check out the official playlist for *BLIND ITEMS AND BRITISH BOYS* on Spotify!

(Scan the following code in the Spotify app on your phone to bring up the playlist!)

For all future updates, be sure to bookmark and check out
melissagreskobooks.com

FOLLOW ME ON SOCIAL MEDIA!
@melissaspeaksdog on TikTok and Instagram
@melissaglovesbooks on TikTok (my "BookTok" account)
@MelissaGresko on X

Penelope and Ricky's love story is next...

Keep reading for an exclusive sneak peek at the next book in the "Thirty, Flirty and Finding Love" Series...*OUT ON LAKE FLOSSMOOR*

CHAPTER ONE

RICKY

Everyone in Ricky Thompson's life abandoned him.

Ok, that was probably a bit dramatic.

They didn't necessarily abandon him in the literal sense - at least not *every* time - but Ricky did become an afterthought in the lives of most people he knew, including his family. Usually the people who ended up leaving him kept in touch, even if it was just in the form of a LinkedIn connection or - when it came to his family - a weekly text message in the group chat. He hated that his strongest relationships were to people who only contacted him via FaceTime, but maybe that was his lot in life. At least they hadn't abandoned him *completely*. That was somewhat of a comfort, but it still didn't make him feel great.

Clearly, it was something to do with *him* as a person. Which he couldn't quite figure out - Ricky loved to take care of people. He prided himself in being the one who was always sober enough to remember to order them an Uber home and take away his friends' drinks whenever they got too sloppy. He loved being the one who was thoughtful enough to bring his boss doughnuts on his last day in the law office where Ricky worked. Hell, he even walked his coworker's dog every other weekend when she went down to Laguna Beach to see her boyfriend. Surely he was someone people would want to keep around?

It was just a fact about his life that he had come to accept - everyone was eventually going to *leave*. It was a sure as the fact that the grass was green and the sky was blue. Everyone that Ricky cared about was eventually going to leave him to fend for himself. At some point, it was inevitable.

He was truly on his own in this world.

It had started in high school. First, during their freshman year, his best friend Kenny moved away after his parents suddenly got divorced. They'd literally packed up and moved over the weekend, and he'd had to find out through *MySpace* of all things. His twin brother Tim had left him to go to a separate college on the East Coast, and that was *after* he'd left him behind in their grade, skipping ahead and eventually graduating early.

His parents had left him to go retire in Florida the second he graduated high school, selling their childhood home before he had even moved all his things out. His sister Erika had left him to travel around Mexico with her new boyfriend as soon as she graduated college, so with all the kids out of the house, Leonard Thompson declared that he wasn't going to stick around in Madison any longer and it was time for him and his wife to get some much needed relaxation. As if raising their children had been a burden on them.

Since no one was bothering to stick around with him and he came to accept the fact that he'd been left behind, Ricky figured he might as well move out of Wisconsin and go somewhere far away for a fresh start. Everyone else was doing it - why shouldn't he?

But his bad luck didn't end there. Everyone *still* left him.

Every girl he ever dated packed up and gently sat him down for the 'it's not you, it's me' talk. *He* never got to break up with anyone - he had always been dumped. Or ghosted. He tried to tell himself that everyone got ghosted when they were venturing out into the dating world, but it certainly didn't relieve any of the sting every time he was a left on read.

Every friend he lived with moved out the second their lease was up. His last roommate had left him to get his own place because he wanted more privacy and to feel more adult. For some reason he just didn't want to be around Ricky anymore. They still saw each other pretty regularly, but Ricky was bracing himself for the fact that eventually, Dean was going to stop calling or returning his texts. It was only a matter of time.

It was why he kept people close, but kept a good arms length of space between them at the same time. Just in case. He was willing to take care of everyone else but sacrifice his own happiness if it meant they at least tried to text him every once in a while like his family did. That seemed to be all he was good for, and he'd come to peace with that. Still, he couldn't help but hold out hope that someday, someone would stick around and be in it for the long haul.

The only person who hadn't physically left him was Holly, his rabbit - and that was probably only because he fed her and kept her safe from coyotes. He was sure that, if given the choice, she'd run far away from him too. Susie, his coworker's dog, *had* actually run away from him last week, so clearly this strange repulsion people had to his company extended to animals.

Thank God he'd managed to get her back, although that mostly had to do with the fact that she was an obese golden retriever who was easily distracted.

So that was why when he first laid eyes on Penelope Adamczyk back in December, he vowed right then and there that he wasn't going to pursue anything romantic with her. Despite the fact that her sheer beauty hit him like a freight train as soon as he laid eyes on her from across the room - he wouldn't allow himself to make a move. She would just leave like everyone else. What was the point in getting involved with the most gorgeous girl he'd ever seen, just for it to end in heartbreak? He wasn't sure he'd be able to come back from that.

Still, dressed in his zoot suit that he'd rented specifically for this ridiculous Gatsby themed party, he smiled and put on a polite face when they met at the snack table, striking up conversation about the decor simply because it was what was expected of him as a guest.

Unfortunately, his anxiety about avoiding any possible romantic encounter with her caused him to forget how to function as a human being. When he introduced himself, he tried to shake using his hand with the glass he was holding, then awkwardly tried to change course and spilled half of his whiskey on the floor. Then his voice had squeaked when he introduced himself, like a kid going through puberty. The interaction had lasted fifteen whole seconds, but he was mortified. He had avoided her the rest of the evening and left the party three hours early.

Ricky hadn't stopped thinking about her since.

The only reason he had been invited to the damn

party was because his former roommate, Dean Coffey, was Taylor's Mullins' assistant, and in an effort to have the biggest and best party for his boss, Dean had invited pretty much every human being he'd ever interacted with in the Los Angeles area. Taylor was an up and coming author who was actually doing pretty well for herself, and Dean worked tirelessly to make sure her life was easy now that she had him as her assistant.

Ricky had debated leaving the party early even before he'd run into Penelope, since it was clear to anyone with eyes that Dean and Taylor were hopelessly in love with each other. Dean had insisted nothing was going on between them, but Ricky knew that whenever Dean was lying, he started to throw around more British slang words than normal. He knew from experience that the more times Dean called him a 'right git' the more he was trying to hide.

Taylor might as well have written 'I'm in love with Dean Coffey' on her forehead under the glittery headband of her Gatsby costume. As happy as Ricky was for his friend to have finally found a girl who was, by all accounts, quite the catch, he couldn't help but feel a slight pang of jealousy.

That was all he wanted. To find a nice girl, settle down, have some kids, eventually go back to law school...the universe seemed to have other plans.

He'd had a grand total of two serious girlfriends in his thirty-one years of life, neither of which had ended well. His first girlfriend, Denise, had taken off with his expensive gaming computer and moved up with Seattle with her yoga instructor. His second girlfriend, Sally, had let him down so easily that he almost forgot how horribly it felt to be broken up with in that moment. Next thing he knew, she had shacked up with her new boyfriend a month after she'd dumped him, and Ricky was alone once again.

But when his eyes had first fallen upon Penelope, her long chestnut hair curled delicately down her back and her bright red dress standing out against her tan skin, he was done for. He was pretty positive she had smiled the entire night, and her infectious laugh was so genuine and girlish that it made her sound like she should be in a Disney cartoon surrounded by talking woodland creatures. She'd somehow managed to find lipstick that matched her dress perfectly, and even from across the room, he could see a spattering of freckles forming a constellation of dots across her plump cheeks as she smiled. He'd truly never seen anyone so radiant in his life. How could anyone focus on the birthday girl when Penelope was in the room?

He had hoped he wouldn't run into her again after that night, but the more Dean and Taylor continued to hang out, the more he found himself in Penelope's presence. Each time he encountered her, he smiled politely, made small talk about the weather, and then inevitably acted awkward and left early. He usually could blame his Crohn's disease and claim he was having stomach problems, which he was sure was the least attractive thing he could possibly do. Still, it was better than the alternative - second guessing every word he said until he felt like dying of embarrassment. He was acting like he hadn't spoken English in years.

His first encounter with Penelope had been over a year ago, and a lot had changed in that time. Ricky was now studying for the LSAT, while still living alone. Dean and Taylor were now officially engaged - and expecting a baby. Penelope was going to be everywhere now. She'd be at the engagement party. The baby shower. The wedding shower. At the *wedding*. He wouldn't be able to escape her.

Ricky found himself actually wishing Dean *hadn't*

stuck around in his life for as long as he had. If he was going to stop calling him and talking to him like everyone else, he kind of wished he'd just get on with it already. For once, he hated being invited to things, because that meant he'd have to be in the same room as Penelope.

He couldn't bring himself to get over the anxiety and stress that came up every time he thought about talking to her. His last date had been almost *three* years ago at this point. He hadn't touched a woman in so long, he was sure that he'd forgotten how to do it correctly. What was the point in dating if he was just going to be inevitably dumped? So he had just... stopped.

Ricky Thompson was a mess, and he was not about to subject anyone to that mess, let alone the gorgeous soul that was Penelope Adamczyk. She was far too perfect for him, and way out of his league. That much was clear.

Yet no matter how hard he tried, he couldn't stop himself from asking about her. Many times. He knew all about her own horrendous luck in the dating game. She'd just gotten out of a five year relationship and was apparently not in any mood to start dating again, which was a slight relief. At least he knew that he didn't have to worry about her reciprocating any feelings towards him - although why would anyone as beautiful as *her* be interested in a lame string bean of a man like him? He had curly brown hair that never sat right on his head no matter what he did. He could barely grow a mustache let alone a full beard. He was tall, his arms were too long and lanky, and the slight muscle definition he did have from his tennis days in high school and college was nothing compared to some of the models who lived in L.A.

He knew that she was a teacher at a local high school, teaching social studies. She lived with her friend Betsy, who taught at the same school as her. She was also, coincidently, from the Midwest, but she'd grown up in Illinois, not Wisconsin. Taylor and Dean were probably sick of his relentless questioning. They probably thought he was some psycho stalker freak. He tried to just work his questions delicately into conversation, and if they suspected anything, neither of them said as much.

He couldn't help himself. When it came to Penelope, she consumed his thoughts more often than not.

Which was highly inconvenient, seeing as how he couldn't do anything about it.

He debated trying to be friends with her, just so he'd have an excuse to see her every once in a while. A morbid thought popped into his head and he wondered if he was friends with her, then *maybe* her exit from his life would come about quicker - perhaps he could speed along the process. There didn't seem to be any rhyme or reason to the way this curse worked. Maybe it was worth a shot?

In fact, he'd finally mustered up the courage that very morning to add her on Instagram, sending her a follow request before taking his phone and chucking it across the room in a panic a few seconds later. He debated taking the request back, but what if she had already seen it? And then he unfollowed her right away? That would look even worse! He knew from the few times he'd seen her that she was chatty, and probably would approach him about it in front of *everyone* the next time he saw her at an event. Taking it back now would only look bad for him. What was done was done...maybe he'd just delete Instagram to avoid the scenario all together.

Thankfully for him, he had an excuse to miss Taylor and Dean's official engagement party that weekend. They'd already had one small party to announce the engagement - and their pregnancy - which told Ricky that Dean and Taylor were going to be holding a *lot* of events as they prepared for their nuptials. At least he had a valid excuse this time.

His brother Tim was getting married, so the whole family was headed back to Wisconsin for the event. Ricky hadn't seen any of his family in person since the pandemic, and he found that he was actually *excited* about getting together with them again, despite the fact that it was likely going to be filled with drama and passive aggressive insults thrown around left and right. They were using the family property out on Lake Flossmoor to host the whole thing - everyone was staying there, they were having the parties and rehearsal dinner there, and the reception itself would be on a lavish mega yacht out on the lake. It was two weeks away from Ricky's depressing life in L.A. and he simply couldn't wait.

So now, Ricky was at the airport, sitting with Holly in a pet carrier under his seat while he waited for the plane to start boarding. He didn't hear his phone ding with the notification from Instagram that Penelope had accepted his follow request, and sent one of her own, because he was too wrapped up in his own thoughts. Two weeks with his family would be rough, but two weeks away from Penelope Adamcyzk would definitely be welcome.

Maybe then he could finally stop thinking about her, and start getting over her.